WITHDRAWN

GREY EXPECTATIONS

A Selection of Recent Titles by Clea Simon

CATTERY ROW
CRIES AND WHISKERS
MEW IS FOR MURDER
SHADES OF GREY *
GREY MATTERS *
GREY ZONE *
GREY EXPECTATIONS *

available from Severn House

GREY EXPECTATIONS

A Dulcie Schwartz feline mystery

Clea Simon

Severn House

This first world edition published 2012
in Great Britain and in the USA by
SEVERN HOUSE PUBLISHERS LTD of
9–15 High Street, Sutton, Surrey, England, SM1 1DF.
Trade paperback edition first published
in Great Britain and the USA 2012 by
SEVERN HOUSE PUBLISHERS LTD.

British Library Cataloguing in Publication Data

Simon, Clea.
  Grey expectations. – (Dulcie Schwartz feline mystery)
  1. Schwartz, Dulcie (Fictitious character)–Fiction.
  2. Detective and mystery stories.
  I. Title II. Series
  813.6-dc23

ISBN-13: 978-0-7278-8134-2 (cased)
ISBN-13: 978-1-84751-412-7 (trade paper)

All Severn House titles are printed on acid-free paper.

Severn House Publishers support The Forest Stewardship Council [FSC],
the leading international forest certification organisation. All our titles that
are printed on Greenpeace-approved FSC-certified paper carry the FSC logo.

Typeset by Palimpsest Book Production Ltd.,
Falkirk, Stirlingshire, Scotland.
Printed and bound in Great Britain by
MPG Books Ltd., Bodmin, Cornwall.

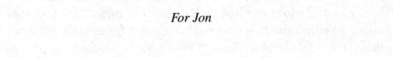

For Jon

Acknowledgements

Heartfelt gratitude to my readers – Lisa Susser, Chris Mesarch, Brett Milano, and Jon Garelick – for all your catches and comments. Thanks as well to Caroline Leavitt, Vicki Croke, and Naomi Yang for encouragement (and basil), and to my agent Colleen Mohyde, editor Rachel Simpson Hutchens, and the wonderfully supportive Lisa Jones, Frank Garelick, and Sophie Garelick. Purrs to you all, folks, and may the spirit of love watch over you.

ONE

*T*he horses thundered on, as if drawn by traces unseen to their destination. Miles beyond the cresting ridge they had carried her without pause, but her thoughts lay elsewhere, lost in the inky night. Writing, she should be writing, and yet she journey'd on this dark path. Propelled to continue on, not by fear or base desire, but from a strange and wond'rous destiny, a dream that so moved her, she traveled. Exhausted, spent in both body and soul far beyond what mortal woman should endure, she clung to the carriage bench, its worn leather no longer soft beneath her hands as the seemingly everlasting night faded into dawn. An hour more, perhaps two, before the horses would be changed. An hour or two before she could—

'Stop!' Dulcie woke with a start. 'Bad Esmé. That hurt!'

If anything could bring Dulcie back to the light of day, it was her kitten. Specifically, her kitten's teeth. Dulcie had been dozing, lost in a dream. Oblivious to the book on her lap, she must have let her hand slide off the page to dangle by her side. Maybe she'd even twitched. At any rate, she liked to think there had been a provocation. Dulcie didn't want to believe the little tuxedo cat would just bite her for no reason.

'No!' She tried to sound firm, shaking her finger in what she intended as a stern gesture. 'No biting. No. Bad kit—' Dulcie stopped herself. The last thing she wanted was for the young animal to develop self-esteem issues. Unlikely, true, but when acting *in loco parentis* one couldn't be too careful. 'Bad *behavior*,' she corrected herself, as well as the young feline. 'Biting is a bad thing to do.'

But the extended digit offered too much temptation, and the kitten grabbed it. And while the claws in her neat white paws were sheathed, her teeth sunk into soft flesh.

'Ow!' Dulcie tried to extricate her hand, all thoughts of socially correct pet parenting momentarily shelved. 'Esmé!' Every move, though, only served to egg on the overexcited kitten, who now had her front legs wrapped around the offending hand. 'Let go!'

The little cat only held on tighter and started to kick with her white hind booties. In desperation, Dulcie pulled back – and knocked the heavy book on her lap to the floor. The ensuing 'thump' finally served to interrupt the kitten's frenzy, distracting her enough to allow Dulcie to free herself.

Deprived of prey, the cat sat back and eyed her person. Like the kitten, Dulcie was on the small side, with a tendency toward plumpness. Unlike the kitten, Dulcie's hair was brown, with a reddish cast and a pronounced tendency to curl, especially as late May brought the first wave of humidity to the city. For a moment, though, the two resembled each other. Esmé hesitating, as if wondering where to pounce next. Dulcie considering her small but rambunctious pet. And then, as if heeding some inner summons, the kitten turned and bounded out of the room, allowing Dulcie to turn her attention back to work.

Instead, with a smile, Dulcie watched the kitten bounce off. Rubbing the red marks those tiny teeth had left, she realized no real harm had been done. It wasn't as if the kitten's antics had interrupted anything productive. The afternoon thus far had been a waste, and the kitten might have even done her a service, waking her from her nap. The warm breeze coming in the living room window only hinted at more dreams to come, and the book at her feet suddenly looked too heavy to lift.

She should get back to work – specifically to the large and unpromising book on the floor beside her. Dulcie knew that. If only the reading waiting for her between those dull brown covers was just a little more exciting. If only, she admitted with a sigh, she could simply dive back into her long-time favorite adventure, *The Ravages of Umbria.* That book might have just as colorless a cover – Dulcie looked over at the well-worn edition that always graced her desk – but its insides were anything but.

Set in a haunted version of Italy that existed in fantasy only, *The Ravages* featured a beleaguered noblewoman who had to save herself from a panoply of dangers, including not only the usual ghosts and monks, but also the sneaky betrayal of an unfaithful friend. And the only tools she had at her disposal were her own wits. Unusual for her era, Hermetria – the heroine of *The Ravages* – was the kind of character Dulcie could really believe in. Only two segments of the book survived, which put off more casual readers, but for Dulcie, the lack of a definitive ending made the novel more compelling. Even more fascinating, the author, who had managed to remain anonymous for two centuries, just might have lived a life that was almost as tumultuous as her heroine's – although probably with fewer ghosts.

And that's where both the excitement and the trouble lay. A graduate student doing her dissertation on the Gothic fiction of the late eighteenth century, Dulcie was not only a fan of the headstrong heroine, she was also hot in pursuit of the author. Recently, she sometimes almost felt like she'd pinned the nameless writer down, that she was on the brink of solving a two-hundred-year-old literary mystery. She'd even begun dreaming about her, although in truth she couldn't be sure if her dreams were about the author, her heroine – or some fevered version of herself as she struggled with her doctoral thesis. Some people – her boyfriend was one – thought she'd gotten a bit too close to the book to retain any kind of academic objectivity about its nameless author. But why spend five, six, even seven years of your life studying something if you didn't love it? Why tackle a mystery if you didn't feel you had some insight into how it could be solved?

These weren't questions Chris, her sweetie, had answers for – but his gentle criticism still had some validity. Which was why she had put today aside for the dull necessity of non-fiction research. Specifically, in this case, textual analysis of decidedly un-fun writing. Over the course of the last year, Dulcie had found some real clues as to who her mysterious author might be – but only clues. So, in an effort to bolster her theories, Dulcie was looking for traces of the author in political writings of the day, in particular some radical pamphlets to which her author might have contributed. Or might not have, which would probably prove something, too, although Dulcie didn't even want to think about that possibility just yet.

Before her unscheduled nap – and Esmé's interruption – Dulcie had already spent the greater part of the day with the book in front of her – a collection of two-hundred-year-old essays from the fledgling United States. To say they weren't the most thrilling reading would be akin to saying Esmé wasn't the tamest of pets, but . . .

Writing a thesis wasn't supposed to be all fun and games. Or even ghosts and goblins, she reminded herself. In fact, it was the discipline of academic life – the rigor – that had first attracted Dulcie. Well, that and the realization that she might be able to make a living with the novels she loved.

Only the week before, Dulcie had finally screwed herself up to begin the actual writing of what was essentially the most important paper of her academic career. She'd begun with discipline on the Monday morning, planting herself and her laptop on the kitchen table. It had started slowly, and she'd spent so much time staring into space that even the cat had seemed bored by her. But the effort had paid off: by Friday, she was blissfully typing away on an early chapter about the novel itself. She'd been so caught up in her work that she still had her breakfast coffee mug by her side when she'd looked up to find her boyfriend watching her sometime after eight that night – but she also had a decent draft of the chapter, the first of a projected twenty.

She'd given herself the weekend off after that, but was determined to apply that same discipline to her next bit of research. Admittedly, Monday had been a bit of a waste. It was hard to change streams, she told herself, from writing to researching once again. But now it was time to put her money where her mouth was. Or, to be somewhat more accurate, to put her eyes where her ideas were. With another sigh and a quick glance around – the kitten still had not returned – she resigned herself to the inevitable. She picked up the bound volume and opened it.

Two pages in, she found her eyes growing heavy again. Out of three hundred pages, she had – she flicked through the bound volume – two-hundred eighty left. For a fleeting moment, Dulcie admitted just how grateful she had been for the kitten's violent interruption. And, as if she had picked up on some silent cue, Esmé suddenly appeared again, standing on her round haunches to bat at the air.

'You know you're not supposed to play like that, kitty.' Dulcie smiled at the sight of the little cat, white belly exposed as she reared up. But she resisted the urge to shadow-box with the cat. 'You know that.'

Esmé tilted her head to look up at her, and for a moment, Dulcie was sure the little tuxedo cat understood her. There were always signs. After all, Esmé had last attacked when Dulcie had been sleeping – and she should have been working. Not to mention that she'd been in a most distressing part of the recurring dream. And now, here the little cat was again, just when Dulcie had been thinking of her. Was Esmé psychic? Dulcie toyed with the idea – and then dismissed it. The little tuxedo cat might not have quite the communicative powers of her predecessor, the late great longhair Mr Grey, but she had revealed an ability to communicate telepathically on occasion. Still that was only when Esmé – short for Her Most Royal Principessa Esmeralda – wanted to make herself heard. Not particularly in response to any cue she had picked up from Dulcie. As much as Dulcie might have hoped the little tuxedo cat would grow into a more empathic pet, it was infinitely more likely that the cat was responding to something more prosaic. Both times, in some subtle, unconscious way, she had probably given the little beast a signal that she was available for play.

Esmé demanded Dulcie's attention when she wanted it, Dulcie realized, nursing her hand. And only when it served her purpose.

'Sometimes I feel like you can talk, when you want to.' Dulcie got up to wash her hand. Telepathic or not, Esmé could bite. 'Listening, however, is a whole different story.'

'Why does she talk like that to me?' While Dulcie hummed to herself in the bathroom, the tuxedo cat watched, wondering. 'Doesn't she know that I'm only doing my job?'

Over the humming and the gurgle of the tap, Dulcie didn't hear the series of small peeps and squeaks that were the kitten's preferred method of communication. A strange sense of well-being came over her, however, as another voice responded. She didn't hear it – only Esmé did – but as she dried her hands and thought, once more, about the tasks of the day, they all seemed feasible somehow, as if she might just get everything done. Once again, all seemed right with the world.

'She doesn't mean to be difficult, little one,' the other voice purred into a set of fuzzy black ears. 'She has great trials coming up, and she will need you – and appreciate your efforts – then.'

TWO

By the time the sun had begun to sink, the warm feeling had faded, replaced by the kind of mind-numbing boredom that would have made the intrusion of feline fangs welcome. However, Esmé was napping by then, her white nose tucked neatly beneath her black tuft of a tail, right in the center of Dulcie's desk.

'What is it about cats and paper?' Dulcie mused. One green eye opened, but the little cat knew better than to venture an answer. She might have known one wasn't necessary, for just then, the front door slammed open, knocking into the wall. And although cats are supposed to be averse to loud noises, the commotion drew the attention of the little beast, who rose in a flash and scampered off toward the tall and lanky young man who stepped in.

'I'm home!' Chris announced, redundantly. 'And I've got dumplings!'

Dulcie rose a little more slowly and went to greet her boyfriend. He was a dear, and she knew those dumplings – from Mary Chung's, if she wasn't mistaken – were a peace offering. Since moving in together two months before, they'd discovered some unpleasant differences. While their tolerance for bookish mess was fairly equal, for example, Dulcie had found herself washing a sink's worth of old and crusty dishes a few times too often. And while Dulcie didn't consider herself a girly girl by any means – her upbringing on an Oregon commune hadn't included training in lipstick or flirting – her love for long, hot showers had made Chris late for class more than once. Plus, it was likely Chris's rough-housing that had made the kitten so wild. A cat, Dulcie had told him more than once, is not a dog.

As the semester wound down, however, they'd both found themselves laughing more than they grumbled. And Tuesday-night dumplings – eaten with recyclable chopsticks – were one of their new traditions. And so she greeted him with a kiss, taking the takeout bag into the kitchen as he shed his jacket and backpack. Placing it on the counter, she opened it. Dumplings *and* . . . she took out a plastic container of spicy soup.

'Yes!' she called out, knowing Chris would understand. This wasn't just for his benefit, however, and with a little more bounce in her step, she quickly gathered the bowls and utensils necessary for their feast. Those pamphlets would go down a lot easier after some *suan la chow show*.

It was with a sinking feeling, then, that Dulcie heard the phone ring. Halfway to the living room, she had bowls in one hand, the takeout bag in the other.

'Chris?' she called. Their phone tended to migrate from the living room to the bedroom.

'Sorry!' he yelled back, and Dulcie heard water running.

Abandoning – for now – their meal, she went in search of the errant phone, finding it just as her boyfriend emerged from the bathroom. She smiled up at him as she reached for it. He'd washed his face, and his bangs were sticking up, making him look more than ever like an overgrown Dennis the Menace.

That smile disappeared when she picked up the receiver. There was nobody on the line. The phone was silent. 'Hello? *Hello*?'

Chris looked at her, concern shadowing his face.

Dulcie shrugged. 'Prank?' She mouthed the word silently, then tried once more. 'Is anybody there?'

She was about to hang up when a sudden sob broke the silence.

'Hello?' Dulcie stood up and, waving Chris off, took the phone into the kitchen. 'Who's there? Can I help you?' At times of stress, even a doctoral candidate's grammar might slip.

'It's me.' The voice, thickened by tears, belonged to her buddy and classmate, Trista. 'I didn't know who else to call.'

'Trista! Where are you?' Dulcie had never heard her friend so upset. 'What's wrong?'

'I'm in trouble, Dulcie. Big trouble.' Trista was usually the tough one of Dulcie's crew; a Victorian specialist with a very contemporary edge. Right now, though, her friend's voice sounded strangled, as if she'd been crying – or worse.

'The cops think I murdered Roland Galveston.'

THREE

Fifteen minutes later, Dulcie was eating cold dumplings and barely tasting them.

'Why did she call you, anyway?' Chris had finished his share and for the first time ever hadn't immediately gotten out the ice cream. Instead, he was sitting opposite her at their kitchen table, absently petting the kitten on his lap – and grilling Dulcie. 'I mean, you're not a lawyer. You're not her mother.'

'I'm her friend, Chris.' Dulcie felt her throat threatening to close up, and she put down the rather leathery dumpling. 'And this is – this is horrible. Roland was one of us – and he's gone. Murdered, she said.' She swallowed, hard. 'Dead.' It came out as a whisper.

'I'm sorry, sweetie. That's awful.' Chris must have heard the tears welling up in Dulcie's voice, and he abandoned Esmé to wrap his arms around his girlfriend. 'Did you know him well?'

Dulcie shook her head. 'He hasn't been here that long. Hadn't.' The tense got to her, and she bit her lip. 'And to think that *they* think that Trista . . .' She shook her head. 'She's scared, Chris. I could hear it.'

'I believe you, Dulce. And I know you care about her. I just meant, well, haven't you had enough going on? This is terrible, I know, but if she's in trouble – couldn't she find someone else to call?'

Dulcie leaned back against her boyfriend with a sigh. He had never met Roland; he couldn't entirely understand. And he liked Trista, she knew that. Plus, Trista's boyfriend was his best friend and former room-mate. He was only being protective – and with reason. Not only was Dulcie in the middle of her thesis, she'd only recently recovered from a crisis with one of her students.

'It's just that . . .' Chris let his protest trail off. He didn't have to finish it. Dulcie knew what he meant. After the turmoil of the previous months, she was still a little off her game; the way those tears had sprung up so fast only proved that she hadn't yet recovered her normal resilience.

'I want you to take care of yourself first,' Chris blurted out.

Dulcie nodded and looked down to see Esmé's green eyes staring up at her. Maybe the kitten was hoping for treats, but Dulcie suspected something bigger. Something about those eyes – which as the kitten had matured had become the same color as Mr Grey's – gave her courage. She began reciting the facts.

'I know, Chris, but Trista is my friend. I have experience with the police. I know the ins and outs of, well, of the local justice system and the law school's legal aid program. And –' she swallowed – 'I've also been accused of murder.'

'Exactly,' he murmured into her curls, but she had a sneaking feeling he, too, was looking at the kitten.

'All the more reason for me to help her.' Dulcie twisted around to peer up at her beau. Now that she had a project to focus on, her eyes were clear and dry. 'Roland is – well, I can't do anything for him now. But Tris isn't a murderer, any more than you or I.'

With that, the kitten landed on the table, knocking over the dipping sauce and putting the conversation to an end.

Dulcie knew what she had to do, even if Chris didn't want to let it – or her – go. 'Sweetie, let me walk with you at least.' He was finishing the clean-up as Dulcie donned her sweater. 'I've got to be in the computer lab by nine, anyway.'

Dulcie glanced at the clock. 'You just got home, Chris. Take some time for yourself.' That wasn't the issue, and she knew it.

Chris sputtered a bit, and then confirmed her suspicion. 'But Dulce, Trista's all the way in the Square.'

Dulcie would have given him a look – *the* look, as he'd named it, the one that ended all discussion – only she had to concentrate on the buttons. Her oatmeal-colored sweater, one of her mother's more creative efforts, had become a favorite as the New England spring began to thaw the city, its nubbly texture making up for the fact that its buttons didn't quite match up. When she was done, she looked up at her boyfriend. 'Chris. I walk it every day. Besides, it's still light out.'

He had no rebuttal to that, but he looked so miserable that Dulcie went over and kissed him again. 'It'll be OK. I promise. Besides –' she headed toward the door – 'I'm just a bystander this time. What trouble can I get into?'

As the door closed behind her, Dulcie heard a crash and then

Chris's voice calling the kitten's name, frustration if not anger tightening his voice. 'At least it isn't just me,' she said to herself as she headed off into the twilight.

Chris's apartment – hers too for the last few months – lay in the bottom of Cambridgeport, an old neighborhood tucked into a bend of the Charles River. Once heavily industrial, a remnant of the college town's blue-collar roots, the area was now largely residential, and as Dulcie walked by the former factories-turned-lofts and into an area of single-family houses, it occurred to her that she could almost forget that she was in a city. That, she suspected, was what Chris had been worried about. Quiet as it was, Cambridgeport still had an urban crime rate, and for all she knew, her colleague's death could have been the result of random street crime. It was hard to be nervous, however, when she could smell someone's lilacs in the cool, damp air.

As she walked, she tried to make sense of what her friend had told her. Roland Galveston wasn't someone she knew well, but she certainly knew *of* him. The young scholar had come from Vanderbilt on a one-year fellowship, and Dulcie, along with everyone else in her department, had gone to hear his fellowship-mandated talk. Roland's specialty wasn't hers; he focused on the late Victorians, who had always seemed somewhat overwritten and, if she thought about it, constipated, compared to her own late-eighteenth-century writers. Still, he'd been a colleague – a young man of promise. To think of him gone, as dead – murdered – sent a chill down her spine. She wrapped her sweater a bit tighter and tried to focus, instead, on the problem at hand.

Her area of expertise – the great Gothic novelists of the 1790s – might not get the attention of the Victorians, but it didn't have the rivalries either. And while Roland's fellowship had come with some kind of cushy research job, she was out there teaching – spreading the word about her author. Crossing Brookline Street to walk on the sunny side, Dulcie relaxed a little and mulled over Trista's words. Why would anyone want to kill Roland – and why would anyone suspect Trista? Galveston was a rising star. Of course, he'd have enemies. But murderous ones? Rivalries existed in the department. They always did, and the recent budget crunch hadn't made things any easier. But people dealt with them in civilized ways. Back-stabbing was metaphorical at the university, and even at the worst of times it would not amount to more than some ill-founded rumor or perhaps a nasty anonymous note.

Maybe that's what had gotten Trista in trouble, Dulcie thought as she made her way down the street. Maybe someone had spread a nasty rumor about her friend – not because of anything to do with Roland Galveston, but to hurt Trista. Only, murder was a pretty serious accusation to hurl at someone, wasn't it?

Under ordinary conditions, Trista would have been laughing at the idea. Somewhat tougher than her curly-haired friend, Trista would have told Dulcie that it sounded 'like one of your books, Dulce. Only, without a ghost.'

The breeze off the river was cool, even in the fading sun, and Dulcie shivered again, pulling the collar of the oatmeal sweater up around her neck. This wasn't a story from one of her books. Dulcie not only had some experience with crimes at the university, she also knew a bit more about ghosts than she'd ever confessed to her friend. But this time, she hadn't been given a clue as to what was really going on. All she knew was that one of her colleagues was dead. And when her friend had called, she hadn't been laughing.

FOUR

T rista had dried her tears by the time Dulcie arrived, but Dulcie almost wished she hadn't. The blonde Victorian had let her in and had been pacing since, despite her friend's repeated requests for her to sit.

'I can't, Dulce,' Trista had said, finally, when Dulcie had gone so far as to take her arm. 'I'm just too freaked out!'

Dulcie looked at her friend, unsure of what to say. Trista had always been a bit of a contradiction. Most of the English department grad students were rather geeky. Dulcie knew that was one reason she was comfortable there, among bookworms like herself. And although the small department was prey to all the usual gossip and intrigues, it was usually a friendly place. If Dulcie hadn't been a confirmed cat person, she'd thought, on more than one occasion, that she could easily see them all as dormice – burrowing away into some dark, private corner of a great library.

Trista, though, had stood out from the start. Visually, her short spiky bleached hair and figure-baring outfits were out of place among their rather shaggy and decidedly unfashionable lot. And her piercings – starting with the gold stud in her nose – tended to startle those who only knew her area of expertise. The contrast went beyond the visual: unlike most of their quiet colleagues, Trista had always been brash. A little louder, a little more outspoken than anyone else in the department, Trista scared a good many of their colleagues – the men especially. But Dulcie, who had suffered with her through qualifying exams and horrendous teaching loads, knew a different side of the slight blonde. Trista worked at her tough demeanor. If she was pacing, it was because she was terrified. Because she didn't dare say so, and because she couldn't make a run for it.

'Tris, please. You're making me dizzy.' As much as Dulcie sympathized, her friend's manic movement was interrupting her own thought process. 'Please, sit here and tell me once again what happened.'

With a sigh that Dulcie hoped let off some of the pressure inside, Trista collapsed on the sofa. That she immediately picked up a pencil and began to twirl it between her fingers was annoying, but Dulcie let that go – for Trista had begun to talk.

'You know about the Rattigan prize, right?' The question was rhetorical, although Dulcie nodded anyway. Everyone in the department knew about the Rattigan – one of the few academic honors that still came with a substantial stipend. 'And you know I'm almost ready to defend, right?' Another nod. Trista had pulled slightly ahead of her friend in the race to finish her doctoral dissertation. 'Well, that's it.'

With that, she clamped her mouth shut, but not before Dulcie saw the telltale tremor in her lips. 'Oh, Tris!' Dulcie's heart went out to her friend, and she moved closer just in time. Trista broke out sobbing once again, and Dulcie patted her back while she tried to piece everything together.

Trista, she knew, had been working all out through the winter, pushing herself past the point of exhaustion. Although her thesis wasn't anything Dulcie cared about – something about architectural details in the mid-Victorian novel – Dulcie had been impressed by how comprehensive Trista's research had been. She had gotten permission to read rare manuscripts – first drafts of books that were now long forgotten – and she had backed this primary research up with supporting material, from diaries to contemporary reviews. The Victorians, Dulcie knew this much, saved everything – and Trista had done her best to read it all, as well as keep up with all the modern scholars in her field. It had been an impressive feat, and anyone who looked over at the slight, pierced blonde and thought 'airhead' was going to have another thought coming once she published.

Trista started hiccuping, and Dulcie reached for the Kleenex. Publishing. That was key, but Trista seemed to have a clear road ahead of her. Once she defended her thesis, she could revise it – two university presses had already approached her, an almost unheard of bounty. And the Rattigan? Nothing in life was ever certain, but Trista was viewed in the department as the likely winner. In addition to the money – a rarity as the university increasingly shuffled to protect its dwindling endowment – the one-year post-doc that came with it was seen as a stepping stone to a tenure track position. And for Trista, Dulcie knew, it meant one more year in Cambridge, where her boyfriend Jerry was finishing his own graduate studies. It meant, in brief, happiness.

Trista's hiccups had subsided, and Dulcie suggested tea. As she made her way into Trista's kitchen, she added Roland Galveston to the equation. The newcomer was smart, sure, but had he been a threat to Trista? Academic positions were few and far between, but Dulcie didn't think she was being too much of a Pollyanna to assume that there might be jobs for both of them.

As she waited for the water to boil, she forced herself to think rationally. That was, after all, supposed to be her forte. What were Trista's chances – and how did Roland affect them? Not everyone became a professor, after all; Dulcie had heard of several doctorates and almost-doctorates who dropped out, overwhelmed either by the pressure or the tide of rejections. That didn't mean the end of the world. Last fall, an all-but-dissertation had made a big deal about going on to business school, and a recent grad had landed a position with a ritzy New York auction house, appraising rare books. Dulcie rummaged through the cabinet, looking for clean mugs. Trista was dedicated. Smart. She was also a mess. Academia hadn't been kind to her.

Was it the wrong path for her friend? No; she shook her head. Trista was no more likely than Dulcie to give up her dream of a scholar's life. But would she have felt threatened by Roland Galveston?

If anything, Jerry had seemed more concerned about the newcomer than his girlfriend had, as the dashing Texan had shown what might have been more than a scholarly interest in his pretty colleague. Could that mean that Jerry . . .? As she returned with two mugs of peppermint tea, Dulcie realized she had to gather a little more info.

'Tris, if you can, would you run through it again?' She sipped her tea gingerly and still managed to burn her lip. Running her tongue over the tender spot, she thought about what Trista had already told her. Now that her friend had calmed down, she was wondering if she had missed something. 'I mean, well, did they find – um – something?'

Another hiccup. 'I'm not sure. There were two of them, both plain clothes. They showed up saying they had questions. Questions concerning "the late Roland Galveston". And the way they looked at me was enough. Dulcie, I think they didn't have enough to charge me, but was clear they thought I had done something. One of the cops was asking about the Rattigan, about my research habits.' She took a swallow of her own tea, oblivious to the heat. 'He even asked about Jerry and our plans. Like, were we hurting for money.'

'That's crazy. Everyone we know is broke.' It struck her that Tris still hadn't answered her question. 'But, Tris, do they even know—' Dulcie was suddenly at a loss for words. 'I mean, did they find a body or something?'

Another shake of the head. 'I don't know, Dulcie. I don't know *anything*. All I know is the way they referred to him – to Roland – and then the way they questioned me. And they told me not to leave town.'

Dulcie was about to dismiss that as so much dramatic nonsense, when it hit her. Trista *had* to leave town – leave the state, actually. She was scheduled to give a lecture at Brown University in Providence in a few days. While Tris was hoping for the Rattigan, she couldn't count on it, and such guest appearances were the academic equivalent of Broadway auditions. If nothing was certain, if Trista wasn't being charged with anything, surely, the police would make an exception for that.

'The Kiplinger Lecture?' She didn't have to say more.

Trista only shrugged. 'I didn't dare ask. I mean, it's just a job. It's not worth getting arrested over. Is it?'

'I don't know.' Dulcie tried her tea again. This was getting serious. 'Have you talked to anyone at the legal clinic? Do you want me to call Suze?' Dulcie's former room-mate would be graduating from the law school in a few weeks, but Dulcie knew she'd make time to help a friend.

If the friend wanted help. Trista only shrugged. 'I don't know. I really don't, Dulce. I mean, what can they do?'

Dulcie opened her mouth – and then shut it. Trista was upset enough. 'Why don't we start at the beginning?' she asked instead. 'Tell me exactly what happened when the police came. Tell me what they said.'

Still sniffling, Trista ran through it all again. From the first knock on her door by the plain-clothes detectives to her panicked call. An ordinary Tuesday evening had been utterly destroyed. The whole visit – Dulcie did some quick calculating – had probably only taken about twenty minutes.

'So, they didn't advise you to seek counsel?' Years of living with Suze had taught Dulcie a few things.

'I don't think so.' The normally sharp Trista was sounding a little unsure. 'Just, you know, that I shouldn't leave town.'

'And tell me again – what exactly did they say about Roland?' Something was bothering Dulcie. Something she couldn't quite identify.

'Just that one phrase – calling him "the late". I don't think the cop was supposed to tell me that; the other guy – shorter guy – gave him a look that shut him up. But it was the way they talked about him, you know? Like they were trying hard not to use the past tense.' She paused. To English majors, this was important. Still, Dulcie wanted to know more.

'And then?' she prompted her friend.

Another shake of her blonde hair. 'They wanted to know when I'd last seen him. What my "relationship" with him was.' Trista used her fingers to make air quotes around the word.

'Relationship?' Dulcie looked at her friend, trying to see beyond her stoic front. Although Trista and Jerry had been living together for months now, they'd gone through a rough patch, and Dulcie knew her friend had gone out with other guys in the interim. 'Tris, were you and Roland . . .?'

'Roland? He's – no.' Trista reached for another tissue, and for a moment Dulcie wondered if her friend was avoiding her gaze. 'He's not my type.'

It wasn't what she'd started to say, of that Dulcie was sure. A horrible thought crept into Dulcie's mind. 'Tris, you don't think that Jerry thinks . . .' She let it hang. Jerry was a computer geek and Chris's best friend. Hardly the sort to act out of jealous rage. However, he did love Trista – and she had led him a merry chase for a while this past winter. 'He wouldn't get in a fight or anything. Would he?'

'I don't think so.' Trista shrugged and turned away. 'Not Jerry.'

'Did the cops ask about him? About Jerry?' Something was wrong. Dulcie wasn't psychic – she didn't believe in that stuff, not really. But something had changed.

'No, just what I told you. They came over. They asked me when I'd last seen Roland and, and . . . that other stuff. Then they told me not to leave town for a while.' Trista had regained her composure now and was dabbing at her nose, which was red against its little gold stud. 'Then they left and I called you.'

'Huh.' Dulcie couldn't place it. And so she finished her tea. Trista seemed calmer – or at least somewhat distracted. Though she was once again walking around, her route – gathering papers, a notebook that had fallen behind the sofa, and her laptop – looked to have more purpose. In fact, as Dulcie stood up to return her mug to the kitchen, Tris followed her. Dulcie had the distinct impression that although her friend had summoned her, she now wanted Dulcie to leave.

'Well, I guess we'll hear more. The department has probably been informed.' She put the mug in the sink and turned to face her friend. Trista was looking at the window. By now the late twilight had faded and her own face, pale and pierced, stared back. 'Tris . . .' Dulcie's heart went out to her friend. 'Do you want me to follow up, maybe, with Suze?'

'I guess so.' She shrugged. Dulcie had never heard her sound so vague. Then again, all the tears must have worn her out. 'Yeah, that would be good.'

Exhaustion, Dulcie decided, and she leaned in to hug her

friend. Trista hesitated a moment, she could feel the slender body tense up. Then she hugged her back and took a deep breath. 'Thanks, Dulce.' The ghost of a smile flickered on her face. 'You're a pal.'

'It's nothing.' Dulcie tried to smile back. Roland might be beyond help; Trista wasn't. 'Now, back to work!'

It was a weak joke, but it relaxed them both. And Dulcie headed out into the night, trying very hard to figure out what had just happened – and why her friend was being so evasive.

Chris was gone by the time she got home, and the kitten was sacked out on the sofa. Looking at the soft white belly, Dulcie had a sneaking feeling that Chris had given the little cat some extra treats. Sure enough, the last of the dumplings had been eviscerated, its dough wrapper lying in the trash.

The kitten followed her into the kitchen as Dulcie made herself a peanut butter and jelly sandwich: open-faced. She'd had enough of carbohydrates for the night. She brought the plate into the living room and sat opposite the couch. Esmé jumped up as if on cue, flopping on her back and squirming a bit. While the little cat didn't seem to be in distress, she had probably had enough spiced pork for a lifetime, Dulcie decided. Well, she wouldn't begrudge her the dumpling now.

Besides, Esmé upside down was particularly adorable, Dulcie thought to herself as she ate. Staring at a cat always helped her concentrate, and right now her brain didn't seem to be firing on all cylinders. The peanut butter was good, salty and rich, but she knew the snack was more procrastination than nutrition. Despite their supposedly radical content, those essays were the driest part of her research thus far – and they were a necessary evil. All of her colleagues had to read material they didn't love. When she thought of what Trista had plowed through, she shuddered.

Another thought made her shiver again, despite the humidity that had closed down the earlier cool evening breeze. Trista. There was something wrong with what her friend had been telling her. Something she couldn't quite put her finger on. Dulcie took another bite and tried to figure out what was bothering her.

There were a lot of options. Maybe, she thought hopefully, Trista had been wrong about the whole thing. Maybe Roland wasn't even dead – or not murdered, anyway. Trista had been so hazy about what had happened – even about what she had been asked. If someone had come to question Dulcie, she'd have remembered his – or her – name, for sure. She'd probably have gotten a badge number. Then again, living with Suze as her friend went through law school might have given her an unusual perspective. And Trista had reason to be preoccupied, didn't she? Dulcie looked at Esmé for an answer, but the little cat remained silent.

The second question was why Trista had been so reticent about soliciting help. Once she'd unburdened herself to Dulcie, she'd seemed ready to forget the whole thing. As Esmé stretched out along the sofa, Dulcie answered that one for herself. Trista had her hands full: the Kiplinger prize, the lecture in Providence, the defense of her thesis . . . there was only so much even a particularly sharp human mind could contain.

Besides, Dulcie had almost promised to ask Suze about it. Trista hadn't come this far without being organized. At some level, she probably considered the problem delegated. She hadn't been charged, not yet, and she'd done what she could, following a first interrogation. When she was a full professor and had a team of graduate students laboring under her that would be a useful skill.

Dulcie, however, could not let go of anything so easily. Maybe that was why Trista had pulled ahead of her in the race to finish. She and Trista had passed their general exams the same semester. They had even settled on their topics at around the same time. But still, Dulcie knew she was at least a year away from finishing, whereas Trista could be gone by September.

The idea of finishing boggled the mind, and – staring at Esmé for answers – Dulcie wondered if that was in fact one reason she wasn't yet done. True, research had been a little easier for Trista: those Victorians documented every aspect of their lives, whereas Dulcie really had to dig to find out about her subject. But that had been a large part of the appeal of Dulcie's topic. She had fallen in love with the nearly forgotten Gothic novel, *The Ravages of Umbria*, in part because of its obscurity. Not only was the author unknown, the work itself – what was left of it – was usually dismissed as so much sensationalist claptrap – yet another goosebump-raising tale of an orphaned heiress trapped in a lonely tower. The ornate – some would say 'overwritten' – prose had wrapped her in its spell and convinced her that there was more to the book, and its nameless author, than just some cheap high-jinks, or another 'She-Author' trying to make some quick eighteenth-century pence.

And it wasn't like Dulcie hadn't made any progress. Through scrupulous textual analysis, Dulcie had just about proven that the wild adventure did have more to it than ghosts and unfaithful knights. Had, in fact, proven that the nameless author had used her fun fiction to lay out a powerful argument for women's rights. An argument that might have caused her to take ship and flee from London to the New World. But to support that initial discovery, Dulcie was now compelled to wade through what felt like an ocean of other political writings, and that's where she'd got bogged down.

'It's like my reward is to read more drudgery,' she complained to the kitten. Esmé flipped her head and pinned her with one green eye. 'You're right, Esmé,' Dulcie told her. 'I shouldn't be worrying about my own work when my friend is in trouble.'

The kitten mewed softly and flipped over, and for the life of her Dulcie couldn't tell if the little beast was reacting to the Chinese food or making a comment on her person's ability to avoid unpleasant work.

'Well, it's not like I don't have the best excuse in the world,' Dulcie said. Esmé watched her head to the kitchen, but wisely declined to comment.

FIVE

'Suze, she's not the sort to panic.' It wasn't really a question where Dulcie's obligations lay, and after a longing look at her papers, she had reached Suze on her cell. Although it was after nine, her former room-mate was in the Coop. She'd been in line to pick up her graduation gown and her requisite Doctor of Laws collar – the student-centric store stayed open late as Commencement drew close – but she'd stepped between the racks to give some impromptu legal advice. 'Trista's as tough as they come.'

'What? Sorry, you go ahead.' Suze tended to multitask, but

this was asking a lot. 'But, Dulcie, you said the police didn't charge her, right? They didn't even say specifically why they were there?'

'No, I mean, yes. That's right.' Even sitting in her living room, Dulcie could get flustered. It didn't help that Esmé had shaken off the effects of the spicy dumplings and was practically doing backflips with her new toy mouse, her white paws acting like little semaphore flags in the fading light. 'She said they just asked her about her relationship with Roland, whatever that means.'

Suze made a noise that suggested she had her own ideas, and Dulcie bit her lip. Especially as graduation grew near, Suze had gotten a little less tolerant of some of her one-time roomie's friends – though never with Dulcie herself. For a moment, Dulcie thought of Esmé and her own impatience, but the kitten had rocketed out of the room, leaving her person in the growing gloom.

'Suze, she and Jerry were just going through a phase.' Ever since meeting Ariano the previous summer, Suze had become a big fan of monogamy. 'And, besides, that isn't the cops' concern.'

'Hang on.' Dulcie heard shuffling and imagined her tall, athletic friend shrugging into the long, black gown. Three weeks, and Suze would no longer be a student. For Dulcie, with at least a year – minimum – ahead, the idea was almost incomprehensible. So much had changed since they'd met in sophomore year. 'Hey, did you hear the Kenyan ambassador is going to be one of the honorees? Sorry, so go through it again. What exactly did she tell you the police said?'

Dulcie noted how Suze had qualified her question. Her friend was going to be a wonderful advocate, but right now it was a little annoying. For what felt like the fourteenth time, she ran through everything that had happened – everything that Trista had said had happened, she corrected herself. Out of the corner of her eye, she saw a feline shape jump up to the window sill and begin to groom. The image was comforting. Some things did stay the same. 'And then they told her not to leave town.'

'Huh.' Suze's tone said it all. 'Somehow, I doubt a police detective said that.'

'What do you mean?' The cat, silhouetted against the window, looked larger than Esmé. In the late afternoon light, the long guard hairs almost glowed.

'I think your friend has an active imagination, Dulcie.'

'But . . .' Dulcie paused. Suze had once accused her of getting carried away by her fancies. That's what happened, she had figured out, when a law student lives with a literature major. 'Would they say anything more if they weren't ready to charge her?'

Another sigh. Dulcie waited, a new thought forming in her head. That cat – it was hard to see in this light – but wasn't the fur longer than Esmé's? The silhouette a little larger and leaner?

'—overdramatizing a situation.' Suze had been talking, and Dulcie had missed it.

'So, you think she made the whole thing up?' That much she'd gotten.

'I'm not saying she made it all up, but if she was really a suspect in a murder investigation there'd be more going on than two plain-clothes cops simply dropping by. Even if they didn't yet have a warrant for her arrest. They didn't even confirm that this guy is dead. Maybe there's something going on with him, something else that they want to investigate. Maybe an identity theft issue, or something with a fellowship or work. I mean, does he have a campus job?'

Dulcie shrugged. 'Probably. I think the fellowship comes with a position – something in the library or one of the conservation labs.'

'Well, maybe there's something going on outside of his studies.' Suze was on a roll. 'Maybe, I don't know, maybe *he's* done something that's making the police talk to his female colleagues. Something that would make them wish he was gone – even talk about him as "the late".'

Suze didn't have to elaborate. The campus had been rocked by a sexual harassment scandal not that long ago. 'Well, why did Trista feel threatened by them?'

'Didn't you say she's defending her thesis next week?' In the background, Dulcie heard a PA announcement. Nine forty-five, the store was probably closing. 'Look, unless somebody shows up with a warrant, I really wouldn't worry about this, 'kay, Dulcie? I've got to run.'

'Bye.' Dulcie let her friend run off. Chris was working as usual; the overnight help-desk positions in the computer lab paid the best. Right now, that was fine. She leaned back on the old sofa and watched the silhouetted cat continue his methodical bath.

'Mr Grey, what do you think of all this?' She had no doubt now. Although the cat on the window sill remained shadowy in the fading light, his shape, his form, even his calm composure let her know that her former feline had once again appeared. But as so often happened, the vision remained silent. Dulcie wondered if there was some rule – she could hear her former pet or see him. Rarely did she experience both, and right now, she longed to hear what she'd come to think of as his voice, soft and deep. Still, the sight of him was immensely comforting. Maybe Suze was right. Maybe Trista had a bad case of stage fright and had made some kind of routine visit larger than it was. It was a stretch, but then again, Trista had spent the last four years embedded in Victorian melodrama.

It hit her like cold water. Like a gust of winter in the warm spring night. Dulcie had sensed something was wrong, and Suze had been sure she was overreacting. If her former room-mate hadn't been so distracted, she would undoubtedly have noticed it herself. As cool and calmly as she could, Dulcie went through it all one more time. What Trista had told her on the phone. What Trista had told her about the police visit. What she had repeated – both back to Trista and then to Suze, with her almost-legal mind. No wonder Suze had dismissed it. Dulcie took a deep breath of relief.

Trista could not have been accused of murder. Nobody had actually said that Roland Galveston was dead.

It was the pressure. It had to be. Dulcie knew how hard her friend had been working. Next week, she'd be facing the ultimate test. Maybe Trista had had a little breakdown – a 'brain melt', as the grad students called it. It happened to all of them eventually, and Trista with her cool exterior was probably a little more brittle than most.

Still, something was up. It was easy for Suze to dismiss Trista's concerns. Dulcie had sat with her, had held her as she cried. Dulcie believed the police had visited her friend and colleague and had warned her about something. The trick would be finding out what was going on – with Trista, with Roland, with the Rattigan, maybe – without disturbing her buddy's fragile equilibrium any more.

'I can do this.' Dulcie reached for the phone. She'd call Trista and reassure her, first off. Then she'd start thinking. Maybe even go back to talk to her. 'I'm a researcher, too, Mr Grey. I bet there's a simple way to get to the bottom of this.' She didn't want to turn the lights on – not while the shadow of her beloved cat kept her company. The movement though – or maybe it was the sudden determined tone of her voice – had disturbed him. As she pulled the phone on to her lap, she looked up to see him arching – his fur bristling and his tail fluffed out to three times its normal size as he stared out at something in the dark.

'What is it, Mr Grey? Is something out there?' She ran over to the window and peered into the yard. All she could see were shadows. 'Is it a dog? Another cat?' She could no longer see her old friend beside her, but she felt the touch of fur against her bare arm, soft as velvet and as comforting.

'It's not something in the yard, is it, Mr Grey?' She turned toward where he had been. By some trick of the light, two green sparks were reflected off the window. Two green sparks that now stared into her own eyes, bright with a warning intensity. 'Suze is wrong, isn't she? There's something dangerous out there.' The sparks flared once – and were gone.

SIX

She wasn't keen on going out again, that was for sure. The night – Cambridgeport – had suddenly grown to seem threatening. However, her original plan still made sense: research usually held the answer. A quick Google search – plugging in 'crime', 'murder', and the university itself – didn't bring up anything of interest, but that wasn't necessarily conclusive, and so she used her laptop to call up the department directory. Then with a deep breath for courage, Dulcie returned to the phone. She'd call Roland directly. That would be the simplest thing. Of course, if he answered, she'd have to come up with some excuse for calling. Well, there was a departmental meeting scheduled for the morning. She could always claim to be unsure about the time or something.

Thinking of that sparked an idea: if she couldn't reach Roland – she checked the clock – she could conceivably call Martin Thorpe, the acting head of the department. The problem was, she'd been ducking Thorpe for days. In addition to running the little fiefdom of bookish scholars, the balding scholar was her thesis adviser. He had already expressed doubt about some of her theories, his own expertise leading him to tut-tut her 'headstrong ways', as he so quaintly put it. And instead of being impressed with the chapter she'd drafted the week before, he seemed to expect her to be more productive. She was working as fast as she could – writing as she researched, even if it did make her feel a little like she was getting dressed before she'd put her underwear on. Still, with Thorpe, she sometimes felt like she couldn't win.

'Less thought and more writing,' she grumbled as she scrolled down the phone list. 'Doesn't he remember what it was like? How hard it is, to pull everything together?'

It wasn't just Thorpe, Dulcie knew. Part of it was her thesis topic itself. No matter how good a case she made for *The Ravages of Umbria* and its nameless author, most of her colleagues would never take the work seriously. To them, all the Gothics were cheap fiction, churned out to amuse a newly literate class of shop girls and merchants' wives. Never mind that these books were some of the first fiction written by and for women, never mind that *The Ravages* – what had survived of it – rose above the conventions of the genre – all they saw were the ghosts and abductions, the exotic locales and the overwrought plots, and, in the case of her favorite, an incomplete plot at that. The fact that these books were meant to evoke strong emotions probably played against them, Dulcie had long ago realized. Nothing that much fun would ever be taken seriously by many of her colleagues.

Her thesis adviser, though – he should know better. 'He could at least *pretend* to like the work,' said Dulcie. The kitten yawned, stretching out one white mitten, reminding Dulcie how late it was. Too late to call Thorpe, she realized with relief. But if she wasn't going to work on her thesis, she should at least clear up this mess.

'Hi, you've reached virtual Roland . . .' Dulcie listened to the voicemail, only realizing at the last moment that she should have prepared something to say.

'Um, Roland? This is Dulcie. Dulcie Schwartz.' She gave her

number and hung up without mentioning the meeting, feeling as flustered as a freshman with a crush. What was it about the visiting scholar? Unlike some of the departmental superstars who had blazed through, the Texan wasn't particularly tall or handsome. Sandy-haired, with more freckles than Dulcie herself would sprout come summer, he had a nice enough face, despite a Chaucerian gap between his two front teeth. Maybe it was that gap – or maybe it was his reputation. Despite Trista's best efforts to engage her, she could never tell one idealized Dickensian waif from the next, so she couldn't tell for sure if Roland was as smart as he was rumored to be. No, it must be the gap.

Chris had a perfectly lovely face as well, Dulcie caught herself. And not only was he brilliant – he'd graduate summa, one day – but he was also kind. Dulcie knew her boyfriend worked the overnight shifts largely for the overnight bonus, but even when he was as sleep deprived as the panicked freshmen who flocked to his cubicle, he was as gentle and helpful as . . . well, as Martin Thorpe wasn't.

Right now, however, Chris was at work. And so, steeling herself, Dulcie reached once more for the phone – only to have it start ringing.

'Hello?' Dulcie heard the hesitation in her own voice. If this was Roland calling her back . . .

She needn't have worried. 'Dulcinea! I *knew* you'd be there.' Her mother's boisterous voice called out from what sounded like the middle of a percussion ensemble.

'Hi, Lucy.' Dulcie relaxed. Her mother had never quite gotten the idea that since she'd gotten a cell phone, she was usually within reach. 'What's up?'

'I think you know.' Lucy's voice took on a sing-song quality that made Dulcie sigh. Despite Mr Grey's continued presence in her life, Dulcie didn't really buy the idea of the supernatural influencing everyday life. Growing up on the commune – the arts colony, as her mother called it – had been enough to make the most romantic New Ager into a hardened realist. And Dulcie had spent enough years scrambling to make sure the utility bills were paid to not have much faith in the benevolence of the universe.

'Why don't you tell me?' Dulcie lay back on the sofa, tucking her feet under the now sleeping kitten.

'Don't you feel the energy, Dulcie? Don't you feel the heat?' Behind Lucy, someone started singing. The communal kitchen, Dulcie figured, conjuring up her memories of the loud, crowded space. 'Can't you just feel it?'

'The solstice,' Dulcie said, as much to herself as to her mother. Of course, even though the beginning of summer was still weeks away, the brethren – Dulcie tried not to think of them as 'inmates' – would be starting preparations already. At least, along with the incantations and midnight yoga, the kitchen would get a thorough cleaning. If Matilda were still there, anyway. 'Is Ma—Sparrowhawk still among you?' She seemed to recall something about the older woman leaving.

'Yes, her soul quest brought her back in February.' Lucy's voice started to fade against the cacophony, and Dulcie missed some of what came next. '—more a voyage of self-discovery.'

So the romance hadn't lasted. Poor woman. Dulcie felt another pang of gratitude for Chris – and affection for her mom. 'Thanks. I was just thinking of her for some reason,' she explained. Lucy would never have asked, Dulcie knew that. To do so would be to deny her sensitivity, as she saw it.

'Of course you did, dear.' Lucy's perkiness had returned. 'She's why I'm calling.'

'Oh?' For some reason, Dulcie suddenly felt exhausted.

'Yes, dear.' Lucy didn't seem to notice. 'Since Sparrowhawk returned, she's been having visions, and last night, we did a circle together.'

Could two people make a circle? Dulcie didn't want to ask.

'It was a full moon, as I'm sure you'd noticed.'

Dulcie grunted something that she hoped sounded positive. She had been having strange dreams, though these seemed more in keeping with her work than with the watery light that seeped through Chris's ancient blinds. Her response seemed enough for Lucy.

'And after we chanted for a while, Sparrowhawk had her vision. Dulcie – you and Chris are going to come out here for the solstice. For the solar energy.'

'Mom.' Enough was enough. Dulcie and Chris both had undergraduates who they had to see through the last throes of finals. Then Dulcie wanted to be here for Suze's graduation. Suze's mother was coming up from New Jersey, as well as a score of cousins who Dulcie had never met. After Commencement, the campus would quiet down for a few weeks. And in those precious few weeks, before the summer-school students flooded the city, Dulcie would finally be able to get some work done. It was true, she and Chris had talked about taking a vacation. Maybe even taking the bus out to the West Coast – and Lucy – during the last weeks of August. June, though? No, it wasn't going to happen. 'Chris and I are working. We're going full out, and we don't have the time—'

'That's it, Dulcinea. You don't have the time.' The uproar around her mother seemed to have died down. Either everyone was eating, or Lucy had managed to drag the phone into a closet. 'Neither of you has the time. The spirits are out of alignment at this. Already, someone close to you has been taken, Dulcie. And I'm not going to let my daughter be swallowed up by evil, too.'

SEVEN

The kitten did her best. Still, after fifteen minutes of concerted play, Esmé was sacked out on the sofa with the kind of graceless abandon that only a cat can make look comfortable, and Dulcie was even more aware of the isolation of the apartment. She couldn't call it quiet, really. Someone's salsa music could be felt, as much as heard, through the walls, just loud enough to reassure Dulcie that there were other people alive in the building. But after reading another long paper explaining why women did not need to be educated, she found herself beginning to agree.

Lucy's call had been distressing for all the usual reasons – maternal loneliness, maternal battiness – but if it had shattered her focus, at least it had also shaken Dulcie from her own paranormal fears. She would work later. Now she needed something. She wasn't hungry, exactly. But it might be time for . . .

'Midnight pizza!' Chris looked up from his workstation, surprise spreading a broad grin across his thin face. 'My heroine!'

'Those dumplings were a long time ago.' Dulcie didn't mention the peanut butter – or the earlier premonition that had still made her a little nervous about setting out. A sweaty undergrad looked up from a nearby cubicle. 'Sorry,' she mouthed silently. He ducked back down without comment.

Chris tore off a slice, and after a moment's hesitation, Dulcie joined him. The two munched in companionable quiet, the few stragglers leaving them in peace for the moment. 'So,' Chris said, finally, as he folded his last slice in half. 'What's up?'

'I couldn't just have missed you?' She was teasing. It felt good to talk to someone who didn't claim to know everything before it was laid out. Since his mouth was full of pizza, she explained. First, the situation with Trista and Roland and her own realization about Trista's flawed interrogation. Then her inability to reach Roland – and the call from Lucy.

Chris rolled his eyes at that. When they'd first started seeing each other, Dulcie had been worried that her unconventional upbringing – and her most unconventional mother – would put off the serious mathematician. But Chris's logical mind had been charmed by Dulcie's past. At times, she'd begun to worry he'd romanticized it, making the commune out to be more idyllic than his own straightforward working-class roots. He certainly failed to see why Lucy's eccentricities bothered Dulcie quite as much as they did.

'This isn't Lucy being all charming and fairy dust,' she said in her own defense, finishing off her own last slice. 'This was creepy.'

'You know she misses you.' Chris picked some cheese off the box. 'She'd probably say anything to get you to come out this summer.'

'Well, scaring me isn't the way to do it.' Comfortably full and sitting with her boyfriend, Dulcie felt the strange edginess begin to fade. 'Though I guess I should call her more.'

'That's not what's bothering you, though.'

'Not really. I mean, Suze didn't take the whole thing with Trista seriously to begin with, and nobody has actually said anything about Roland being dead. I mean, no text message from the department, nothing. But . . .' She let it hang, unsure of how to continue.

'You don't know if Trista knows something that hasn't been made public yet, that she can't talk about, or if there's something else going on,' Chris said, finishing the thought. 'And it's too late to call Thorpe now, or anyone else in the department, right?'

Dulcie nodded.

'And I'm stuck here working, and when you go home, you'll be alone.'

'I've got Esmé.' She could almost laugh about it now.

'Who, if I guess right, will be asleep when you're awake – and rampaging around the house when you're finally ready to conk out.'

Dulcie nodded in agreement.

'Do you want to work here for a while?' His voice had become gentle with concern. 'I can hook you up with an empty terminal.'

'Nah, I'm OK now.' Dulcie stood and picked up the pizza box. 'In fact, I should get going. Maybe I can get through these stupid essays and bash out an outline for this chapter. Then I could get back to the real stuff tomorrow.'

The grin became wider now. 'That's my girl.'

He took the empty box from her and helped her into her sweater. 'Do me one favor, Dulce?'

She turned, buttoning those oversized buttons. 'What?'

'Let's not push our luck, OK? Take a cab home?'

EIGHT

Writing, she should be in her cabin, locked away, writing. And yet, she stood on the deck, peering into the inky dark, trying in vain to see her way through the impervious blackness. Like a storm unending, the sea itself heaved and tossed. Even in the dark, she could sense its enormity, the mighty and yet mindless strength of it, upon whose mercy she among the other ship-bound souls must rely. She tasted salt, the spray bitter on her lips. Or were those tears? In the cold dark fullness of the night, she could no longer tell. Could barely discern where the ship ceased to be and the ocean began on this wild night, wind toss'd and bitter. She brushed an errant curl aside, realizing the full intent of her words. Her worlds were colliding – the real and the unreal, once again. The ship reared up, a mere scrap

upon the back of this heaving beast, and she reached for the rail,
spray slick and icy. And as it must rise, so too must it dive, down
into the beast's belly, the trough of the wave. Would it be so
difficult then, to simply let go – to release her hold on the rail,
on this frail and broken life?

Dulcie woke with a start, disturbing the cat, who had managed
to wedge herself under Dulcie's chin. Illuminated by the light of
the moon, Dulcie's bedroom looked ghostly, cool and blue, but
calm. Even the cat, she recognized, had been sound asleep – until
her own sudden movement had woken her.

'Sorry, kitty,' Dulcie apologized to those blinking eyes. In the
light of the waxing moon they almost glowed. 'I had a dream.'

The little cat stretched, and Dulcie reached over the smooth
black back for her glass of water. Water. An ocean crossing. She
took a sip, grateful for the cool fresh taste, and lay back on the
pillow. The cat, clearly assuming that the night's disturbance had
been completed, started kneading.

It could have been the pizza. She'd only eaten one slice. OK,
two. But she'd gotten Chris's favorite – pepperoni and sausage
– and on top of the dumpling and the peanut butter, she'd felt a
little uncomfortable. The cab had probably been a mistake: a
walk would have shaken the food down. But she'd been touched
by her boyfriend's concern and just a little spooked.

Besides, she'd been having dreams like this for a while now.
Even on those rare occasions when she had gone to bed almost
hungry. Dulcie would never admit anything about her dreams to
Lucy; her mother was too quick to attribute everything to some
latent familial psychic powers, whereas Dulcie saw them as her
subconscious at work, piecing together connections she had
missed in the light of day. But sometimes, she had found, these
vivid nightmares had proven to have an extra smidgen of the
truth about them. And as much as she tried to dismiss the idea
– arguing with herself that everything in her dreams could be
traced back to the day's reading at some level – she'd learned
to trust them, no matter where they came from. Or how disturbing
they might feel.

'What do you think it is, Esmé? Can you tell me?' Dulcie
looked down at the little cat, but she kept on with her work,
pushing one paw and then another into the blanket. 'I'm as certain

as I can be that my author emigrated. I mean, those later essays, from America, seem to prove it.'

This wasn't new ground for Dulcie. Even Martin Thorpe had agreed with her on this point. By identifying certain phrases, Dulcie had been able to trace the unknown author of *The Ravages* across the ocean. She'd found certain images – illustrating strikingly modern ideas about women and their role in society – first in the London papers, then *The Ravages*, and ultimately in some of the more incendiary newspapers of the new American republic. Dulcie had found one piece that she was sure was by 'her' author that dated from 1795. But then the trail had gone cold.

It wasn't enough. Thorpe, she knew, was waiting for her to dig up more essays – maybe even something that would give the author a name. But Dulcie was beginning to despair.

She looked over at Esmé, but the little cat appeared to be sound asleep. Reaching over to stroke her soft fur, Dulcie tried to rally. After all, she told herself, there were reasons for her author to stop writing. That last piece – with its plea 'to bear the Mind as treasur'd as the Virtue of her sex' – was fiery stuff, coming as it did on the heels of the French revolution. And while the United States had a built-in affinity for France – the sworn enemies of England had helped the fledgling colonies win their own independence – by the middle of the nineties, this friendship was fading. America had made peace with England, and even Lafayette, the hero of the revolution, was in trouble with the new French Republic. Dulcie wasn't sure if folks in Philadelphia would know about the Terror, or that the Committee of Public Safety had thrown the marquis in jail. But she'd read enough political papers to know that her author had landed just as the political climate was turning conservative.

'Maybe she just couldn't get published any more.' Dulcie addressed the cat, who sniffled and readjusted without waking. 'It happens.'

Dulcie didn't want to think about how often it happened. A job at an auction house might be fine for some, for those who could deal with the fickle fashions of wealthy collectors. Dulcie had incorporated too much of her mother's anti-materialist sentiment to ever feel at home in that setting. If she could just find one or two more examples – just enough to prove her theory – she would have enough evidence to make up a chapter of her thesis. And even if Thorpe had insisted that she posit the author's movement as speculative, she'd already drafted a paper for the graduate students' journal on the writing. 'Cast Upon the Sea: The Transmission of Feminist Ideas to the More Fertile Ground of the New World' was almost ready for publication, and Dulcie felt sure it would turn some heads. At least, she'd thought she felt confident about it.

'Maybe that's all it is.' She turned toward the cat. 'Maybe I'm a little more worried about my paper than I'd thought.'

The small cat didn't respond, and Dulcie realized she was second-guessing herself. Maybe it was anxiety, but she couldn't shake the feeling that the dream was about more than the voyage. What had gotten to her – what had remained after she awoke – was that awful feeling of being trapped. Of despair. Had her author considered suicide? The idea was chilling, and not just because of the vivid images of the wild waves. In her heart of hearts, Dulcie had suspected – hoped might be the better word – that the author was more than a literary forebear. Dulcie's mother's family had come from Philadelphia, from much more established and respectable stock than Lucy's hippie lifestyle would suggest. And Lucy had always told Dulcie that their female ancestors had been independent women. Was it too much to hope that maybe, just maybe, the reason Dulcie had bonded so strongly with *The Ravages of Umbria*, the reason she had found her purpose in studying this author, was because of some long distant family tie?

'What do you say, Esmé?' But the kitten was fast sleep. And so, with a little shuffling and pillow fluffing, Dulcie followed suit.

NINE

When she next awoke, the moon had been replaced by bright sunshine, the kind that makes nightmares seem silly. A quick glance at the clock, however, reawakened that sense of dread. Sometime during the night, she must have hit it, turning the alarm off. Or – no, Esmé was nowhere to be seen. Whatever had happened, Dulcie had no time for breakfast. The departmental meeting would begin in fifteen minutes, and especially as she still had no new evidence for her thesis, she really didn't need Thorpe on her case.

'Whoa!' Chris had been unlocking the front door as she rushed out, and she spun on her heels to give her boyfriend a quick kiss.

'Gotta run. Meeting.'

'Call me!' His voice followed her down the stairs. *One of these days*, Dulcie thought with a twinge of regret, *we'll have a normal life*. For now, trotting up the street, Dulcie tried to organize her thoughts. First, the meeting, which promised to be dull but necessary. At least Nancy, the departmental secretary, made good coffee, and Dulcie had had the forethought to grab her oversized travel mug before she'd bolted.

Dulcie hurried toward Mass Ave, realizing that she hadn't even bothered to button her sweater. The Pacific North-West had been damp and cool, but the winters never seemed as bitter as they did here in New England. Here, from late October on, Dulcie piled layer on layer. Now, between her steady trot and the bright sun, she was actually warm. She smiled up at the sky, at the little fluffy clouds making their way across a clean, fresh blue – and walked into a wall of wool.

'Watch it, why don't you?' The harsh Boston accent, akin to a seagull's caw, took Dulcie aback. It couldn't totally destroy her mood, however, and she looked up with a smile.

'I'm sorry.' She tried to make eye contact with dark eyes, buried deep under bristling brows. 'I was distracted by this beautiful weather.'

'Nutcase.' The large wool-clad person – a man, Dulcie thought – said, loud enough for her to hear, before turning and stalking off.

'Friendly,' Dulcie replied, a little softer, and followed. It was true – she hadn't noticed that the light had changed, and had the man not stopped her with his bulk, she might have stepped into traffic. He might have saved her life. 'Sorry,' she said again, sending the apology into the space where he had been. If she had inherited anything from Lucy, it was a sense of karmic balance. Maybe she deserved that verbal slap for being so inattentive.

'I wonder if that's what Esmé needs,' she asked of a passing

sparrow. Mr Grey had come to her fully grown and had been a
gentle cat from the first. 'Or maybe it's just Chris.' Whatever
she didn't know about training a kitten, she knew that his genial
rough-housing was wrong and would only lead to tears.

That, however, was a problem to be tackled later. As the high-
rises and storefronts of Central Square gave way to the red-brick
of the university, Dulcie returned to planning her morning. First,
the meeting – the thought of that coffee made her mouth water,
and she found herself swallowing. If she were lucky, Roland
would be there. She might have to make up some kind of story
about why she'd called, but she could handle it. If he wasn't –
and, really, there were a million reasons why he might not be
– she'd ask Thorpe about him. Or, no, even better – she'd ask
Nancy. Just a casual question thrown out there to let her know
if the jovial Texan had gone missing or, worse, turned up dead.
Odds were, that would take care of the whole problem.

Either way, she thought, she might be able to get more out of
Trista. Her friend had been so upset the night before, as close
to hysteria as Dulcie had ever seen her. A visit from the cops
could do that, what with their usually gruff manners and refusal
to explain anything that was going on. But even Suze had thought
that Trista had blown it out of proportion. And even if she was
still nervous – or suffering from exhaustion or whatever – Trista
would be more approachable this morning, after a night's sleep,
and especially after a departmental meeting. In keeping with her
hip look, Trista liked to present a cool facade. No matter what
it cost her, she'd be rational in front of the rest of the department
– and Dulcie might be able to get a little more sense out of her,
starting with why she'd decided that their imported colleague
had been killed.

She looked at her watch. Ten twenty, she just might make it.
And if all went according to plan, she would put this curious
incident behind her. She might even be able to duck Thorpe after.
If she could get into the library by noon, Dulcie thought, turning
off Mass Ave, this would be a most beautiful day.

An hour later, it registered with Dulcie that she had not even
gotten coffee. It wasn't that Nancy hadn't made it. As soon as
she'd skipped up the steps to the old clapboard house that served
as the departmental headquarters, she'd smelled that marvelous,

ever so slightly burned aroma, the result of too many drips left on the institutional coffee-maker.

But before she could even step from the front hall into the former sitting room that now served as an all-purpose office-cum-gathering space, Dulcie was grabbed and hustled into the conference room opposite.

'Dulcie, thank God.' It was Trista, looking a little frantic. 'Do you have a minute?'

'Hey, Trista. Yeah, I talked to Suze—' Dulcie tried to respond, but her friend cut her off.

'There's something going on – something I hadn't thought of. It might . . . well, we should talk.'

'Miss Schwartz, there you are.' Martin Thorpe had walked in. 'I was wondering when you'd get here.'

'The meeting's not till—' She checked her watch. Ten thirty-five. 'I'm only five minutes late.'

'These are not ordinary times.' Thorpe looked at her over his glasses. 'Your presence is requested immediately.' He looked up, as if seeing Trista for the first time. 'Yours, too, Miss Dunlop.'

'What?' Dulce mouthed the question silently to Trista as they trekked up the stairs behind their leader.

Trista shook her head. 'Not here,' she whispered, looking down behind them.

There wasn't time for anything more. Dulcie ducked instinctively as she watched Thorpe stoop under the lintel that led into the upstairs conference room. The building dated to the Revolutionary War, and as far as its current inhabitants could tell, it had barely been renovated, except for the addition of electricity and a flush toilet that could be temperamental. That made it almost contemporaneous with the author of *The Ravages*, a fact that usually pleased Dulcie, who liked to imagine the scenes the old wood must have witnessed. Only, today, Dulcie didn't have time for such fantasies. She made it up to the doorway and stopped short, until Trista, behind her, gave her a small shove.

'Ladies, please.' Thorpe motioned to two chairs in the far corner. He himself had not taken his usual seat. That was occupied by a man they all knew well, the man whose unexpected appearance had caused Dulcie to stop so suddenly. Even as she scurried over to one of the empty chairs, his image stayed with her and set her mind racing.

He was big, for starters. Big enough to make the little room seem claustrophobic, and his grey hair – thick and swept to the side – and substantial salt-and-pepper moustache did nothing to soften features that could have been carved out of granite. Like a nightmare version of Theodore Roosevelt or some dyspeptic walrus, he looked as substantial – and as tall – as Thorpe, even while seated at the conference table. Almost as tall, Dulcie noted, daring a glance at the visitor, as the university police officer who stood behind him to his right.

What he was doing here was a mystery, but his presence had subdued the usual hum of speculation. She stole another peek at the big man. Yes, it was whom she thought: Dr Gustav Coffin, head of Widener's rare book collection and university legend. Dr Coffin, rumor had it, had built the priceless Mildon rare book library through a combination of charm and bulldog-like tenacity, bullying donors and experts alike to contribute to his own personal climate-controlled fiefdom. Immune to the vagaries of the stock market, which had played such havoc with the university investments as a whole, he had emerged from the jet-setting world of private philanthropy and commanded respect far beyond the halls of academe. It was said he had his own personal keys to the Mildon Collection rooms, set deep within Widener's stacks. And that when he did emerge, it was to fly to New York or London to secure some new prize, or to consult for the Met, the Louvre, or the Hermitage.

Every day he worked with the kind of treasures Dulcie and her colleagues only dreamed about, she realized, swallowing hard. But they never seemed to make him happy. Whether it was because of a graduate student disturbing him with another request, or because he was in the midst of dismissing yet one more university request for tighter budgeting when it came to conservation or restoration, he was known as much for his temper as that stone-carved scowl. This morning he looked positively thunderous.

Now he turned and glowered at Dulcie and at Trista, who had taken an extra few seconds to scuttle to her seat.

'They're all here now,' Thorpe said, and Dulcie heard a slight tremor in his voice.

A silent nod appraised them all. The cop took a step forward, but Dr Coffin raised his hand. The cop froze.

'I have assembled you this morning because of a serious

breach.' Coffin, the descendant of Puritan preachers, had a voice of fire and brimstone. Never mind that the librarian hadn't actually called the meeting. It was his now. 'A very serious breach.' His gaze traveled slowly around the table, and Dulcie swallowed again, aware of how dry her mouth had become.

'All of you have access to the Mildon Rare Book Collection in the Widener Annex.' The gaze continued, like a lighthouse, making its way from face to face. 'All of you have utilized that access within the last semester.'

Dulcie felt a wild desire to look around. Had they all been in the collection? Was the entire department in fact here? Was Roland? She hadn't had a chance to check.

'And so all of you are, of necessity, suspects.' A pause, during which Dulcie heard at least one of her colleagues also try to swallow. 'At least one of you knows whereof I speak. Perhaps more. For we will uncover the truth and recover—'

'Professor Coffin?' The spell was momentarily broken as the cop spoke. Maybe it was just the contrast, but Dulcie noticed he was quite attractive. Young, with sandy hair and an athlete's build. 'Maybe we could get to the point.'

Coffin's glare made it clear he did not share Dulcie's appreciation. It did serve to silence the cop, however, and the large man turned back to the students.

'There has been a breach of trust. Of security, and of everything we respect and hold dear.' One more scan of the room, and the cop was forgotten. 'The Dunster Codex,' he said, finally. 'The Dunster Codex has been stolen.'

TEN

'The *what*?' Ethan's stage whisper broke the stunned silence around the table. Coffin turned toward him with the kind of look a hawk would turn on a small and not particularly tasty rodent.

'The Dunster Codex,' Thorpe repeated, emphasizing each word, as if hearing, not comprehension, were the grad student's problem.

'I haven't seen it, but I know it's an ancient manuscript,' Lloyd, Dulcie's office mate, said, stepping in to explain. 'Old English. Pre-Norman, anyway. Something to do with the king's grant to a monastery.' He looked around for confirmation. Dulcie shrugged. She knew of the treasure, but its era was way before hers.

'It's eleventh century, actually, and a real treasure. A king's grant for a monastery to collect taxes, or tithes, to be accurate.' Darien, a medievalist, was probably the only one there to have read the parchment. 'Access is extremely limited.'

'Of course access is limited.' Coffin's voice made them all look up. Dulcie thought again of mice. Scared, grey mice. 'The Dunster Codex is a priceless piece of literary history, undoubtedly the most valuable acquisition the collection has made during my tenure. It is also extremely fragile. All of you have been in the rare book collection. All of you know the protocol.'

Heads bobbed around the table. They'd all surrendered their pens for soft-pointed pencils. They'd all donned the white cotton gloves, lightly dusted with some kind of non-reactive talc.

'And because you've all been ticketed within the past month, you are all persons of interest.'

'Ticketed?' Dulcie couldn't help it. The words were out before she could think. All eyes turned toward her, and she remembered: in addition to the regular library security, the special collections had its own appropriately archaic entrance ritual. Those admitted signed a large ledger and were given the blue carbon copy as a receipt. That ticket and two pencils were allowed in, nothing else. In theory, scholars were responsible for showing this 'blue ticket' if questioned and were supposed to turn it in to reclaim their bags and coats. In reality, the quiet collection got so few visitors that whoever was staffing the front desk could easily keep an eye on everything – and most of them ended up holding on to the little blue slip. It made a handy bookmark.

'Never mind.' Dulcie couldn't remember the last time she'd gone into the sealed room. Surely it hadn't been in the last month? Most of the Gothics just weren't considered that rare – or that valuable. The only novel from her period she'd ever seen there was a moth-eaten copy of *The Wetherly Ghost*. Still, odds were, if she ever completely emptied her bag, she'd find one or two of the blue slips crumpled on the bottom.

'We will be investigating.' Coffin's eyes made a circuit, chilling

each student in turn. 'And we will get to the bottom of this.'
With that he nodded – once to Thorpe and once to the officer
beside him – and left the room, taking, as far as Dulcie was
concerned, all of its oxygen with him.

Once they'd all been able to breathe again, the startled students
had tramped downstairs to raid the coffee pot and talk. Everyone
had questions, but answers were in as short supply as coffee
filters. Nancy, as usual, tried to supply both.

'They're just looking for information,' she said in her motherly
tone as she set up a fresh pot to brew. 'I'm sure it's nothing.'

'Nothing? How can it be nothing?' Bill was sweating, his face
an unhealthy pink. 'The Dunster Codex is missing!'

'Didn't we trade, like, a Gutenberg Bible or something for it?'
a voice in the corner said, prompting groans.

'Not a *Gutenberg* . . .' someone started explaining. 'But almost
as thick. Still, it was one of the priciest acquisitions in the collection's history.'

'Persons of interest . . .' A female voice rose above the crowd,
tight and anxious. 'Does that mean we're all suspects?'

'It was bound in leather at some point.' The explanation
continued. 'Though I gather the binding is pretty much in shreds.
There are still traces of gold leaf on the front, probably a later
addition . . .'

'Are they talking to the staff, too? The cleaning crew and
security? I mean, why just us?' More voices chimed in, and
Nancy had her hands full trying to calm the crowd. Dulcie simply
listened and tried to remember if she'd ever seen the missing
book.

'What is the Dunster Codex again?' Ethan didn't seem to get
it. 'Is it like one piece of parchment, or is it bound or what?'

Nobody answered him. Partly, Dulcie acknowledged with a
twinge of guilt, because it was Ethan. He never did pick up on
new things, whether it was grading standards or the latest forms
for ordering texts. But partly it was because in the momentary
lull following Ethan's outburst, Lloyd voiced the question that
blew the others away: 'Coffin said "in the last month", right?'

Nods all around.

'Well, does this mean that the Codex has been missing for a
month – and they've only now noticed?'

After that, the buzz came back louder and stronger. Dulcie felt a headache coming on. Something was wrong. *Very* wrong. Before she could flee, however, Trista had grabbed her arm and dragged her down the hall.

'It's tied up with Roland,' her friend whispered, leaning in close to be heard. 'It's got to be.'

'You think Roland stole it?' Dulcie looked up at her friend. Something wasn't making sense. 'Or died trying to defend it?'

'I don't know.' Trista looked around, her pale face strangely stern. 'I don't understand what's exactly going on, but he did have a job in Widener last semester, and this semester he's been working with rare book conservation. There's something else, too – too much to be mere coincidence.'

'Wait a minute, Tris. What do you mean – something else? What else is going on?' Dulcie watched Trista as her head swiveled, taking in the crowd. Being a Victorian, she'd been steeped in the moralistic and heavily plotted novels of the period. As a fan of the Gothic, Dulcie knew different. 'And, Trista, about Roland—'

'You believe me – that I didn't have anything to do with him. Don't you?' Trista turned back and grabbed Dulcie's hands, her blue eyes fierce.

Dulcie resisted the temptation to shake her friend off. 'Trista, I meant to say.' Her friend was acting so strange, Dulcie was a little afraid to confront her. 'What you told me? The cops never mentioned *murder*. They never even actually said he was dead.' She paused. 'Right?'

'Look, it's more complicated than you know.' Trista eyes could have shot sparks. 'You've got to believe me.'

'I believe you wouldn't kill somebody.' Dulcie was at a loss. 'But maybe your imagination—'

'Look who's talking!' Trista's voice had become a hiss.

'No, it's not that I don't believe you.' Dulcie back-pedalled furiously, trying to figure out what had happened. 'It's just that *you* said murder. They didn't. And there hasn't been any kind of announcement – no student alerts or anything. Maybe . . . maybe he's just a suspect in all of this?'

'I think . . . well, I can't explain here.' Trista glanced around. The old clapboard had a cozy porch out back, and Dulcie was turning toward the door when her friend stopped her. Their colleagues were all still talking; nobody was paying attention to them. That didn't seem to make Trista any more relaxed. 'Not . . . in this building. Not today. Look, Dulcie.' Trista bit her lip, nodding. 'I can't explain it all right now. I don't have – I've got to talk to some people. Figure something out. Can you just – just don't do anything, OK? And don't *say* anything – to anyone.'

'Uh, sure.' Dulcie looked down. So did Trista. And as if she'd only just noticed that she had her friend's hands in a death grip, she loosened it. 'But Tris?'

'What?' Trista's hands tightened again, just a little, on Dulcie's.

'I've already talked to Suze – and to Chris, of course. I mean, I told them what you said—'

A little squeeze. Dulcie fought the urge to pull away. 'Can't be helped.' Trista turned one way, then the other, checking out their classmates. 'Look, just, nobody else. I'll explain. I promise.' Another squeeze. 'Please?'

'OK.' Dulcie wasn't sure about any of this. But Trista was a friend. And whatever else was going on, Dulcie was pretty sure she was not a murderer.

'Thank you, Dulce. It means the world to me.' Bending slightly, she let go of Dulcie's hands and gave her friend a quick hug. 'Look, I've got a make a phone call – and I can't do it here. Want to meet at the Brew House in fifteen? Double latte on me? I'll explain everything. I promise.'

Dulcie responded with a weak, but well-intentioned smile. On top of everything, she still hadn't had any coffee. At least she'd get to sit down with Trista and tell her what Suze had said. She'd have to find some way to soft-pedal Suze's theory – that her friend was overreacting due to thesis stress – but she'd find a way. And so it was with a somewhat lighter heart that she watched her friend maneuver around the edge of the mulling crowd and slip out the front. And, with a sigh designed to breathe all the envy out of her body, she went in search of Martin Thorpe.

She found her adviser in the upstairs hallway, apparently on his way to the tiny office where, for all intents and purposes, he lived. Trying not to stare too jealously at the large mug of steaming coffee in his hand, she asked for a word. But instead of inviting her in, as was his custom, her balding adviser looked up with a start. 'Miss Schwartz?'

'Yes, is everything OK?'

He seemed as nervous as his students. Instead of ushering her in, he stood there, blinking.

Dulcie figured this was as much of a cue as she would get. 'I was curious, Mr Thorpe, if you could tell me. I didn't see Roland Galveston here today. Is he— Is everything OK with him?'

He blinked again, and Dulcie imagined a terrified rodent. Some kind of hairless mouse, perhaps.

'Roland Galveston?' she tried again, raising her voice slightly to make sure he heard. 'Texan? New guy?'

'What? Oh, of course.' Another blink, and Dulcie turned to look at the wall behind her. Whatever the balding adviser was staring at, Dulcie couldn't see it.

'Who wants to know?' The booming voice of Dr Coffin broke in, startling Dulcie, who spun back around. Thorpe actually jumped, his coffee sloshing over the brim of his mug, as the man himself appeared behind him. Coffin hadn't left at all, Dulcie realized. He must have commandeered Thorpe's private office the better to confer with the senior tutor – or to spy on the students. Now he stood in the doorway, behind Thorpe, who had turned to stare up at him, and glowered like a thundercloud. 'Why are *you* looking for him?'

'I'm Dulcie Schwartz.' She gathered what was left of her shattered courage. He might look like some evil giant, but she had right on her side – and a minor mystery to solve. 'Sir. And I'm not looking for him, I just . . .' This was the part she hadn't figured out yet. What to say that wouldn't betray Trista's confidence or get either of them in trouble. 'I would like to speak with him.'

Coffin made a sound somewhere between a snort and a grunt. In happier circumstances, Dulcie would have seen him as a walrus. Here, he was just scary.

'Excuse me?' She called on her last ounce of nerve. A fair lady could be brave. Had to be, sometimes.

'Well,' he grumbled, 'I assume it will soon be common knowledge, what with your Facebooks and your Twitters. You may as well hear the truth.'

He paused. Dulcie suspected it was for effect, but it was almost more than she could stand. Trista had been right; Suze wrong. Roland had been murdered.

'Is he . . . gone?' Her voice squeaked, and she felt particularly mouse-like.

'I'll say.' That grumble again. The hall walls began to spin. 'And about time too.'

Dulcie grabbed at the frame of the door behind her for support. None of this was making sense.

'At any rate, once we find him, this young man – I cannot call him a gentleman – will be called to account for his misdeeds.' Coffin gestured, raising his hand to the sky – or to the dying light-bulb that flickered above them. 'He has been a dark stain on the university's history. The sooner erased, the better.'

'So, he's not – dead.' Her voice was so low, she didn't even know if he heard her. At any rate, he paid her no heed and kept talking, addressing the hallway as if it were the pulpit of Memorial Church.

'To start with, that name? Roland Galveston? If anybody in admissions had been half awake, she or he would have recognized an obvious pseudonym.'

Now that the blood was returning, Dulcie felt a flush of irra-tional disappointment. She'd loved Roland Galveston's name. It had been perfect for the cheery Texan.

'He had not been graduated from Vanderbilt.' Coffin was still talking, listing sins each greater than its predecessor. 'We do not even know if he matriculated! Foolish of him, really, to have chosen a relatively respectable institution. So easy to check. And we have every reason to believe he is involved with the disap-pearance of the Dunster Codex.'

Dulcie stepped back – and into the wall. The way Coffin was looking at her, she was sure he suspected her personally of something.

'Roland? A thief?' Was this what Trista had been about to tell her?

'We suspect he had an accomplice.' Coffin's eyes were as grey as his hair and as steely.

'Here? In the department?' She couldn't help it. She'd been thinking of Trista anyway, and now – no. Not Trista.

'Yes.' Coffin was staring at her most intently. 'Sound familiar?'

With a start, she saw what he was implying. 'Me? No way!' If she could have backed up more, she would have. But Coffin had either grilled her enough – or assumed that she was sufficiently terrified that she would confess without further prompting. The latter wasn't that far off, Dulcie realized, and it was with great relief that she saw him lean back on his heels and then, with another grumble, turn back into Thorpe's office. Only then did she realize that her thesis adviser had already disappeared. It was not, she thought, a bad idea.

'Coffee.' She stumbled down the stairs and into the front room. The crowd had begun to thin a bit, but one look at her face and they parted to let her at a blessedly full pot.

She was pouring, already savoring the rich aroma, when the crowd closed back up around her. She heard Lloyd, her long-time office-mate and friend. Ethan, who, although clueless, was also guileless. She took a sip and relaxed. When she opened her eyes, Nancy was smiling at her. All would be right again with the world.

And then she heard a voice, female, that she didn't recognize. Coming in a lull in the communal hubbub, it sounded as clear as an emergency broadcasting announcement.

'What I want to know,' the voice said, 'is who would *want* to steal the Dunster Codex? From what I hear, that horrible old thing is haunted.'

ELEVEN

Dulcie was out on the street before she knew it, the concerned voices of her friends fading behind her. She knew she had blanched, had sputtered into the coffee, but she'd had no time to explain. Air had suddenly seemed more important than caffeine, and in the spring warmth, the crowded coffee room had become unbearably close.

Halfway down the block, she stopped to think. Haunted? Was the Dunster Codex haunted? Something had been tickling the edge of her mind since that horrible meeting, but she didn't think that was it. She tried closing her eyes, but when she did all she saw was Dr Coffin's face, stern and looming. Maybe it was that moustache. 'But I always found grey so comforting. And whiskers!' She opened her eyes to see a squirrel looking on suspiciously. If Mr Grey were here, his tail would be lashing in excitement, she knew. Esmé, on the other hand, would probably see the fuzzy rodent and then turn to bite Dulcie's foot. Displaced aggression. Dulcie understood the theory, but that knowledge didn't help her miss her gentle old cat any less.

'Mr Grey, can you help me with this?' Even though Esmé had shown signs of being able to communicate, Dulcie never thought of asking her for advice or aid. In life, Mr Grey had been a quiet cat, mature and contemplative. Since that awful day, nearly a year and a half before, his occasional presence had only become more so – and if the spectral cat's advice was often cryptic, well, Dulcie was willing to overlook that. Or, to be honest, blame her own lack of comprehension. Esmé, though, would never be anything but a kitten to her. Especially, she thought ruefully, if Chris kept encouraging her worst habits.

This bright morning must not have been cut out for ghosts, however, because her plea remained unanswered. But she had other, more ordinary, sources of information. And so she took another sip from her travel mug for courage, hiked her bag higher over her shoulder, and headed off to meet Trista.

The Brew House was everything a student hang-out should be: cheap, accessible, and filled with friendly faces. Trista probably hadn't counted on the latter when she'd suggested it, Dulcie decided, and so she waited outside for her friend. She'd quickly finished the departmental coffee, but she'd take Trista up on her offer. The Brew House double latte was more of a milk drink, anyway, she reasoned.

Ten minutes later, she was wondering if her friend had had second thoughts. Juggling her empty mug, she fished her phone from her bag. No, no messages. No missed calls, either. She started to type in Trista's number – there had to be an explanation – when a pack of undergrads barreled into her.

'Sorry!' one of them had the grace to yell over his shoulder, as the five – or was it six? – hurtled down the sidewalk. Shouldn't they be gone already? Dulcie wondered. Each year, they seemed to linger longer and longer into what Dulcie thought of as her private time: post-exams and pre-summer session. She turned to look into the coffee house. It was still crowded. Well, exam period lasted till the end of the week. Maybe some of the hunched-over bodies in there were studying.

'Goddess be!' Dulcie could have smacked herself. Almost did when she heard Lucy's favorite exclamation come out of her mouth. Of course, she'd been waiting out here, when Trista must have been inside, buried in the mob. She waved through the window at the slim blonde.

'Trista!' Her friend hadn't seen her and was staring into space. 'It's Dulcie!' At that, the woman turned around, and Dulcie saw that, despite the resemblance, it wasn't her colleague. 'Sorry, I thought you were someone else.'

The young woman – almost a girl, really – kept staring. Dulcie shrugged. She hadn't been that rude. Then she grabbed her bag and pushed by Dulcie, out the door. Dulcie watched as she hurried, head down, toward the corner. Exams were hard on everyone. She remembered them well. But Dulcie was willing to bet that it wasn't academic worries that made that girl run so fast. That pale face had been splotchy, the nose red. That girl had been blinking away tears.

'I wonder—' But Dulcie shook off the thought. She had her own friends to worry about. Walking into the coffee house, she waited while her eyes adjusted to the lower light. Five dark heads were crowded around one small table. A paper slipped to the floor, and two of those heads bumped as they bent to retrieve it. Study group. Three other tables held laptops, but none of the heads bent over the keyboards – bent to avoid eye contact with someone who might dare to want to share their table – were blonde. Dulcie made her way to the back. Two more groups had grabbed all the seats, and none of their members looked familiar. On the remaining tables, three more singles hunched over papers or laptops – except for one man, whose face was planted in a book, clearly asleep.

Dulcie turned. She'd been wrong. Trista wasn't back here. Unless – no, the bathroom key still hung from the side of the counter. And when Dulcie stepped back out into the sunlight, she saw no sign of her friend there either.

This was getting ridiculous. 'Trista?' Her call had gone direct to voicemail. Maybe that phone call Trista had mentioned was simply lasting longer than she had expected. 'I'm at the Brew House? We were going to meet?' She looked around. No sign of her friend on the street. 'Call me.'

She clicked her phone shut. Trista had a poor sense of time.

Dulcie should have known that 'fifteen minutes' really meant more like a half hour. At least.

Well, there wasn't anything she could do here. And truth was, with the adrenalin surge from the meeting, she didn't need any more caffeine. Trista would call her back. For now, she'd head to the library.

It was reflex, she knew that, heading to the library whenever things were going wrong. It wasn't a bad reflex for a scholar; Dulcie had made some fantastic academic discoveries while fleeing the pressures of everyday life. The majestic granite building before her was as much a sanctuary as a workplace, she acknowledged as she climbed the stone steps: a hiding place where she felt safe. In truth, with its more than five miles of books stored primarily in its underground stacks, the giant library had more than a little in common with a rabbit's warren. And she, Dulcie, was beginning to feel a little like a timid bunny.

For a moment she flashed on Mr Grey, and how he'd pounce on a rucked-up blanket, his feline instincts urging him to flush out any prey that was hiding in its tunnels. Maybe that's what Esmé was trying to do – flush Dulcie out of her routine and into trying new things. The thought of her young cat warmed her; the little animal wasn't trying to be disruptive. It was her nature to be young, playful, and fierce.

'We can't fight who we are,' Dulcie murmured to herself as she dug out her ID. Flashing it at the guard, she felt her spirits lift. A different setting might help her to finally get through those hated essays. She might even take a break from that one collection and see what else she could read. All she had to find were one or maybe two more good literary examples. Never mind the beautiful spring weather, what Dulcie needed to get the sap flowing was likely right here in front of her.

'Hey, darling.' In true Mona fashion, the librarian's greeting rang out through the entrance hall, almost deserted on this balmy day. 'How's that handsome man of yours?'

Dulcie felt herself blushing as she rushed over. Mona was a dear, but her voice was as large as the rest of her, and the two guards were making no effort to hide their broad grins.

'Chris is OK,' she said, more to Mona's multicolored nails

than to the librarian's broad mocha-colored face. 'We're getting used to the new situation.'

'Getting used to it?' Dulcie looked up and saw concern dampen the grin. 'Girl, you should be on your honeymoon with him.'

'No, it's great. Really.' Dulcie cast about for a less sensitive subject. 'How're things by you?'

'Well, you probably heard about the robbery, right?' Even leaning close, Mona's voice boomed.

Dulcie nodded. So much for getting away from her problems here.

'They've had us going over the records. Who had access; who used that access. Royal pain.'

Dulcie had to smile. Of course, to Mona, it was a bureaucratic hassle. 'I'm sure they'll figure it out.' A thought hit her. 'Is it possible that it wasn't stolen? I mean, if they're checking records, maybe it was just . . . mislaid?'

Mona rolled her eyes. 'With the security they have on that thing? No, I think it was spirited away.'

'You mean, a professional job?' Thieves had attacked the library in the past. While books might not have quite the cachet of art, there were collectors out there willing to put up money to obtain rarities.

But Mona didn't even give her time to follow up on that though. 'Pros? No, I mean magic, Dulcie. If you heard some of the stories I've heard . . . . Believe me, no collector would want that nasty old thing. It's cursed.'

TWELVE

Dulcie let her smile fade as she descended into the stacks. It was a relief, really, not to have to pretend any more. Mona meant well, but all this talk about curses and hauntings just gave Dulcie the creeps.

'Words cannot conjure bad luck,' she muttered to herself. 'Words are simply tools for communication.' After a lifetime of Lucy, whose vaguely Wiccan faith tended to absorb just about any supernatural belief that caught her fancy, this ethos – the

creed of the scholar – was Dulcie's defense. It was also, sometimes, a little hard to believe when everything seemed to be going
wrong all at once.

'A text, any text, is a vessel.' She let herself wax lyrical as
she emerged from the elevator, three levels below the yard. 'A
way for a story to be carried – and a means by which a reader
can be carried away.'

She'd meant to cheer herself up. After all, how many times
had she enjoyed being transported by a good book – by *The
Ravages of Umbria* in particular? But as she pictured the two-
hundred-year-old novel, she couldn't help thinking of its author.
Where had the author been heading on her own journey? And
why was it surrounded by such a sense of dread?

Only a few months earlier, Dulcie had been sure she had the
key to this particular mystery. The unnamed author had emigrated
from England to the fledgling United States, of that she was sure.
Essays in her distinctive style had been published in Philadelphia
less than three years after she had 'disappeared' from the London
scene, and Dulcie had a sneaking suspicion that the émigré had
found love, or at least started a family, on this side of the Atlantic.

That was before the latest series of dreams, though. In these
dreams, the author seemed to be fleeing something – or someone.
Even worse, she seemed to be filled with despair. Dulcie had
been shy about sharing these nightmares. Chris, rational thinker
that he was, would have attributed them to too much late-night
pepperoni pizza. And Lucy, she was sure, would over-interpret
them and try to involve her daughter in some complicated herbal
exorcism. Nobody else would understand at all, and so Dulcie
had kept them to herself.

She dropped her books on the carrel with a thud. Had she just
said to herself that nobody would understand? She sat with
another thud, letting her head sink to the molded plastic desktop.
Nobody – and no cat. Just when she needed him again, Mr Grey
was absent. Leaving her alone with a recalcitrant kitten and the
daylight world of clueless humans.

It was pointless. Dulcie made herself sit up and open a book.
Chris wasn't clueless. And he'd even heard Mr Grey speak – her
former pet's wise, warm voice advising them both to embrace
their future together with open hearts. But Chris, as was befitting
a computer sciences scholar, was more concerned with the

practical here and now. Plus, he had never known her long-haired
pet in life. To Chris, Mr Grey was a story and a voice. He would
never be the comforting presence that the real cat had been, not
that long ago.

A drop appeared on the page, spreading as it soaked into the
paper. Dulcie sat up. There was no point in crying. Mr Grey had
been a great cat. He'd set her up with Esmé – she was convinced
of that – and he still visited occasionally. She had a living cat
as well as a living boyfriend. Beyond that, Mr Grey's silence
didn't bear thinking about; she had work to do.

Moving quickly, before her melancholy returned, Dulcie found
herself in front of a row of collected journals. There she paused
for a moment, deciding between two books. The one she opted
for – another collection of political essays – was fairly new to
her. It wasn't a new book, far from it, but this particular volume
was one she had never bothered with before. Pulling it from the
shelf, Dulcie wondered why. It wasn't much to look at: blue-dyed
leather with its title, *Early American Dissenters,* impressed in
small gold type. There was something appealing about it, however.
Maybe, she realized with a chuckle, it was simply because she
hadn't opened it before. And so she took the volume – filled, as
it was, with the promise of brilliant discoveries – back to her
carrel with a lighter step than before.

Sitting with the book, Dulcie indulged in a little private ritual.
Eyes closed, she leaned over the blue binding and inhaled,
enjoying the almost imperceptible woodsy-dusty smell of old
paper and leather: the aroma of a well-preserved book. Along
with the smell of fresh brewed coffee, that subtle earthy smell
always perked her up, just as the baby-powder smell of a clean
cat could calm her down.

'Maybe it's just as well you aren't here with me, Mr Grey,'
she whispered to the empty air. 'Between the two of you, I'd be
too blissed out to work.' Instead, she settled in to read, looking
for those distinctive phrases that set her author apart.

It was almost like a treasure hunt, looking for nameless essays
from the author of *The Ravages*. Granted, Dulcie admitted, most
of her colleagues wouldn't see her findings as treasure. That just
made her current tack all the more promising. Through her
research, Dulcie had not only come close to proving that *The
Ravages*, so-called sensationalist trash, had a very real and very

witty message about the role of women. She had also linked the nameless author with the burgeoning feminist movement of the time. Two hundred years ago, women writers were staking a claim in literature – and their lives – and Dulcie was only now, retroactively, figuring it out. When she published . . .

She paused. Her breath catching in a way that had little to do with the atmospherically controlled setting. When she published, she'd be in the same situation Trista was: competing for post-docs. Hoping for a teaching job . . . somewhere. And Chris? Well, as a computer guy, he had a little more flexibility about his career. Still, it was the one thing they hadn't talked about.

'*You could, you know.*' The deep voice, quiet, but no whisper, sounded right behind her ear.

'Mr Grey?' Dulcie sat up, but resisted the temptation to turn around. Although she could now feel the tickle of whiskers on her left ear, she knew that if she looked, she'd see nothing but shadows.

'*He's been thinking about this, too.*' The voice had a slight edge to it, admonishing her, she knew, for her timidity.

'You've talked to Chris?' She didn't know why, exactly, but that thought sent a twinge of jealousy pinging through her. And just like that, she knew the presence – Mr Grey – was gone.

'I should be happy. My cat and my boyfriend get along.' She bit her lip and tried to return to her book. 'I mean, it's a lot to ask.'

She started reading again, but her thoughts were elsewhere. Only recently had Mr Grey, her spectral visitor, revealed himself to Chris. The idea that the two were having discussions without her was a little disturbing. He wouldn't leave her, would he? Maybe now that she had Esmé . . . maybe he always wanted a male human . . .

'*Now, now, little one.*' The voice was barely audible, an under-tone on the hum of the air conditioning. But it was enough. Dulcie smiled to herself, and got down to work.

A half hour later, Dulcie wasn't worried about her career prospects any more. An hour later, she wasn't even worried about Mr Grey. *Early American Dissenters* was a mother lode: disor-ganized – the volume didn't even have a table of contents – but full of exactly the kind of radical essays she had been hoping to find. Whoever had edited it had cared more about being inclusive than about presenting any kind of structured argument. Which was, to Dulcie's mind, perfect.

Here was an essay trying to revive the Levellers – a proto-socialist school that had its heyday before the revolution. '*Justice and Inequality cannot abide* . . .' the essay ran, before a list of such horrible disparities that Dulcie's sympathies as well as her intellectual curiosity were raised. Following that piece was a discussion of liberalism and the republic that sounded almost like it could be current. How far should government be involved in everyday life? What rights did the individual have against corrupt power? It was as timely as anything in the *Crimson* op-ed pages. Except, of course, that the '*Government, as limited as the Men who Decreed it*' consisted entirely of white men. Women and people of color – many of whom were enslaved – were not invited to such lofty debate.

Well, that would change, she thought. And her author would help change it. She skimmed ahead, browsing for familiar phrases: the 'woman question', that's what she was looking for. That, as well as education, were the two areas her author cared most about.

Dulcie's stomach grumbled, reminding her that even the heady combination of intellectual discovery and coffee were not suffi-cient for survival. She checked her watch. It was after noon. She looked back at the bound volume. Without a table of contents, it was hard to know what other topics its papers might cover. Then again, that made the volume more of a treasure trove, one filled with possibilities. She'd read one more essay . . .

She didn't stop. She couldn't. The piece on the limitations of government had been followed by one on the definition of 'liberty'. It had not only raised the question of slavery – already a hot topic during the Constitutional debates – but even the issue of whether a person needed to own property to deserve full rights under the law. To a contemporary reader, Dulcie knew, this would sound incredibly restrictive, arcane and unfair. To her it was, well, revolutionary.

Her stomach grumbled again, but she had to continue. If only she could find her author in this group . . . .

In truth, Thorpe had been more impressed by Dulcie's latest discovery about her author than he had been by the writer's big novel. That the author of a 'minor, and fragmented, Gothic' – his words – had been an early feminist activist had impressed her balding tutor. He'd even asked her if she'd consider rethinking her thesis to focus on these later, political works. At the time, Dulcie had rejected his suggestion out of hand. Now, with this blue-bound volume in hand, she was tempted. Post-revolutionary social theory was hot right now, and that meant a thesis on an early émigré feminist might be more likely to land her a post-doc or even a tenure track position. Problem was, it would also mean shifting the focus of her work away from that one great novel, *The Ravages of Umbria*. That book, even in the incomplete form that survived, had been what had drawn her in in the first place. Was it worth giving it up?

'Follow your spirit guide,' Lucy had told her on more than one occasion. Of course, for Lucy, that usually meant letting your whim decide which incense was appropriate for the occasion. But even her old thesis adviser, now retired, had said something similar, if less poetic.

'You're going to live with this. Breathe it. Even eat it for the next few years,' Professor Bullock had told her, early on, before his declining health had muted his famous brain. 'Choose something you really love, Ms Schwartz. Because otherwise you'll hate it – and yourself – by the time you're done.'

She'd taken those words to heart, hitching her academic wagon to a book that few had read – and even fewer respected. And it had paid off for her. Surely, the fact that that original wonderful novel had led her into a new direction didn't mean she had made the wrong move, did it?

She turned to the next essay, hoping for an answer and finding an argument about landholding and the public trust. The next was on term limits. Things really didn't change, and as her stomach rumbled once more, she reached with one hand for her bag, using the other to close the leather cover. But the volume was heavier than she remembered, and it was with dismay that she saw the tissue-thin pages begin to flip in a disorderly fashion, falling, folding as they fell. She grabbed at the volume – even if it had disappointed her, it was a fine, old book. That's when she saw it – one phrase on the bottom of the page: '. . . *a delicate issue of the Female mind . . .*' And then it was gone.

'What? Where . . .' Dulcie opened the volume again and began looking through the pages, turning the delicate paper as quickly as she dared while she scanned the lower right corners. 'Who was writing about the female mind?' No table of contents meant she had no clue as to which essay that phrase had come from. Starting again from that piece on the Levelers, she speed-read. Congress. Term limits. Nothing . . .

The buzzing almost made her jump out of her seat, her hands pulling back from the pages by reflex so as not to rip them. 'What the . . .?' That buzzing again, and Dulcie came back to earth. Her phone, deep in her bag, was vibrating. It must, she thought, digging for it, be up against something – a pen, the metal case of her laptop. Although she had turned the ringer off, it sounded like an angry bee, desperate for attention.

There, beneath a hair tie, she found it – and at that moment it fell silent, as if it really had just wanted her touch. Phone in hand, she looked around guiltily. Cell use was prohibited in the stacks. Even having the phone on could get her a reprimand, not to mention dirty looks from her colleagues. She leaned out of her carrel, ready to apologize. No stares greeted her, though. No frowns peered around the edges of the other carrels or from the stacks. Feeling like she'd gotten away with something, she reached for the switch on the small phone. Then she looked back at the volume. This would not be, she could see, a quick study.

'Sorry,' she murmured, to any stray scholars who studied on, unseen. Her concentration broken, she shoved her notebook into her bag. It was way past time for lunch.

Her phone started buzzing again as she was checking out the blue volume, vibrating against something in her bag and earning her a raised eyebrow from the rotund security guard.

'Sorry.' She smiled as she silenced it. 'I thought I'd turned it off.'

He sniffed, staring down his pug nose at her, and she noticed how much like a bulldog he looked. Well, maybe it went with the job.

He finished checking her out and waved her through, and she reached for the phone. It wasn't likely to be Chris, though she could hope. More likely it was Trista, with some excuse for blowing her off earlier in the day. Well, if that were the case, she would exact compensation in the form of company for lunch. She didn't think it would be difficult: Lala's three-bean burgers were justly famous, and if Trista joined her they could chew over the latest revelations together.

The light was with her – and she was famished – so she was already in line by the time she checked her messages. Rather to her surprise, the missed call had come from Chris.

He answered on the first ring, and she yelled over the din, 'Hey there! I'm waiting for a seat at Lala's. Want to join me?'

'Dulce, did you listen to my message?' Her boyfriend sounded unusually serious.

'No, I just saw that you'd called.' With a nod to the person behind her, she stepped aside. Up against the wall, it was easier to hear. 'I was in Widener. I'd thought it was going to be Trista.'

'So, you haven't spoken to her today?'

A place at the bar opened up and Dulcie went for it, ignoring the pointed look from the customer behind her. 'Not really.' She pointed to the menu to order and kept on talking. 'She was at the departmental meeting, but then she ran out. We were going to have coffee.'

Chris exhaled audibly, and Dulcie realized her boyfriend had been holding his breath. She leaned forward, as if she could get closer to him through the phone. 'Chris, what's up?'

His voice was soft, and the restaurant loud. 'Look, I'm just glad you're not involved in this. Not really.' That much she got. 'No matter what Mr Grey says.'

'Mr Grey?' The waitress put a burger down in front of her, but for once Dulcie hesitated and didn't automatically reach for the house-made hot sauce. 'Did you say Mr Grey, Chris? Mr Grey spoke to you? About me?' She couldn't help the tone of her voice. She just couldn't.

Chris seemed to understand. 'Yeah, he – uh – he came to me this morning,' he said, a little abashed. 'I mean, I think he did. I was sleeping. But I thought I felt him jump on to the bed, you know?'

Dulcie nodded, momentarily unaware that her boyfriend couldn't see her reaction.

It didn't seem to matter. He kept talking. 'So, I may have been dreaming. But then I heard this voice, deep and low, telling me to watch out for you. That you were going to be dragged into something. That it wasn't safe to be too trusting.'

Dulcie swallowed, her appetite gone. 'He said that?'

'I think he did. Like I said, I might have been dreaming. And I'm not entirely sure that he meant you were too trusting. Just that there was danger in being too trusting, and that I should watch out for you.'

'Oh.' Dulcie didn't know what else to say. Mr Grey was talking to Chris. Not to her. *About* her. It was only when she heard Chris say her name that she realized he had something more to add.

'Dulcie?'

'Yeah?' This was going to take a while to digest.

'Um, sweetie, that's not why I called. I mean, not entirely. In fact, I might have thought it was all a dream, but before I could go back to sleep – or maybe because the dream woke me up – the doorbell rang.'

She made some noise. She must have, because he kept on talking.

'It was the cops. Dulcie. They had come to the apartment. That's what I was calling about. They want to know what's going on.'

Dulcie roused herself. This was something she could handle. 'They came to the apartment and woke you up? How rude. I'm sorry, honey. Do they want me to call them back?'

'Worse than that, Dulcie. I wanted to warn you. I mean, I'm sure it's nothing, but I thought you should know. They've looked up your schedule. They're coming to campus to find you.'

For a moment, Dulcie considered flight. Not back to Chris – the cops knew where they lived. Besides, the idea that Mr Grey had spoken to her boyfriend, instead of coming to her directly, was something she didn't want to think about. Not now.

Dulcie's dream came back to her, crashing over her like an ocean wave, with its feeling of hopelessness. Is this how the nameless dream figure had felt? Had the dream woman – Dulcie just knew it was her anonymous author – been hounded by authorities, forced to flee her home – even her country?

She slumped on the counter stool, letting the weight of the day drag her down. The burger no longer looked appealing, and she pushed it away. But just as she was about to put her head in her hands, maybe even let some of those tears loose, she felt something. A swipe, a sting, like the rake of claws across her face. The shock made her sit up straight, and when she realized what was happening, she took a deep breath.

'Thank you, Mr Grey.' Maybe he was no longer exclusively

her pet. For now, this was enough. Warmed by the conviction that she was not alone – that someone (well, maybe two some-ones) was looking out for her, she felt her fear begin to spark into anger.

She had plenty of tinder to fuel the fire. After all, the idea that the police were looking for her was ridiculous. She was no criminal. She wasn't fleeing anybody. And no matter what Professor Coffin implied, she was no thief.

Plus, she was busy! Dulcie looked down at her burger with a new determination. She reached for the hot sauce and let it pour, only noticing afterward that it looked disturbingly like blood. But it wasn't. She took an angry bite. She hadn't hurt anyone. The pepper spurred her on. She had done nothing wrong, and she had nothing to say to the police. All Trista had said—

Trista. That must be why her friend hadn't showed up. She was probably talking to the police now; she had probably let the time get away from her. That was OK; this was all serious enough that Dulcie could forgive her friend. Roland Galveston might be mixed up in something, but he wasn't dead – and so Trista couldn't be charged with murder. She'd get everything cleared up.

Nobody had been killed. Dulcie found she could eat again and took another satisfying bite. Lala was the best. Another mouthful, and she remembered how hungry she was. Which was just as well, because the three-bean burger was really a two-fister, and there was no point in putting it back on the plate once it was dressed with all that lovely hot sauce.

So when her phone rang again two minutes later, she looked at it with longing – but not too much. Probably Chris again. He probably wanted to apologize for scaring her. Maybe he wanted to make plans for later. But when she had chased a particularly spicy mouthful with some of Lala's limeade and wiped her hands as well as she could, she didn't find the number she expected on the phone. Neither their apartment nor Chris's phone started with the familiar '495' exchange. Whoever had called had been using a university phone, and it was with a bit of curiosity – and still-sticky hands – that she dialed voicemail.

There was no message, and as she once again raised the messy burger to her lips, Dulcie mulled over the possibilities. Was there something happening at the departmental offices that Nancy

wanted her to know about? Was it Thorpe? She could try the
number – later. Lala's was too busy for her to claim counter
space for anything but the serious work of eating. As she chewed
another mouthful, she considered what else to do with her day.
She *could* head back to the library. Something about the underground atmosphere was conducive to serious reading. Or she
could go to her office. She had the blue volume in her bag, and
if she needed a break, the last of the final exams waited for her
red pencil.

Maybe it was the thought of grading, or maybe it was that,
now she had quelled her cravings, she could see that the day
outside was golden, the sky beautiful and bright with promise.
Or maybe, to be honest, it was that she was creeped out by what
Chris had said. Dodging the looks from waiting patrons, she
picked up the phone again. That last call was weighing on her.
If only she had recognized the extension. If only the caller had
left a message.

Then it hit her: she had called Roland last night and asked
him to ring her. She'd called the number listed in the student
directory – a home phone or cell. But maybe his own phone was
broken. Maybe his cell had been stolen and he was catching up
from a university extension, holed up in some office on campus.
That had to be it. And because her own message had been so
vague, he hadn't left a message of his own. Maybe he even knew
that he'd been outed by Coffin. Maybe he was on the run, reaching
out to a colleague . . .

Wiping her hand one more time on the greasy napkin, she hit
redial and waited for two, then three rings. Roland had just called
her; he had to answer. Four rings, and the phone picked up.

'Roland?' Finally, all this mystery would be put to rest.

'University Police. How may I direct your call?'

Dulcie sat there, the café buzzing about her, frozen.

'Hello?' Something brushed against her, hard, and she
nearly fell off her stool. A woman muttered as she squeezed
in beside her.

'Hello? University Police.'

Fumbling with hands that had suddenly turned to ice, Dulcie
hung up.

THIRTEEN

'**M**r Grey, are you there?'

Dulcie had run out to the street, leaving the last of her burger behind. Not even Lala's surprised face, looking up from behind the counter, could stop her, so desperate was she to get out – to get away.

'Mr Grey? I could really use some help here.' She'd run out of breath halfway through the Yard. Out of ideas, too. Dropping the phone back into her bag as if it were contaminated, she had wanted to get away. Now that she had calmed down a little, it registered that her first panicked thought – that the police could somehow trace her, that they would be converging on the sandwich shop within seconds – had faded. Trista's odd experience had left her spooked, and the mix-up with the Dunster Codex seemed to threaten them all. Still, her initial destination – the basement office she shared with Lloyd – no longer seemed like such a good idea. While it was unlikely that the police would track her to a Harvard Square eatery, they very well might have someone waiting at her office. Especially – she looked at her watch – since her office hours were supposed to start in twenty minutes.

'Are you out there?' She glanced around the campus, which resembled a park more than ever now that the grounds crew were getting it ready for Commencement. 'Mr Grey?' A movement behind a tree caught her eye, but it was only a squirrel. Stepping over a string barrier – the grounds crew were serious about their reseeding efforts – she leaned back against a tall elm. At least the Yard was quiet and shady, the tree bark scratchy through her cotton shirt. With her eyes closed, she could almost pretend she was back home.

'*Home, little one?*'

'You know what I mean. The commune.' For a moment, resting there, this conversation seemed like the most natural thing in the world. Then it hit her, and she jerked herself up. 'Mr Grey!'

'*Now, now.*' The voice came from behind her, as if she had

been reclining on the sofa and the graceful grey cat had come walking along its narrow back. She waited for the brush of fur as he settled behind her. Instead, she felt a slight breeze, as if he were moving away, and heard a low rumble, almost more growl than purr.

'I'm sorry.' She slumped back against the tree. 'I'm just scared. The department has us all thinking we're guilty until proven innocent, and now the police are looking for me. And—' She swallowed, the lump in her throat making her pause as much as her fear of chasing her dear friend away. 'And, well, you hardly talk to me any more, Mr Grey. You talk to Chris.'

She hadn't meant it to sound like that, to sound so jealous and petty, but as soon as the words were out of her mouth, she regretted them. Maybe Mr Grey sensed that, because instead of the claw swipe she half expected, all she heard was a quizzical, '*Mrup?*'

'You warned him, but not me. You always seem to be talking to him.'

'*He's part of your life now, little one. Don't you trust him?*'

Dulcie swallowed again, the unshed tears going down hard. 'I do, Mr Grey. You know I do. I just—' She paused, trying to find the right words for the confused flood of feelings washing over her. Her voice had shrunk to just above a whisper. Even so, her own words embarrassed her. 'I don't want to share you.'

The truth out, she held her breath. Either he would comfort her, reassure her of his continued presence in her life – and of the specialness of their relationship. Or he would rebuke her. But instead of his gentle voice, or the touch of fur or fang, she heard a louder, human voice.

'Dulcie! There you are!' It was Lloyd, coming from the direction of the office. Of course, he would have vacated it so she could meet with her students. 'I was hoping to catch you.'

'Hey.' Plastering a smile on her face, she nodded at her friend. 'What's up? Are they lining up for my sage advice?'

'Sorry.' He shook his head, and she felt her heart sink. 'Nothing so pleasant. A cop came by and checked out when your office hours were. He was asking me about your habits, your friends. Like *you'd* know any dealers!'

'Dealers?' This wasn't making sense. 'Like, drugs?'

'Dealers, collectors. The kind of people who would pay big

money for something like . . .' His voice dropped. 'You know, the Dunster Codex.'

'Oh, this is ridiculous.' Dulcie's head spun. 'I can't even remember the last time I was in the Mildon room.'

'I pretty much told him that. Told him that your area of expertise didn't usually take you into special collections, but he kept asking.' Lloyd glanced over his shoulder, and Dulcie could tell he was spooked. 'But there are other things, Dulcie. Strange things.' He wiped away the sweat that had suddenly appeared on his upper lip. 'Things I think you might have some, um, unique insight into.'

'What?' Dulcie felt her stomach sink. That burger might not have been the best move.

'You know I used to work in Circulation, right?'

She nodded.

'I know the girl who got my old job, and she said—' He looked around again and licked his lips. 'She said the Codex had moved recently.'

'So, maybe it was just misplaced, not stolen.' She heard the relief in her voice, and heard it fade as Lloyd shook his head.

'Dulcie, listen: I didn't say it *had been* moved. I said "moved". You know they keep it in its own case?'

Dulcie nodded. 'A humidity-controlled, fireproof casket.' That last word caused her to stumble, but her friend didn't seem to notice.

'Well, twice now, when they've opened the case, the Codex hasn't been there, where it was supposed to be.' His voice was low now, confidential. Dulcie had to lean in to hear what he said next: 'And *The Wetherly Ghost* has been in its place.'

'That – that makes no sense,' Dulcie sputtered. She knew the classic Gothic too well. '*The Wetherly Ghost* doesn't need that kind of protection, not their copy. It's only about two hundred years old, and it's paper – not parchment, or whatever the Codex is.'

'I know.' Lloyd was meeting her eyes now. 'And there's always some excuse for the Codex not being there. It's being treated for mold, or there's some new decay-preventative process or something. But you know what they say about it – and about the *Wetherly.*'

'Oh, come on.' Dulcie felt the frustration building. 'The book may be *about* a haunting. But the thing itself is *not* haunted. It's not even that good!' She turned around, as if looking for help, but if Mr Grey was anywhere in the Yard, he was not prepared to debate the relative merits of eighteenth-century novels. 'Look, I've seen the Mildon *Wetherly*. I've even read a copy of the book. It's a perfectly ordinary Gothic by a perfectly ordinary author, Geoffrey Thomas. Thomas was the Earl of Richmond or something, so it was a big deal when he wrote it, but it's not any great shakes as a novel. And the Mildon copy is a first edition, sure, but just a printed book. The only reason for it even being in the Mildon is that it may have belonged to Thomas Paine. *May* have.'

'They say he was reading it when he died. Imagine, a total rationalist – a father of the country – reading a Gothic novel.'

'He was a sick old man. Maybe he wanted something diverting.' Dulcie was getting worked up. 'Of course, I'd have thought *The Ravages* would have been a better choice.'

'So, you don't believe . . .?' He left the rest of the question unspoken.

'No, I don't.' She took a deep breath. 'Look, I do believe that sometimes the spirits of those we love may linger.' She chose the word carefully, hoping that Mr Grey would not take offense. 'And, yes, the popular novels of that era do delve heavily into the supernatural. But, no, I do not believe that *The Wetherly Ghost* or any other books are themselves haunted.'

Even as she spoke, Dulcie thought of her strange dreams. If some spirit didn't linger, then what was the connection? Were her nocturnal visions simply the result of her scholarly immersion? It was too much to explain now to Lloyd, so she simply repeated herself. 'Neither the *Wetherly* nor the Dunster Codex is haunted.'

Something in her voice must have gotten through to Lloyd. He looked calmer now. 'OK, then. I'm glad I don't have to deal with it though. But Dulcie?'

'What?' She couldn't stop thinking of that dream. Something had been troubling the woman. Haunting her.

'Maybe you shouldn't tell the cops about the *Wetherly* when you talk to them. I mean, Coffin obviously thinks it's a big deal, or it wouldn't be in the Mildon to start with. And it is wrapped up in this, somehow.'

'Maybe I just shouldn't talk to the cops at all.'

He winced at that, and Dulcie wondered just how much the university police had pressured her timid office mate. 'Shouldn't you just clear this up?' he asked. 'I'm sure they're grilling everybody.'

'Have they questioned you yet?' She tried to catch her friend's eye, but he was staring at the new sod that carpeted the ground.

'Well, no. But I'm sure they just haven't gotten to me on their list.' He turned back toward her and held so still that she was sure he was lying. 'You know, the longer you evade them, the worse this will be.'

'I'm *not*—' She stopped herself. She had been evading them. Not by not being home, but by not returning that call. 'Look, I just want to find out what's going on before I talk to anyone.' The beginning of a plan began to form in her head. 'Would you do me a favor?'

Lloyd's pale face blanched a bit more, and two distinct lines appeared above his brow. To his credit, though, the word that finally came out of his mouth was succinct. 'Sure.'

'It doesn't have to do with any hauntings. Just – would you go back to the office and post a notice that I won't be able to make my office hours today?' Obvious relief washed over his face, but he still looked quizzical. 'There's someone who I think knows something about what is going on,' she explained. 'She was supposed to fill me in, but we didn't meet up. If I can only find her, I'm sure I can get to the bottom of this.'

'Find the Dunster Codex?' His high forehead wrinkled up even more.

'Well, probably not.' She smiled. Now that she had a clear plan, anything seemed possible. 'But I am sure that there is a rational, reasonable explanation for everything that's been going on. At the very least, I want to find out why the police are interested in me – that will be enough of a solution for one day.'

FOURTEEN

Once Lloyd had set off, Dulcie took a moment to plan her next step. No matter what everyone kept whispering, she didn't believe for a minute that the Dunster Codex was haunted. It was a valuable object, and it had been stolen. The idea that one of her colleagues was involved was unfortunate, particularly because the likely suspect was the missing Roland Galveston. That didn't mean there was anything supernatural going on, however. Merely criminal. And for better or worse, she was being dragged into it – just as Trista had been.

Trista had known something, though. She'd been about to tell Dulcie after the meeting, but she hadn't shown up. In the back of her mind, Dulcie could hear Suze's voice. She knew what her former room-mate would say: Suze would want Dulcie to go to the police and tell them everything that had been going on with Trista. But Suze was all ready to graduate. And she'd only had to pass a bunch of exams. For all of Suze's smarts, she didn't know the pressure of writing a thesis, of defending it.

As Dulcie saw it, the odds were good that Trista had already spoken with the cops. She had probably gone to them right after the departmental meeting. Maybe she was with them still. One thing Dulcie knew for sure: with everything that was happening, the last thing Trista needed was to have her friend calling up the university police to add her two cents and complicate the situation. No, Dulcie would find out what was going on first – and *then* take the information directly to the police. But to do that, she had to find Trista. The question was: how?

Like the rest of their colleagues, Trista also shared an office in the basement of Memorial Hall. And while it might be possible to sneak in, and slump past her own office, the risk of running into the police was just too high. After all, if the cops had bothered to look up her schedule, they almost certainly had a picture of her as well – the departmental facebook would have provided that, even if she wasn't well remembered from her previous run-ins with the law.

If it had been term time still, Trista might have been leading a section or some other kind of study group. This late in the spring, though, most of their tutoring duties were over. And since Trista was up against it with her defense, she'd probably be holed up reading. Which meant, really, she could be anywhere.

Dulcie pulled out her cell. Didn't this new age of communications mean that everyone was accessible all the time? But as her call went to Trista's voicemail once again, she realized that by itself might be a clue. Trista, Dulcie knew, had a secret hideaway deep in the bowels of the science library.

'It's the best,' Trista had confided in her only a few months before. 'The only books I can read are the ones I bring in with me. And nobody knows where to find me.'

Nobody but me, Dulcie thought, and headed up Mass Ave.

Half a block away from the shuttle stop, Dulcie caught herself. If, in fact, the police were looking for her, might they have alerted the university drivers? With a shiver, Dulcie stepped back and waited while the crimson and white bus pulled up, disgorging three tired-looking undergrads. The little bus paused for a moment, and Dulcie weighed the risk against the walk. But, no, it was a fine day – and the twenty or so blocks would do her good.

Cambridge prided itself on being pedestrian friendly. And while Dulcie had joined her colleagues in cursing the brick sidewalks each February, when they seemed particularly slick with ice, in these last days of May they were as picturesque as a postcard, glowing red against the explosion of spring green. Above her, the sky was a soft, full blue, the color broken only by the kind of clouds that children draw, white puffy things gamboling across the sky. The lilacs were already fading, dropping their tired blossoms on the ground, but the sweet scent lingered, and Dulcie was almost skipping as she passed by the Common and headed up to the Quad.

Then she saw it: brick, but not friendly. Not warm at all. How could she have forgotten that a walk up to the Quad, where the science library was located, would bring her right past the main university police headquarters? Dulcie mentally kicked herself and looked around. If she darted across the street, she could avoid passing right in front of the building. But wouldn't she then be more visible from those upper windows? The ones that looked out like so many unblinking eyes? What if she put her head down and hurried past. She could pretend she was late for a section or, better yet, an exam. An exam that – she looked at her watch – started at three p.m.? Well, maybe the university police weren't as conversant with the exam schedule. Maybe they didn't have all their forces out looking for one particular curly-haired grad student. And maybe she should give up her search for Trista. Wait for her friend to surface and explain herself. Go back to her own academic bolt hole and make her way through those essays. If she could glean one kernel from them, well, maybe she could have that part of her thesis done within the week.

The thought was enough to almost turn her around. Then she stopped. What had Mr Grey said, about friendship? If Trista was in some kind of a jam, Dulcie owed it to her to help – even if her friend didn't think she needed help. And even – Suze's words rang in her head – if Trista seemed to be afraid of shadows.

Besides, that was all she was afraid of, wasn't she? So the cops wanted to talk to her. She should have expected that after Professor Coffin's bombshell at the morning meeting. And the science library was only two blocks away. Two very long blocks.

In front of her, a garage door began to groan and creak open. A university cruiser pulled out and paused, and Dulcie found herself cringing, taking one step back and then another. But the car had only paused for traffic, and then pulled out, driving up the street without any sirens or any apparent hurry. As Dulcie watched, the door cranked close, shuddering a bit as it hit the driveway, and she shuddered with it. A breeze had picked up, and one of those fluffy clouds had passed over the sun. She closed her eyes and felt her curls blow around her face. Almost as if she were on a ship's deck, facing a dreaded future.

The key, Dulcie repeated, was that she had done it. Whatever fear she had felt, whatever dread had caused her those horrible sleepless nights – and no matter what Dulcie may have told Lloyd, she did believe that those dreams were psychic gifts – the nameless author had gone through with her plan. Dulcie might not know how yet, but she had the textual proof. The author of *The Ravages*, the woman in her dreams, had made the long and arduous journey from London to the New World and had lived to write again.

So, too, would Dulcie. So what if Dulcie had been temporarily derailed, stuck searching for that final essay – that last bit of political writing that would prove her point. She'd been throwing herself into *The Ravages* for more than three years now. She still loved the book, what there was of it. It was only now, when she was stuck reading these later works, these possibly – no, probably – peripheral essays, that she was beginning to feel the drag that all her colleagues talked about. Not yet four years in, she finally had thesis fatigue.

And only today she might have broken through. That one phrase, surfacing from the blue volume, might be the key to everything. Dulcie paused on the sidewalk: what she'd give to just be able to dive back into that collection, to find that sentence, that essay. But, how could she concentrate with what was going on? No, she decided, better to talk to Trista. Clear things up. Then she could get back to work with a clear conscience and nothing hanging over her. And without further ado, she marched right by the police station.

As soon as Dulcie entered the science library, she understood why Trista had chosen it. When last she'd dropped by, it had been winter, and not only had the Quad seemed horribly distant from everything in the Square, but the modern library had also looked – and felt – cold. Now, with the sun shining, it was an entirely different building. Its translucent stone walls glowed, lending a soft ivory light to the interior. And its modern fixtures – recessed lighting, spotless carpeting – made Widener look, well, shabby. Plus, Dulcie noticed with a touch of satisfaction, the science library was empty, or almost. A work-study student seemed to be catching up on his own reading at the checkout desk, while a uniformed guard stared out the glass door. The result was almost pure silence.

'Hi.' Dulcie found herself whispering as she presented her ID to the guard. He nodded, and she swiped through, marveling at the lack of bluster. Maybe she should start coming up here, too. Once she was done with her research and had started writing for real. The reading room, off to her left, looked cool and calm, its blue-grey carpet muffling any sound from the array of computer terminals.

Dulcie paused to check it out, when a slight sound – barely a whisper – disturbed her reverie. *Dulcie!* She started and looked

around. But, no, either her imagination was getting the better of
her, or Mr Grey was urging her on. Either way, she had come
here with a purpose. Two minutes later, she was in the elevator,
ascending to the modern building's top floor. And three minutes
later, she was staring out at a view of Cambridge she had never
seen.

'Wow.' Her voice was the only sound, but even it was hushed
in wonder. She was facing, she quickly figured, east: a quilt of
green foliage and red-brick was broken by a small tower, the
'castle' of Mt Auburn cemetery that served as much as a park
as a memorial. Built of granite on a man-made hill in the middle
of the cemetery, its oversized grey blocks made it stand out in
style as much as height. She and Chris had taken their bikes up
there a few times and hiked around, looking for famous names,
and once they had climbed the tower, enjoying the view over
what essentially served as the city's own arboretum. Not until
now, however, had she noticed how much the tower looked like
something from one of her novels. She could almost imagine
Hermetria, the heroine of *The Ravages*, imprisoned there. The
well-manicured grounds of the cemetery were hardly rocky crags.
But the idea was right.

And suddenly the modern library seemed sterile. Time to find
Trista and get back to work. With a certain reluctance, Dulcie
turned from the window. As she remembered, Trista's hideaway
was a cubicle over behind the stacks.

'It's all COBOL texts. Ancient history,' her friend had told
her. 'Nobody even uses it any more.'

Dulcie had smiled and nodded. Clearly, Trista picked up more
computer lingo from her boyfriend Jerry than Dulcie did from
Chris. She'd been worried, briefly, that this meant she didn't
listen to her boyfriend, and had brought it up to him that evening.

He'd only laughed. 'Sweetie, if I wanted to talk code, I'd go
hang out with Jerry.' He'd hugged her, then. 'Really, Dulce. With
you I can get away from all of that.'

She hadn't felt entirely easy at his explanation. After all, by
now he was thoroughly versed in the uses of metaphor and simile
in the late-eighteenth-century novel. Shouldn't she reciprocate?
But the incident had stuck in her mind, and finding the bookshelf
was easy.

'Knock, knock!' Dulcie felt a twinge of guilt. A secret study place should not be disturbed. But when nobody answered, she peeked around the shelf to Trista's hideaway. Tucked between the shelves and what appeared to be a utility cabinet, the niche had a chair, a small table that would do for a desk, and enough natural light to make one forget one was indoors. What it did not have was Dulcie's blonde-haired friend.

'Tris?' It was pointless. Dulcie could see that nobody was there. The desk held no books, and the chair was neatly tucked in. On a whim, Dulcie pulled it out. No, the seat felt as cool as the rest of the climate-controlled building. Trista had her phone turned off, but not because she was in the library.

Dulcie turned to leave, when a thought stopped her. Mr Grey. He'd prompted her when she'd hesitated. His voice had gotten her past the police station. Although her spectral pet could be enigmatic, he didn't do anything without a reason. Surely, he'd known that Trista hadn't been here. Maybe, Dulcie thought, she was on her way right now. Besides, the walk had been a little tiring, especially as she'd hurried those last few blocks. And the library was cool and quiet.

Dulcie pulled the chair out further and sat, facing the blank wall. This little niche certainly had no distractions. Then again, it just might be too out of the way. Dulcie ran her hand over the table; a thin layer of fine dust came up, white, on her fingers. Almost like talcum powder.

She rubbed her fingers together, the sight of it on her fingertips sparking a memory. Powder, on her hands . . . fine, white powder. Dulcie found herself thinking about the Mildon, trying to recall the last time she had been in the rare book library – and why. It had to have been about *The Wetherly Ghost*, she decided, and it all came back.

She remembered donning the special cotton gloves the collection required. Coated with some kind of non-corrosive powder that made slipping them on and off easier, more sterile, they were supposedly expensive – and expensive to clean. That powder alone was rumored to cost as much as gold dust, and though Dulcie had serious doubts about that, she'd heard that they were the real reason scholars were required to leave their bags up front when they entered the collection. Whatever the powder was made of, she had noticed how it lingered as she'd left, wiping one hand on the other to cleanse her hands of the fine grains.

Could this be what Mr Grey had wanted to show her? It seemed awfully thin. More likely, the white powder was ordinary dust. Perhaps – she looked up at the utility closet – someone had been drilling. If the walls were plaster, this dust could come from them. But the wall in front of her looked pristine. Above her, the lighting fixture appeared untouched, its light clear and warm. Perfect for reading.

She couldn't resist, she really couldn't. She had done what she could to find Trista, and now she was here and, well, maybe this was what Mr Grey had in mind. Dulcie brushed the remaining white powder from her hand, reached into her bag, and pulled out the blue volume, *Early American Dissenters*. Somewhere, a machine started a low hum, and Dulcie was aware of the slightest shift in air currents. A bit of a chill in the air, perhaps. Well, that would keep her from dozing as she read through the rest of the essays.

It took a while, and Dulcie was grateful for Lucy's sweater by the time she found it. Since so many of the essays were not signed – or were signed by such obvious pen names as 'A Gentleman of Sound Mind' or 'A Partisan Party-Goer' – she had felt it necessary to at least skim each one. By the time she found the most promising – 'On Reading' by 'A Lady of Letters' – her fingers were getting cold.

But it wasn't the air-conditioning that sent goosebumps up her arms. It was the opening phrase: '*The education of young ladies, of virtue undimm'd, must be of concern to all . . .*' That was it – the very phrase that she had found in an article from London, published in 1792. '*The bookish mind, far from challenging the finer qualities, shall enhance them . . .*' That exact passage had been in *The Ravages*, one of the arguments that the heroine, Hermetria, had made to her much more traditionally feminine nemesis, Demetria. '*Learning shall be the setting for her jewel'd countenance . . .*' The missing link! She'd found it.

She rummaged in her bag for her notebook, dropping her pen in the process. Pushing the chair back, she got down on her knees. From this vantage point, the housekeeping in the science library left something to be desired. One gum wrapper – Juicy Fruit – had been kicked over in the corner, its foil balled up against the wall. Dulcie had to smile. If Mr Grey had been here, that bit of junk would have metamorphosed into a toy, and instead of picking it up, she'd have batted it out to him, starting an impromptu soccer match. On a whim, she flicked the little ball and watched as it bounced unevenly on the carpet, stopping over by the wall.

And that's when she saw it, tucked into the edge of the carpet, up against the wall, where the neat installation had left only the slightest gully between the deep pile and the wall. A tiny slip, its faded hue almost camouflaged against the industrial weave. If it hadn't been for the white powder on the table top, she might not even have noticed. But that – and the thought of Mr Grey – had made her think about the special collections. About the missing Dunster Codex. What she saw, half hidden against the wall, was most definitely a blue ticket.

'Oh, Trista.' She sat back, pausing a moment before reaching for it. In reality, it could be anyone's. Many scholars used this library, not all of them science majors. But, realistically, the odds were slim. How many scholars would have had reason to access both the Widener special collections and the science library? How many of them had made a habit of coming to just this secluded corner?

There would be an explanation. There had to be. And with that thought, Dulcie reached over to pluck the ticket from where it was lodged. 'Trista, what are you involved in?' She turned it over, dreading the name she expected to see there. And sat up so fast, she smacked her head on the bottom of the table.

The blue ticket – the one that allowed access to the rare book collection – didn't bear the name of her friend. Instead, in block letters, it bore another's. Spelled out, clear despite the usual carbon fuzziness, was a different name. Her own.

FIFTEEN

Her head no longer hurt where she'd smacked it against the table. In fact, she couldn't feel it at all. But somehow, her legs weren't functioning, and it took forever for Dulcie to scramble out from under the corner desktop, grab her bag, and head for the elevator. This must have been what Mr Grey had wanted her to see. The question was, what did it mean?

As she waited for the elevator to appear, Dulcie tried taking some deep breaths. There was no point in panicking. Only when spots began to appear before her eyes did she realize that hyper-ventilating was a possibility, too, and so she leaned back against the wall to wait – and to try to calm down.

That ticket: when was it from? Dulcie opened her clenched fist just as the sliding metal doors parted in front of her. The elevator was as deserted as the rest of the library, but she still did not dare to do more than peek at the blue paper as she descended toward the first floor. The line where the date should have been was, of course, smudged. If this were something from a novel, she might suspect foul play. In reality, she suspected the failings of outdated technology. Considering that this was a carbon copy, it was a wonder she could read the name on it.

Maybe . . . She opened her fist for one more peek. No luck. That was, in fact, her name written on the dotted line.

The doors slid open as she was peering at the crumpled blue slip, and Dulcie jumped. Over at the checkout desk, the reader looked up and smiled. Dulcie did her best to smile back. Making eye contact with a fellow student helped her ignore the guard, who had turned in her direction. If she could just keep walking . . .

'Miss?'

Dulcie froze, halfway past the guard. If she ran, could she make it to the doors before him?

'Miss?'

Probably not. She turned, that smile turning stiff on her face.

'I have to check your bag.' He looked almost apologetic.

'Of course.' She hadn't even been aware that she was holding her breath till then. Still, it was difficult to open her bag with one hand clenched tight. The guard didn't seem to notice, though, and after a cursory poke through her things, looked up with an answering grin of his own.

'Thanks, miss. Have a nice day.'

She nodded, unable to respond in any more articulate sense, and was out the door.

Five minutes later, Dulcie found herself sitting on a bench in the Radcliffe Quad, trying to figure out what to do next. The police were looking for her, and now she knew why. Or thought she did. Carefully, her hands trembling, Dulcie spread out the little slip to examine it more closely. DULCINEA SCHWARTZ, it said, clear as day. That made sense: on anything official, Dulcie would use her full name. By now, she'd even become inured to the smiles her mismatched monikers produced. The date, however, defied her closest examination; the sweat of her nervous hand hadn't made it any clearer. The only thing she could make out, she thought, was a '5'.

Dulcie wracked her brain. Had she visited the Mildon collection in May? On the fifth of a month prior? In truth, she couldn't quite remember when she'd last used her access. The segregated area – a specially secured library within a library, tucked into the corner of one of the lower floors of Widener – kind of creeped her out. The rumors that its state of the art fire-protection features involved a special vacuum to suck out all the oxygen in the room didn't help.

She looked back at her name, written out large in block letters. Would she even write her name like that? For a moment, she felt a flood of relief. Maybe this was a forgery. After all, she really did have no memory of visiting in the previous month. Maybe she was being framed, an innocent patsy for an international ring of thieves.

No. Dulcie shook her head. As much as she'd like this all to be a story, that theory was as fantastic as any in her novels. She was merely one graduate student among many. Even if she couldn't remember the last time she'd gone into the rare book room, she had visited it, several times. And even if she couldn't recall her most recent visit, she hadn't forgotten the instructions, repeated every time, to press down hard enough to make all the copies legible. All of which probably accounted for the smudged date – and for the thick block letters in which her name had been recorded for all time, like a guilty secret. If she was going to question something, she should be asking about this ticket: how did this little blue tag get from the Mildon – or more likely, from Dulcie's own bag – to Trista's secret hideaway in a secluded corner of the science library? Had Trista been holding on to it for some reason? Had she – Dulcie paused – taken it?

Dulcie punched in Trista's number and again heard it go to voicemail. 'Trista, call me.' She was getting angry now, which at least beat being afraid. Where was her friend? On a whim, she tried Lloyd.

'Hey, Dulcie, are you coming in?' Of course, he was back at their basement office.

'No. I mean, I don't think so.' Somehow office hours seemed like a foreign concept. 'I was wondering – Trista didn't come by, did she? Or call?'

'Funny you should ask.' Lloyd sounded as distracted as always, so Dulcie waited. 'No, she didn't. One of your students did.'

'And that was it?' She didn't even want to mention the police.

'Yup, nobody else. I guess the term really is winding down.'

'About time.' Dulcie suspected her sigh was audible over the phone. That was fine; Lloyd would assume she was grateful not to have a dozen calls to make. Only a week or so ago, when exams were in full force, Dulcie had found it necessary to turn her phone off even when she wasn't in the library. Students were a necessity – teaching paid the bills – but when they panicked, as they seemed to do every exam period, they were truly the bane of a grad student's existence.

Still, she felt a little bad for leaving one of her charges in the lurch.

'Which one?' She ran through her current crop. 'Lisa C.? The one with the purple hair and no concept of sentence structure? Tom the procrastinator?'

She heard a chuckle. 'I'd swear those were my students, Dulcie, but no. This one didn't leave her name.'

'And she wants me to call her back, right?' Undergrads. They thought they were the center of the universe. Or at least of their section leaders' lives.

'Probably. I'm sorry, I should have pressed, but she seemed upset and just kind of turned on her heel. And I've been trying to get through the notes for the Gryzinski paper.'

'That's OK.' Dulcie hoped the irritation in her voice didn't come through. 'I really appreciate you covering for me.'

She prepared to hang up, when Lloyd came back. 'That's fine. It was useful to have the office for another hour, especially after the kerfuffle this morning.' He paused, and Dulcie could almost see him blushing. 'I was a little flustered, I know. But I have gotten a lot done and, well, I know you're in writing mode. So if you want to come in, I'll get lost. Just let me know.'

She considered. It wasn't like she was going to get anything else done, and if she had just a few minutes of quiet, she could finish that essay. Still, if the police were looking for her . . . 'No, thanks. I mean, enjoy.'

'Cool. Oh, Dulcie? I don't know if it helps at all, but that student? The one who came looking for you? I thought she was Trista at first. Could be her younger sister, right down to the nose stud.'

SIXTEEN

I t was a coincidence. It had to be. Still, Dulcie was wondering about the mysterious visitor as she walked, the long way, back to the Square. None of her tutees looked like Trista, not even remotely. An image came to her of a girl, blonde and slim as Trista, whom she had seen in passing. The girl had been upset, maybe over finals. But she wasn't anyone Dulcie had known.

Had the girl been interested in Dulcie – or in one of Dulcie's classes? Dulcie knew she was clutching at straws. Undergrads popped up for a million reasons. Maybe this one was considering concentrating in eighteenth-century British fiction. Maybe she had heard that Dulcie would be offering a junior tutorial in the fall. Maybe she was hoping to get a head start with some summer tutoring. Actually, that last option might not be so bad. Chris had taken on some private tutoring students, and the money had come in handy. If Dulcie could scrape a few hours out of her week, maybe they could go on that vacation they'd been talking about.

As much as she usually loved Cambridge, right now the idea of getting out of the city was appealing. A car whooshed by, and for a moment, she substituted the sound of a wave. She and Chris, on the Cape, reading on the beach . . . Now that would be a vacation. Of course, they'd have to find a place to stay, and it was a little late to get in on anyone's group rental. That wouldn't be a problem if they went cross-country for a change of scene. They could take the bus and spend a week or so at the arts colony. No; she shook her head. That would never work. While Lucy

would love to have them both there, Dulcie knew that bringing
Chris into that environment would be akin to animal cruelty. The
very idea of Chris participating in a moon circle made her laugh
– and the ritual sharing? Not a good idea. Besides, who would
watch over Esmé?

Thoughts of the rambunctious young cat made Dulcie pause.
Usually, she managed to get back home during the day. Not that
the kitten needed her to be present, but Dulcie liked to be. The
sociable little cat certainly never minded the company or a little
extra playtime. Today, though, had just gotten away from her,
and she found she'd been walking with the most direct route to
the apartment on her mind.

That's what had tripped her up. She'd meant to walk around
this area – take one of the old streets with its brick sidewalks
and discover another part of the city. Somehow, she had ended
up back on Mass Ave – and once again, ahead of her, the police
station loomed. In this light, with the late-afternoon shadows
darkening its modern front, it really did loom like some forbid-
ding mountain keep. She thought of the blue ticket in her bag,
about the Dunster Codex and the rumors surrounding it. Then
she thought of her kitten. It had been a tiring day – and a long
one. Esmé would be waiting. It was time to go home.

Head up, as if she truly had nothing to fear, Dulcie strode
right past the police station. Halfway past its brick front, she
heard a grinding noise, like some giant machine, behind her.
The garage door was reeling up, the nose of a cruiser already
visible. That was it. Her courage was shot. Tucking her bag
under her arm, Dulcie ran.

'Honey, I'm home!' Twenty minutes later, Dulcie pushed open
the apartment door to be greeted by the excited chirps of the cat.
'Kitty!' Dropping her bag, she scooped the round feline up in
her arms. A wet nose pushed up against her face, the chorus of
mews replaced by a hearty purr.

'I know. I've missed you, too.' Dulcie leaned her face into the
soft fur. Mr Grey had always greeted her, although his statelier
manner usually meant something a little quieter and more refined.
'Maybe this isn't all bad,' she told the kitten's black back, only
to find those round green eyes suddenly staring up at her.

'What?' Dulcie felt a stab of disloyalty, but she'd been

complimenting the kitten, hadn't she? 'You're both very different kinds of cats. That's all.' It didn't matter. The little animal squirmed to be put down, and Dulcie obliged. As she watched the tuxedo march off, though, she was almost sure she heard the ghost of a chuckle.

'Mr Grey?' No, there was nothing more, and Dulcie went into the kitchen, where a cereal bowl and mug rested in the drying rack. At least Chris was making the effort to clean up after himself, she thought as she reached for the bowl. He hadn't left a note, though, and for a moment, Dulcie wondered why. Was he afraid the police would see it? Had Mr Grey advised him against it?

The idea of her boyfriend and her former pet having private conversations was still unsettling and disturbing, even if Dulcie knew she was being silly. The whole incident with the blue ticket had freaked her out, but she would get an answer to it tomorrow. At the very least, she'd be able to talk it over with her boyfriend soon enough.

'Maybe it is just a girls' night, Esmé,' she called over to the cat. 'Just the two of us, on our own. So what will it be: pizza or Chinese?'

In response, the cat started to wash.

SEVENTEEN

*T*he wind howled, and the ship, storm-toss'd, pitched as if a wild thing, its deck slick with the ocean's spray. Her hand was icy, pale and wet, as she pushed a long curl back. Chill'd to the bone, she wrapped her shawl around her, its thick wool a scarce cover 'gainst the storm. She should retreat, take cover in the cabin that awaited. And yet beneath the deck, she sensed the oppression of all above her. Of all that awaited her at journey's end. Of what she must do . . . She should be writing, laying down these last thoughts before her perils o'ertook her, stole her dreams as they had her life, her home behind. She should take up pen and ink, capture on the paper the thoughts that flew before her, driven on petrel's wings, cloud-driven and

furious. She turned, to her cabin, to the travel desk that ever
accompanied her. To write into the night, as bells began chiming,
furious and loud.

'The reef!' Beyond the mast, lost in the inky black, a lone
seaman cried. 'The reef!' His voice battl'd with the wind, a wail
both mournful and fierce. 'Beware, lest we be dashed upon the
rocks!'

The bells, the bells. Their chiming, fierce and desperate, woke
Dulcie, who sat up, gasping with fear. But as she blinked, the
sound changed from that wild, tinny alarm to the ordinary ring
of her phone. She checked her clock: it was early, too early for
anyone to be calling unless it was an emergency. And so she
dragged herself over to her desk.

'If this is Lucy, calling about a vision,' she mumbled into the
predawn dark. She reached for the phone, blinking, but she was
too late. Whoever had called had hung up again, and when she
checked voicemail, there was no message. She was tempted to
leave it at that – maybe someone had dialed a wrong number.
Maybe it was Lucy, and her poor mother had, too late, figured
out the East Coast time difference. There had been too much
going on, however, and so she checked the incoming calls, hoping
for Lucy – or even Trista. No such luck; the number came up
'restricted', and she was left to lie there, wondering.

It wasn't like she'd been having a restful sleep. Still, the idea
of getting up seemed painful, and the inky black outside was far
from inviting. She checked the clock again. It shouldn't be this
dark, not at this time of year. A storm was brewing, maybe the
first thunderstorm of the season. That would explain her dream.
She closed her eyes, waiting for the sound of rain to lull her
back to sleep.

Dulcie hadn't meant to stay up so late. She'd known Chris
was working and had figured she'd make an early night of it, in
the hope that a good eight hours of sleep would leave her better
prepared to figure out the tangle of the last two days. She'd toyed
with finishing that essay, the one by 'A Lady of Letters'. After
all, it might be the last piece in her thesis puzzle. But despite
her excitement over her discovery, by the time she got home,
Dulcie just didn't feel up to working on something new. Things
had been so crazy lately, she couldn't shake the feeling that

anything new might not necessarily be good. That was silly, she knew, but knowing didn't help. Instead, she told herself that she would be better able to appreciate her new find in the morning, when she was fresh.

Besides, she didn't feel like taking notes. Didn't even, really, feel like thinking, and so, on the grounds that she really needed to refresh her sense of *The Ravages*, particularly the second of the two extant sections, which she didn't have quite by heart, she'd allowed herself a night of reading. Esmé hadn't disagreed, exactly, though Dulcie noticed the little cat prowling around more than usual.

It should have been a relaxing night. She should have slept, though the three-meat pizza – pepperoni, sausage, and meatballs – had probably been a bad idea, arriving as it did after she had scarfed a bowl of Raisin Bran for an appetizer. And just when she'd found her eyes closing, Chris had finally returned her dinner-time call. He'd been swamped, she knew that. But going over the events of the day after midnight had not been conducive to sleep. Especially when he started questioning her memory of the blue ticket – was she sure that was her handwriting? – and wondering out loud what Trista's motives could have been to hang on to it.

'Maybe she wasn't the one who dropped it, Chris.' Dulcie had found herself making excuses for her absent friend. 'Maybe it was just some strange fluke, like it stuck to something that I lent to Tris.'

'Which would be what?' Chris's question left her open-mouthed. He didn't wait for an answer. 'You two never even read the same books. And you don't go up to the Quad, I know you, Dulcie. You're always in Widener – or your office. No, I want to know why Trista had that ticket – and when it is from. When did you last go into the Muldoon or Milltown, or whatever it is – the rare book area – anyway?

To her frustration, and his, she couldn't answer. Not definitively. The Mildon wasn't on her normal rounds. Still, she knew she had been in at some point that year. And she had access.

Chris wasn't happy with that, but there wasn't anything she could do. Besides, she couldn't argue with him when she was exhausted and he was wide awake. She didn't want to. After a day like this, all she wanted was to be held. And he wasn't there.

'I'm sorry, honey.' He must have heard something in her tone.
'I know you don't want to think this way about your friend. But
face it, she's acting strange. And you know you didn't steal the
Dunster Codex.' He paused. 'You didn't, did you?'

'Chris!'

'Sorry, sorry. Bad joke.'

'No, it's OK.' She sniffed, more for effect than anything. 'Truth
is, I don't think I've ever even seen the Codex. And it's not the
first thing I'd have taken, I mean, if I were going to steal anything.'

'Oh?' His voice was softer now, conspiratorial, but Dulcie
knew they were both trying to make light of the day.

'Definitely. If I were going to take anything . . .' She stopped
to think. 'I'd take *The Wetherly Ghost*.' The silence that greeted
her confession showed her she'd lost him. 'It's my period,'
she explained. 'A Gothic. I mean, it's not a great book or
anything. In fact, it's definitely inferior to *The Ravages*, but
it's worth a lot.'

'A Gothic novel worth something?' She heard his joking tone.
At that time of night, it was hard to laugh along.

'It's a first edition in very fine condition. And –' with a reluc-
tant sigh she gave up the secret – 'it comes from the personal
library of Thomas Paine.'

'Wow, well, that's something.' Chris was trying. 'I mean, he
was one of the leaders of the Revolution, right?'

Dulcie didn't respond. When would people recognize it was
the writing, not the book's owner, that mattered? Even if the
owner *had* made history with his own prose.

'So if the cops start asking about that—'

'Chris!' She'd had it, but he laughed, and when she didn't,
he apologized. The rest of the conversation passed without any
more teasing. But the strange mood hadn't been completely
dispelled, and it thickened like a fog as she read into the night.
It didn't help that Esmé continued to act odd. After that first
affectionate greeting, the little cat had been restless, roaming
around the little apartment and chirping to herself. Sometime
after one, Dulcie found her in the kitchen, staring at the corner
of the refrigerator.

'What is it, Esmé?'

The cat didn't move.

'Esmé?'

Not even a tail flick. If it had been Mr Grey sitting there, Dulcie liked to think she'd have gotten an answer. Her former companion would have given her a clue – or explained why he was staring like that. He might even have incorporated a lesson into his vigilance: maybe he was on guard to show her that she should be, too. The longer she watched the young cat, however, the more convinced she became that Esmé was simply exercising her animal instincts. And that brought up a whole other issue.

Dulcie didn't like to think of herself as squeamish. Ghouls, mad monks, and haunted castles didn't faze her. But a mouse? What place did a mouse have in their apartment? In her life? Better not to dwell on it, Dulcie decided, and, leaving Esmé to her studies, she had gone to bed.

EIGHTEEN

O *pposing forces then met, with violence profound. Above heaven itself crack'd and opened, flinging its last battery o'er the ship as the heaving sea flung itself o'erhead to meet the tumultuous sky. She, beleaguered lady, toss'd and beaten, would be dashed between Scylla and Charybdis. Staring into the void, she considered such a fate and shivered. Not for her, though 'twere her very soul lost – but for that which awaited: a life washed away as ink, not yet dry, doused by the frigid waters. A life, unfulfilled. A story unfinished, its words unwritten, haunting her. Soaked by frigid salt, as well by pelting rain, she raised her face to the blackness, unwilling to bend, to beg mercy, to . . .*

When Dulcie woke for the second time, the rain beating against the window almost made her believe she was still on-board the ship, soaked and freezing. It must have been the thunder that had woken her, she realized, checking the clock. And even as the wind whistled through the slight opening she had left, causing the shade to rattle and thrash, she lay still. She didn't have to get up for a few hours yet; the storm had come at the right time.

'What a dream.' She shook her head. 'Now, that was a storm.'

Her dreams were often vivid, springing as they seemed to from what her subject had lived through. Recently, however, they had ratcheted up in intensity. Before, Dulcie had felt like a witness, spying on the author. Dreams like this one, though, were more terrifying. This dream set her on the lonely ship. She closed her eyes and, instead of the warm wind, felt the salt spray and the icy rain. Felt, as well, the despair that threatened to sink the woman's spirit, if not her ship – that threatened the promise of . . . what? Sitting up in bed, Dulcie covered her face with her hands. Right now, alone in the dark, she could not find any answers. Could not see how the woman could survive, could fight back against the forces allied against her. Could not conceive of how she would continue, how she would—

'Mrup?' With a thud that belied her small size, the cat landed on the foot of the bed. Dulcie looked up, grateful for the interruption.

'Did the storm wake you, too, Esmé?' She paused to listen. The first real thunder of the season boomed on, and Dulcie saw a flash of lightning illuminating the sky.

Outside, the wind was dying down. 'I think it's over,' she said to Esmé.

'Mrup.' The tuxedo cat seemed to agree and began to knead the blanket on Chris's side of the bed.

'Want to come up here?' Dulcie patted the pillow. Now that the storm had moved on, the breeze coming in was chilly. Dulcie tucked her feet up under her, which was easier than getting up to close the window. 'Esmé?' Her boyfriend wouldn't be home till near dawn, and on a night like this, she could use the company.

The cat ignored her, to continue working the soft mound of blanket into something that was conceivably somehow softer and more appropriate for her plump body. Then she collapsed rather gracelessly, with only the black back of her head turned toward Dulcie.

'Well, thanks for showing up.' Dulcie leaned back on her own pillow. At times like this, she couldn't help thinking of Mr Grey. Even as a living cat, the large grey had been more responsive. For months after he had died, she had slept with one arm outstretched, trained by all the nights when he had come to sleep in the crook of her arm. And since his mortal demise, he had rarely appeared without commenting. True, Dulcie often found his comments confusing. A ghost cat could be even more enigmatic and insular than a living feline. But at least he responded to her and didn't turn his back on her like . . . like . . . this kitten did. It was like the flip side of living with Chris. He loved her, she knew he did, and she loved him. Only, it was hard to wake up from a nightmare and not have him here. Hard to only have this *cat*.

'*Now, now, Dulcie.*'

She was imagining it, she knew that. Her spectral friend was not in this room with her. He would certainly not appear to mediate between her and Esmé, or between herself and Chris. Especially not – she turned on to her side – when he had most recently preferred talking to Chris than to her. Facing away from her boyfriend's pillow wasn't the revenge she had wanted though, and instead she flipped back, punching her own pillow a bit aggressively to fluff it up. Somehow, the room had grown warm again.

'*Now, now.*'

She knew that she was acting out of a fit of pique, and she knew what Mr Grey would say to that. She could almost feel the prick of claws ever so slightly unsheathed, the edge in his usually warm tone: there was a lesson here. Something for her to take away about sharing, about growing. About love. But sometimes she didn't want a lesson. She shifted again, the bed somehow simultaneously too big and too hard to be comfortable. Sometimes she just wanted to be held.

At her feet, the kitten stirred and looked up. 'Sorry,' she muttered as those green eyes blinked and the white part of the nose once more sank down in sleep. 'I know. I should be happy you're here.'

The little cat did look very peaceful. And if she kept her distance, really, whose fault was that? More often than not, their interactions took the form of Dulcie disciplining the young cat. She should be grateful Esmé slept with her at all. Dulcie shifted, kicking at the cover. It had become a warm night again. Humid. And lonely.

'Come here, kitten.' Dulcie reached down to the kitten, lifting her to the top of the bed. 'We can have some good times together, can't we? You can be comfy here, can't you?'

For a moment, she regretted the move. The little cat had been disturbed and now stood, stretching and looking around, as if it were she who had been awakened by a dream.

'Please?' Dulcie began stroking the smooth black back as the cat sat and then settled into a Sphinx pose. 'Esmé?' She tried for even strokes, aiming to relax the cat and ease her toward sleep. The effect was hypnotic for her too, the soft warm body slowly beginning to vibrate and to purr. Dulcie had an image of the sea, calmed, the night-colored swells heaving slowly and gently as a ship moved onward. Moving toward where, she wasn't sure, and for a few seconds she remembered the fear, the dread. The voyage had happened, though. The ship had met its fate, for good or ill, and now the night was still.

Dulcie lowered her own head to the pillow as Esmé's eyes closed, and soon only her fingertips were moving, brushing against the few white guard-hairs that stood out against Esmé's dark back. Soon the fingers were still, leaning slightly against the black fur that heaved softly up and down. Dulcie's own breath barely moved that fur, and neither of them noticed when a shadow landed noiselessly beside them, curling up on the empty pillow to watch until the morning light.

NINETEEN

Despite the late night interruptions, Dulcie slept soundly, only coming awake to hear the ringing of her phone on the nightstand. Sitting up, she found herself once more alone. Chris – she checked the bedside clock – wouldn't be home for another hour yet. And Esmé had removed herself to the window sill, where she peered out at the world like a voyager hoping to spot a distant shore.

'What?' The phone was still ringing, and Dulcie reached for it. Unless – she roused herself – maybe she should let it go to voicemail. No; she checked the number. Tris's home line, not the cops – and not some strange restricted caller. So maybe something had happened to her friend's cell. Dulcie flicked the phone on, trying to remember the last time her buddy had called from the apartment she and Jerry shared.

'So, what happened?' She propped herself up on the pillow and waited. Finally, she'd get to hear whatever it was her friend had meant to tell her yesterday – as well as an explanation for why she'd failed to show. Trista could spin a tale out, but that would be OK if she at least had a good explanation. 'Don't tell me you got lost.'

'What do you mean, what happened?' Whatever she was expecting, it wasn't the voice on the other end. Male, and decidedly worried. 'Dulcie, do you know something?'

'Jerry!' Dulcie sat up and tucked the sheet around her. 'I thought you were going to be Trista.'

'I was hoping she was with you.' A thud interrupted her. Esmé had jumped to the ground. Jerry kept on talking. 'She's not?'

'No, but it's early, right?' Dulcie reached for her clock. 'I was just getting up.'

'I'm sorry. I know it's early. It's just – Trista didn't come home last night.'

Dulcie took a deep breath. That did sound serious, but not necessarily in the way Jerry meant. Trista and Jerry had had problems earlier in the spring, and Trista had gone on a few dates with different men. She loved them both, but if her friends were going through another rough romantic patch, she didn't want to get in the middle of it. Still, there was a note in Jerry's voice that she didn't recognize. Nerves, or—

'I'm really scared. She didn't call. Do you know where she is? What –' he swallowed, loudly enough for her to hear – 'happened?'

Dulcie shook her head, then remembered that he couldn't see her. 'You didn't, I don't know, have a fight or anything?'

'No, nothing like that.' The prevailing note in his voice was sadness now, and she felt bad for asking. 'We've been good, Dulcie. That's why I'm nervous. And, well, it sounds like she stood you up?'

'Not exactly.' Dulcie tucked her knees up and tried to reconstruct the events of the previous day. 'I saw her at the department meeting yesterday, in the morning. That was, well, that was crazy. There's a lot going on.' She paused. Did Jerry know about the police visit? She cast about for a polite way to bring it up.

'Did she tell you anything about our Roland Galveston?' she

said, finally settling on a safe middle ground. 'He's this guy in our department.'

She heard Jerry sigh and realized what this must sound like to him. 'He was – they are friends, Jerry. Just friends.' She hoped she was telling the truth. 'But something is going on. He's gone missing, and he might be involved with, well, with something else that has gone missing – a rare book from the Widener special collections.'

The disappearance of the Dunster Codex might not be general news yet, but Dulcie didn't want to explain. Besides, Jerry didn't care about the Dunster Codex. He cared about Trista. 'We had a big meeting about it, yesterday morning. Everyone in the department. But even before then, Trista had wanted to talk. We were going to get coffee after the meeting, but she said she had to do something first. And then she never showed up.'

'I know you two were going for coffee. She texted me, like, around eleven.' Dulcie relaxed a little. At least her two friends had been communicating. 'She had this crazy day planned and was telling me she might not make it home for dinner. So I didn't worry. Not at first. I even went out to the computer lab for a while around midnight. By the time I got home, it was almost four. There was this huge thunderstorm happening, but the bedroom door was closed, so I figured she'd managed to sleep through it, and I went to sleep on the sofa.'

Dulcie bit her lip. She would hate it if Chris came home and didn't come up to bed. She hated it when he didn't come home. Then again, when he didn't come home, she knew he was at the computer lab. And, she reminded herself, different couples have different rules.

'Maybe she got up early? Didn't want to wake you?' Dulcie heard the question in her own voice. Trista was not a morning person.

Jerry knew it too. 'Trista? No way. Besides, she wouldn't have. She always wakes me up. We have breakfast together.' That detail made Dulcie smile, but it proved the last straw for Jerry. Dulcie heard him sob as he choked out the words: 'She didn't come home last night. And I haven't heard from her. I can't reach her. Dulcie, she's disappeared.'

TWENTY

Dulcie did her best to calm Jerry down, but it was next to impossible to do over the phone. Yes, he knew Trista was defending her thesis next week. How could he not? But he'd called everywhere before trying Dulcie. She wasn't holed up cramming. She was gone – and Jerry's nerves were fraying. Dulcie was worried too, though she had a better sense of Trista's ability to take care of herself.

With a few quick calculations, Dulcie mapped out her day. Classes had ended for the semester, so she had no ten o'clock appointment. She didn't even have office hours, she thought with a twinge of guilt. She'd been thinking that today she'd finish reading that essay, maybe track down enough proof to start writing the next chapter. But friends came first. Besides, even though she'd dodged Chris's questions, she wanted to talk to Trista about that ticket. It had gotten to the science library somehow, and that was most likely related to her friend. Not that she'd bring that up to Jerry; he sounded too upset. Her stomach rumbled, and she suggested meeting for breakfast, at least to plan what to do next.

'I don't know. Maybe I should stay here.' She heard the edge in his voice and decided that was the last thing he needed. Food and caffeine wouldn't solve his problems – not unless Trista walked in while he was refueling – but staying in their tiny walk-up wasn't healthy for anyone. Besides, some things were better discussed in person.

'No, you should get out. Get some air.' She thought quickly. 'Look, leave a note for her someplace obvious. You know she's always losing her phone. And make sure your phone is on. We'll figure this out.'

She sounded more optimistic than she felt, and she looked longingly back at the bed once she had gotten up. Chris would be home soon. She hadn't been in the best mood last night, and his teasing hadn't helped. In the light of morning, however, some of his questions had been valid. He'd be wiped out when he came home, ready for sleep. Still, she'd have liked to bounce all this by him. Even the cat had absented herself, and so she showered and dressed and tried to put her own concerns away.

'Esmé, there you are!' As she reached for her sweater, the round cat appeared, rubbing against the closet door. 'You probably want some breakfast, too.'

The little cat sniffed delicately at the dish, but then sat down and looked at Dulcie.

'What? Wrong flavor?' Those green eyes could be a little unnerving, and Dulcie tried to make light of her unease. 'You want some coffee?'

The cat stared at her without blinking.

'OK, not that.' She bit her lip. Lucy, she knew, would tell her to listen to Esmé. She'd say that the little creature was a messenger, or that she was carrying portents or something. As much as Dulcie tried to distance herself from her mother's *mishegas*, right now she wondered if there might be something in it.

She sat on the kitchen floor and faced the small cat. 'What is it, Esmé? Tell me, please.'

The cat blinked once.

'Esmé, I know you can speak. I've heard you.' She looked around. No sign of her boyfriend. 'We both have. And the way you're looking at me, well, I feel there's something going on. Something besides a mouse.' She shivered at the thought and tried to dismiss it. 'Something important.'

If any of her friends could see her right now, they'd think she'd lost it. Any of them but Chris. Then again, Chris didn't need to plead with the kitten. Chris, by his own account, was getting regular updates from Mr Grey.

Esmé turned toward the table, and Dulcie's heart leaped. Was it Mr Grey? Her former pet might be both enigmatic and elusive, but he'd always come through when she needed him. Maybe Esmé needed him, too. Needed him to translate, at least. She turned toward the table, too. But all she saw was her bag, which she'd dropped there while reaching for her sweater, and some crumbs, highlighted in the morning light. No grey cat; not even the shadow of one.

She turned back to the little cat, just in time to see Esmé stand and walk over to the table. With one neat leap, she made it to the surface, where she sat in the middle of the pile of crumbs and began to wash.

'Great.' Dulcie hauled herself, a little more laboriously, to her feet. 'Was that all to alert me to my lack of housekeeping skills?'

The cat didn't comment, as she was now involved in washing her white belly fur, and so Dulcie reached for her bag. 'Thanks a lot, Esmé.'

Feeling a little disappointed, and a little silly for letting herself get let down, she reached to pet the cat. Esmé looked up from her toilette, and for a moment, Dulcie felt it again. That piercing stare – the cat had to be trying to tell her something. She paused. At this rate, she was going to be late. Whatever it was would have to wait till later. Shouldering her bag and buttoning the first two buttons of the oversized sweater, Dulcie braced herself to meet Jerry and the day.

Chris's apartment – Dulcie still thought of it that way – was on the fourth floor of an old brick building, and the carpet on the wide front stairway was permanently stained. But even though its color had changed from some industrial solid to a messy incoherent plaid over the years, it did serve to muffle the sound as Dulcie clattered down to the sidewalk. Still, the dull thud of her feet was enough to rouse someone, who ducked out of the building as she descended, and then stepped into the alley as Dulcie pushed open the glass front-door.

She looked up as she did to see that, sure enough, Esmé had abandoned her bath for a post at the kitchen window. She waved at the little cat, the white chin and neat bib clearly visible from the sidewalk, and told herself the cat nodded in response. The idea of someone looking out for her was cheering as she headed off to meet Jerry.

But as she turned toward the Square, the cat continued to stare at the sidewalk out front. She watched as a figure stepped out from the side of the building on to the sidewalk. She mewed, helpless, as the figure watched Dulcie walk away, her curls bouncing against the collar of her oatmeal-colored sweater.

'*I tried to warn her. I did my best.*' The words whispered through the empty apartment as the little cat watched her person disappear down the street. '*I can't just say anything out loud. Not and be her pet.*'

'*I know, little one,*' another voice answered. '*I know.*'

TWENTY-ONE

J erry looked half frantic by the time Dulcie saw him, huddled over a corner table at the Greenhouse. His phone in hand, the skinny redhead was staring at it as if the technology had somehow outwitted him. *Disappointed* him, she mentally revised her thoughts. It had, of course. Neither of them had heard from Trista. Then again, she thought, at least the police had not called her back. Which simply meant she could focus on helping her two friends.

'Hey.' She greeted her friend with a hug. Under his T-shirt, he felt like skin and bones. 'No word?'

He shook his head, confirming what she already knew. The waitress appeared with a coffee pot, turned over her cup and filled it. That's what she loved about the Greenhouse. Nobody here would try to make conversation before they'd given you coffee.

'Jerry, did you order?'

He shook his head, and she bit her lip. He was always on the slim side, but worry was taking its toll. 'I think you should eat. At least try to.' She looked up at the waiting server. 'Feta and spinach omelet, please. With hash browns.'

The waitress turned toward Jerry. Dulcie did, too, silently willing him to order. 'I'll take a bagel,' he said, finally. She wasn't optimistic about him eating it.

Dulcie sipped her coffee and considered her next move. She didn't want to upset Jerry any more, but it was pretty clear he didn't know what was going on. She didn't either, really, but she knew about Trista's visit from the police – and her friend's conviction that she was wanted for murder. She was going to have to tell him about that, and about Suze's take that Trista had blown the whole thing out of proportion. That she'd had a little breakdown – brain freeze – that would blow over. Maybe he'd have some insight; maybe he'd been worrying about Trista, too. At any rate, it would all be better in person than over the phone, and if she could get him to eat something first, that would be better still.

Twenty minutes later, she had spelled it all out: that first call from Trista, Suze's rational takedown, the meeting at the department – and then Trista's promise to talk after she spoke with someone. As an afterthought, she wound up by telling him about the call from the cops. She didn't want him to take Trista's fear – that the police were after her – too seriously. Jerry's reaction was not what Dulcie expected.

'Dulcie, you've got to go to the cops right away.' Although Dulcie had been talking too much to finish her own breakfast, Jerry had been distracted enough to eat, and now he focused all his renewed energy on her. 'You have to! I bet that's why they want to talk to you. Trista's in trouble. I *knew* it.'

'But, but . . .' Dulcie bit her lip, the half an omelet she'd managed feeling like lead in her belly. 'I think someone's setting me up.' She'd explained about the meeting – and about the blue ticket – but in consideration of Jerry's feelings had skimmed over her fear that Trista had been the one in possession of that ticket. That left her without a good excuse now, and she pushed her plate back as if it could explain for her. 'I mean, for the theft.'

Jerry didn't pause. Without thinking, he dug his fork into what was left of Dulcie's hash browns and made his case. 'I can see what you're saying, and I'm sorry, Dulcie. But that's obviously a mistake. And it's only about property – an old book. Trista may be involved in a murder, and now she's missing! That's got to take priority.'

'But . . .' Dulcie had told Jerry what Suze had said. It didn't matter; he wasn't listening. At least he was eating, Dulcie thought, watching the thin redhead hoover up the rest of her breakfast. She certainly didn't feel like it.

'So, we'll go to the university police?' He scraped up the last of the fried onion with his fork and signaled for the waitress. 'Now?'

'Sure.' Dulcie didn't know what else to say. When her phone started to ring, she reached for her bag, hoping for deliverance. 'Maybe that's Trista now.'

It wasn't, although she recognized the extension. The university police were calling again.

TWENTY-TWO

Rather than try to explain on the phone, Dulcie had let the call go to voicemail. And soon after, she and Jerry were at the front door of the station.

'Maybe I should go in alone.' Dulcie turned to her friend. 'I mean, they have been calling me.'

'No way.' Jerry held the door open. 'If Trista's involved, I'm involved.' It wasn't exactly a vote of confidence for Dulcie, but she managed a smile and led the tall redhead in.

'Hi, I'm Dulcie Schwartz, a graduate student in—' She was doing her best, gripping the edge of the counter that ran the length of the room. Her voice, she knew by the way the receptionist was straining toward her, was barely audible and sinking.

'Dulcie!' A deep voice boomed like thunder, if thunder could have a brassy Boston accent. 'Miss Schwartz! There you are.'

She looked up to see a man as big as his voice moving toward her, and her initial dismay began to fade.

'Detective Rogovoy.' He wasn't a friend, exactly, but in the past, he had proven to be less of an ogre than he looked. 'Um, good to see you?'

'And you. Especially since we've been trying to get hold of you for more than twenty-four hours now.' He leaned in, and the resemblance to an ogre became more apparent. Despite herself, Dulcie shuddered. 'But never mind that. You're here now. Come on. I've got coffee.'

He put a big paw-like hand on her back and propelled her away from the desk, toward a door. 'Wait, Detective Rogovoy? Do you know Jerry Hannafin?'

She turned toward the redhead. He'd gone a bit pale, but looked up with a brave smile.

'He's sort of involved in all this.' It was the best Dulcie could do on short notice.

'Is he now?' The large detective squinted at Jerry, not a pretty look, and Dulcie saw Jerry grow a shade whiter, which made his freckles stand out. 'Wait here, young man. Miss Schwartz and I have some catching up to do.'

'Please,' Dulcie whispered, willing Jerry to stay. At this point, he seemed like her last tie to the real world. He nodded – at least, she thought he did – and then she was whisked away.

'So, Ms Schwartz, you probably know why we wanted to speak with you.' The portly detective made it sound like a statement, but she nodded sadly, staring at the coffee in front of her. He had promised it was fresh, when he'd brought in the two mugs. To her, it looked too bitter for words.

'Good.' He'd taken the seat opposite her, managing to tuck his knees under the table. 'Why don't you catch me up, then?'

That was a question, Dulcie knew it. She also knew what Suze would say: don't volunteer anything. For that matter, Suze would have told her not to go in, not without a lawyer – or someone as near to the thing itself as her former room-mate – by her side. But between Jerry's insistence and her own nagging feeling that she'd already bugged her about-to-graduate friend beyond the limits of tolerance, she'd found herself here, alone. Besides, she sort of trusted the burly detective. And she did want to make a clean breast of everything.

'Here.' She dug into her bag until she found the blue ticket and put it on the table. 'Here it is.'

The detective looked down at it and back up at her. She reached over and pushed it toward him, willing him to look at it. To respond somehow. 'The ticket.'

'I see.' He picked it up carefully, his sausage-like fingers dwarfing the crumpled paper. 'This is the ticket?'

She nodded, misery choking her. 'Yeah.'

'I see it has your name on it.' He held it so close, she wondered if he was nearsighted. Then he turned it over and examined the back.

She couldn't feel more miserable, and so she continued to address the mug. 'It's real. I mean, I don't remember filling it out, but I'm pretty sure I must have.'

He nodded.

'But I didn't steal the Dunster Codex. I swear I didn't. I don't know why that ticket has surfaced now, or why Trista might have had it. But it doesn't mean what it looks like.'

The mug didn't respond. Neither did the man across the table.

'And I would have asked Trista how she came to have it, only she disappeared before I could and I don't know if she's in real trouble or if she's just hiding because someone was questioning her.'

A thud alerted her to look up. The detective had dropped his meaty hand and was looking at her, not the slip of paper that now lay on the table.

'Hold on, Miss Schwartz. Let's start at the beginning here, shall we?'

She shook her head, overwhelmed. 'I'm not even sure where the beginning is.'

To her surprise, he chuckled. 'Maybe it will help to know that I didn't want to speak to you today about the Dunster Coupon, or whatever this is.' He fingered the blue ticket. 'I've got insurance geeks breathing down my neck about that library thing, but I do things my own way, and I'll be dam— I'm not going to let them rush me. But you're saying that this ticket thing relates to the theft – and that you think someone is trying to make it look like you're involved? That's interesting.'

'I don't know about that.' Dulcie felt the blush creeping up her neck. 'I mean, I haven't spoken to anyone about it – about that ticket. I could be totally wrong about all of that.'

The detective raised his eyebrows. The look did not inspire confidence, and Dulcie swallowed. This was what Suze had warned her about. This was what happened when she started talking without advice. 'I think I spoke too soon,' was all she said.

The big man smiled, and for a moment, Dulcie felt worse. But the smile broadened into a grin, and he shook his head slowly, and she began to hope that maybe, just maybe, her neighborhood ogre was going to take pity on one small student.

'Dulcie Schwartz, you really do have a knack for this, don't you?' He didn't wait for her to answer. 'Getting into trouble, that is.'

'Well, you said—' She managed a weak smile and a shrug. 'You kept calling.'

'And you thought . . .' He shook his head and handed her back the blue ticket. 'Look, we're working on the theft. That's a whole different kettle of fish. We wanted to talk with you about something different though. One of your colleagues, another graduate student—' He shuffled through some papers.

'Roland Galveston.' She finished the sentence. 'Or whatever his real name is.' He looked up at that and waited. 'We heard.'

'You heard what?' His voice had grown soft. Dulcie knew that this was a warning of some sort. She could almost feel Mr Grey beside her, the fur along his spine beginning to fluff up. But she was so tired of being afraid. She wanted to trust someone, to clear the air.

'That he went missing. That nobody knows where he is, and that he came to the university under false pretenses.' It all came tumbling out. 'We had a big department meeting yesterday morning, and one of the senior faculty showed up. That's when I heard all about the Dunster Codex – it's a manuscript, by the way, an ancient manuscript – and that one of us graduate students might have been involved. And because nobody knows where Roland is, everyone seems to be thinking he was involved, and Trista was friends with him. Well, we all were really, but Trista probably knew him better than anyone. And she—'

'There you are.' The door behind her burst open, letting in Jerry and an annoyed looking woman.

'I tried to keep him out, but he was irate.' Dulcie recognized the receptionist from the front desk. 'He said he had to be here.'

'I need to know what's going on with Trista.' Jerry stepped into the room, facing Rogovoy. 'I have to know.'

The detective seemed to take it all in stride. 'It's OK, Miss Sonnabend. I think I'll be OK with two students.'

Muttering, she retreated.

'And you are again?'

'Jerry, Jerry Hannafin. Third year, applied sciences.' Reaching forward a little awkwardly, Jerry shook the detective's hand. 'Trista's my girlfriend, and so ever since she's gone missing, I've been worried about her.'

Too late, Dulcie recognized that Jerry was going to make the same mistake she had. She stood up, hoping to interrupt. 'Jerry—'

'No, Dulcie, it's OK. I don't need you to defend me – or Trista. Officer – sir – you have to tell me what's going on. I mean, I've known Trista Dunlop for years now. I don't know what's going on with the missing manuscript or any of it. All I know is my girlfriend isn't a murderer.'

Dulcie sat back in her seat. Jerry had done it, brought up the one element she had managed to keep secret. She looked from her friend to the detective. The little eyes that squinted out were sharp and focused.

'Murder, you say? Well, isn't it interesting that you bring that up.'

TWENTY-THREE

D ulcie stared at the big man. Beside her, Jerry swallowed, and Dulcie remembered her initial impression of the detective. He was an ogre. A terrible, huge monster – and he was about to devour them both. She swallowed, too. Hard.

And then that impassive boulder of a face split into a grin, and the grin opened into a laugh that showed terrible, huge teeth. Dulcie couldn't help it. She closed her eyes.

'You kids.' The voice sounded friendly, and she dared a peek. He was shaking his head. 'I ask you to come in to talk, and the next thing I know, you're confessing to stolen treasures, conspiracies, and murder. I'm not sure it's a good thing you read so many books.'

'But didn't you want to ask about Roland Galveston?' Dulcie found her voice. 'And if Roland Galveston is missing, isn't it possible that he's—' She paused, afraid to say it. 'Dead?'

'Who says I'm talking about Roland Galveston?' He leaned forward, pinning her with a look. She turned to Jerry, who only shrugged. 'And what kind of name is that, anyway?'

'Well, it might be a *nom de plume*.' Rogovoy raised one eyebrow, and Dulcie felt herself color. 'A pen name, a fake name.' Nothing. 'I mean, we heard at the departmental meeting that there are some questions about his credentials.'

'Not my department.' Rogovoy shook his head. 'Though I do have this Mr Galveston on my list of people to contact.'

'Then you *have* heard from him.' Relief washed over Dulcie.

'Did he tell you about Trista? Is she with him?' She'd almost forgotten Jerry was there.

'Now, now, calm down. Both of you.' Rogovoy patted the air

between them as if he could lower the volume with his hands. 'You're getting ahead of me here.'

'You didn't talk to him, then,' Dulcie guessed, her voice dropping, and when the detective failed to correct her, she felt her mood sink with it. 'He's still missing.'

'*He* is not the object of my questioning.'

Both of the students looked up at the deliberate choice of pronoun. Jerry even started to talk: 'Trista—'

'Nor is anyone named "Trister".' Rogovoy's booming voice cut him off, his brassy accent changing Trista's name to something not quite right. 'What I called you in to speak about, Ms Schwartz, is something a lot more prosaic. And since you're here, Mr Hannafin, you may as well hear it too.' He cleared his throat, and Dulcie was struck by the impression that he was about to recite. Sure enough, his diction cleared up as he intoned: 'The university police have received information that prompts them to alert the student body about certain issues with online security.'

'Hackers?' She turned toward Jerry. He was sure to know a lot more about anything computer related than she was. 'Because Jerry here, and my boyfriend, Chris—'

'No, no, nothing so sophisticated.' Detective Rogovoy was making that motion with his hands again. Dulcie was beginning to get the impression that she made him nervous. 'Just, you know, we've heard something about identity theft among the grad students.'

'Identity theft? Like someone using a fake name?' She was about to bring up Galveston again when the big man shook his head.

'More likely the other way,' he said. 'People getting access to your PIN codes and passwords. Stuff like that.'

'You know who's doing this?' Jerry butted in.

Rogovoy almost laughed. 'If we did, Mr Hannafin . . . No, truth is, we're not sure if it is happening at all, or if it is something being planned. But one of your colleagues, someone who identified himself as a grad student, called and said there was something hinky going on, that we should check the security clearance of off-campus students, the ones who have a certain level of access. Considering how serious these things can get – and that some of you, and I do mean you, Ms Schwartz, have been victimized in the past – we felt we should reach out to you. We're calling about a dozen of your colleagues, too.'

'Well, I'm safe.' Dulcie relaxed. 'Ever since the big hacking scandal, my boyfriend has gone over all my systems. Chris is a doctoral candidate in computer sciences, and he even made me change my passwords. They'd all been the same thing, my birthday, and he said that wasn't safe.'

'And how often have you changed them since?' Rogovoy's voice was soft.

'Well, that was only last year.' Dulcie saw him turn. Saw the detective and Jerry exchange a look.

'Look, this may all be a storm in a tea kettle.' Somehow, the detective's quiet voice was scarier than his loud one. 'All I know is that the forensic computer guys plugged the info into their systems and came up with a bunch of names. We're doing our best to clean this up quickly. But it's the end of the semester and, frankly, we're kind of overloaded. Did you know the ambassador to Kenya is coming to speak? So all we ask is that if you notice anything – charges on your credit cards. Emails from people or companies you never heard of, assuming you've bought into something. Whatever. Just let us know, OK?'

'Sure.' Dulcie was a little stunned. Jerry, however, was not.

'But what about my girlfriend?' He leaned on the table. 'About Trista Dunlop?'

'What about her?' Rogovoy met Jerry's eye, and Dulcie wondered which would give first. 'Do you want to file a report?'

'Maybe.' Jerry looked up at him. 'Yeah, I do.'

'OK, then.' Rogovoy sighed like a bellows and reached for a pen. 'So, I assume she's been missing more than forty-eight hours?'

'Well, no.' Jerry's face knit up. 'Not yet.'

'Not yet?'

He shook his head. 'She didn't come home last night, and she's not answering her cell. Or returning messages.' He looked to Dulcie for confirmation. 'And she was supposed to meet Dulcie for coffee yesterday, only she never showed.'

'It's true, Detective.' Dulcie came to Jerry's defense. 'Something was going on, something she couldn't talk about in the departmental offices. So we made plans to meet and then – nothing. I haven't been able to reach her, either.'

'And is there anything else going on in this young woman's life?' He looked from Dulcie to Jerry. She could almost see his suspicions, and she willed Jerry to keep his mouth shut.

It didn't work. 'She's defending her thesis next week,' he said. 'But that's not it.'

'Wait a minute.' Rogovoy had put the pen down. 'You're telling me that after how many years, this girl is finally finishing up her degree. She's got what's basically the biggest exam of all, and so now she's acting a little weird. Maybe –' he shot Jerry a look – 'she doesn't want to spend every night with her boyfriend. Maybe she doesn't want to schmooze with her girlfriend. Has it ever occurred to you that maybe she's locked herself away someplace quiet? Like, maybe she wants to study?'

'She's not in her favorite super-secret study nook, either.' Dulcie was proud of that one. 'I checked.'

'And if you know about it, how secret can it be?' Rogovoy put the pad away and looked like he was about to leave, when Dulcie played her trump card.

'But it was Trista who told us that Roland Galveston was missing. She said you questioned her – and that you implied she was a suspect in his murder.'

It did not have the desired effect. 'Miss Schwartz. Look. I know you're under a lot of pressure, end of the term and all. And maybe your friend, maybe it's been too much for her. But we don't have any open murder cases here on campus. Believe me, I would know.'

'But—' She paused, unsure of what to say.

Rogovoy looked at her and shook his head. 'Maybe your friend needed some help. It happens, you know. Have you tried asking for her at the health services?'

Dulcie looked at Jerry. This was what she'd been trying to tell him. What Suze had suggested, too. Now he looked defeated. 'No,' he mumbled.

'Well, why don't you try there first.' Rogovoy leaned back in his chair. 'If she's not locked away studying, I'd put money on a nice, restful cot.'

TWENTY-FOUR

'**R**estful cot, my . . .' Jerry was mumbling to himself angrily as they left. Dulcie didn't mind. He'd looked so defeated as they'd been escorted out, she'd been a little worried that he might be near a breakdown himself.

'It doesn't mean she's crazy, Jerry.' Dulcie bit her lip. Chris had gone for counseling, following his mother's treatment for cancer. Did he ever tell his friends? 'And she has been under a lot of stress.'

'So have *you*.' Jerry turned on her with a glare. 'And I don't see you checking yourself in anywhere.'

'I have been having really weird dreams.' It was a peace offering, the best she could do.

Jerry wasn't impressed. 'Checked herself in.' He was still muttering.

Dulcie, however, found herself considering something else the detective had said. 'Hey, Jerry, maybe there is something in the whole identity theft issue. I mean, maybe someone stole Trista's ID. Maybe someone pretending to be Trista is involved with Roland Galveston's disappearance.'

'Maybe he's behind it.' Jerry turned toward her. 'After all, if this Galveston guy's not who he says he is, maybe he's involved with *her* disappearance.'

'It's possible.' Dulcie looked at her friend. 'But what the detective said might make sense too.'

'Trista isn't crazy.' Jerry had his shoulders hunched up as they walked. 'She's not.'

'I know that, and you know that.' Dulcie was trying to calm her friend down and think at the same time. 'Detective Rogovoy doesn't know her. We do. Still . . .' She paused, trying to piece a thought together.

'What?' Jerry barked. 'You think we should go to the health services?'

'It couldn't hurt.' She turned toward the redhead. 'I don't think she's crazy, Jerry. But she has been under a lot of pressure. Maybe

she did have some kind of a collapse.' She saw him about to
protest, so she hurried to get the words out. 'Exhaustion, or
something. I mean, they'd take her phone away if she was checked
in for exhaustion, right?'

He shrugged, and she saw how miserable he looked. 'Try to
think of the bright side, Jer.' She summoned a smile. 'At least
we know she won't really be accused of murder.'

The two walked in companionable silence then, toward the tower
that housed the health services, basically an on-campus hospital
for the university population. The walk took a little longer than
usual; Commencement brought not only visiting dignitaries but
also thousands of family members and alumni, and the sidewalks
were full of pedestrians, many of them stopping at every corner.

'This *is* Mass Ave,' she heard someone say, and she smiled.
'We're *on* it.'

'What if that detective is right?' Jerry's voice was so low, she
almost didn't hear it. 'I mean, about Tris?'

'That she's had a breakdown?' Dulcie watched her friend.
This was what Suze had suggested, and she had wondered, too.
The pressure – and Trista's habit of keeping everything inside
– must have been intense. Add in that talk about a non-existent
murder . . .

Jerry nodded. 'She has been, well, sort of distant at times.
But, I thought . . . I mean, I didn't want to push . . .'

'I'm sure it wasn't anything you did.' Trista's thesis adviser, on
the other hand, was a different matter. 'She's had her hands full.'

'Yeah.' Jerry looked sunken into his own misery. 'And then
for the police to hassle her.'

'But they didn't. Unless—' She stopped short, and Jerry took
a step or two more before he turned to face her. 'Jerry, could it
have been the city police who came to talk to Trista? I mean,
that doesn't make sense.'

He shook his head. 'Nah, it doesn't. If there was a murder –
especially of a student – you'd think they'd involve the university
police. At least they'd let them *know*, you know?'

'Yeah.' Something buzzed around the edge of Dulcie's
consciousness. Trista under pressure. Trista threatened. 'You
know, I could see Trista breaking down and crying. But I can't
imagine her hallucinating a visit from the cops, Jerry. You know

how Rogovoy was talking about identity theft? About hacking? What if someone is impersonating a police officer for some reason? What if that person wanted to scare Trista?'

Jerry paused, his face momentarily lightened. Then he shook his head, frowning. 'It's just unlikely, Dulcie. You know, logically, "when you hear hoof beats, think of a horse, not a zebra".'

Dulcie shrugged. She never understood that computer talk anyway, and they proceeded into the health services.

'No, I'm sorry. No way.' The receptionist, a young man in button-down shirt, was losing his buttoned-down manner. 'And if you keep on insisting, I will call security.'

'All right.' Jerry put his hands up in surrender. 'No need to get bent out of shape.'

'We take patient confidentiality very seriously here.' After fifteen minutes of repeating the same line with numerous varia-tions, the receptionist was looking a little crumpled, his pink face growing pinker up to the roots of his cropped blond hair. 'You have to go.'

'Gotcha.' Jerry backed up a step, and Dulcie grabbed his arm.

'Jerry, no,' she whispered up to her friend. They had been standing by the long, white reception area since stepping into the center, but there was really nothing blocking their access to the bank of elevators farther in. Dulcie didn't even see any secu-rity guards. The young man had sounded like he was reading a script from the moment they'd asked about Trista, and so he had most likely simply advanced to the next page. Still, Dulcie didn't want Jerry to test that hypothesis.

Her hands firmly wrapped around Jerry's forearm, she pulled him away from the desk, more or less in the direction of the front door. He was too big for her to move by brute force. 'Besides –' she had to convince him – 'she probably isn't in here. You said so yourself, right? Trista's not crazy.'

Jerry glared. The receptionist picked up a phone and glared back. More bluff, probably – but Dulcie really didn't want to get into it. 'Jerry!' She tugged at his arm. 'Come on. This isn't going to get us anywhere.'

The logic of her words must have sunk in. Jerry snorted – there was no other word for it – and tossed his red bangs in the direction of the starched young man. Then he turned and led Dulcie out.

Once they were back on the plaza Dulcie could see how upset her friend was. 'If only I knew,' he said, as much to himself as to her. He turned so the shade of the building hid his face. It didn't matter; she could hear the worry in his voice. 'If only she had told me what was going on.'

Dulcie bit her lip. That was the crux of it, wasn't it? Trista hadn't told anyone what was going on – not really – and now they were left worrying.

As if on cue, Dulcie's phone rang. Jerry turned, his whole face lighting up, and Dulcie had to disappoint him. 'Chris,' she mouthed to him as she answered.

'Hey, sweetie,' Chris said. Her boyfriend sounded half asleep. It was a little past eleven and had turned bright and sunny, but he had probably only gotten home a few hours before. 'What's up?'

Dulcie rolled her eyes and thought about how to respond. 'Well, I'm here at the university health services with Jerry.' She paused, unsure how to phrase it in a way that wouldn't upset their mutual friend more. 'Trista has gone missing, and, well, there's a chance that she might have checked herself in. Only, nobody will say anything. Patient confidentiality and all.'

'Huh.' Her boyfriend was waking up. 'Put him on, Dulce?'

She handed the phone to Jerry, who listened for a few moments and then turned away. Dulcie leaned against the wall and tried not to feel insulted. Jerry and Chris had been friends since freshman year. Plus, they were guys. In fact, if Chris took over, he'd be doing Dulcie a favor. It wasn't like her own life hadn't become more complicated recently. Besides, she did need to finish that essay. Now that her morning had been eaten up, she regretted not diving in when she'd had the chance. In fact . . .

Dulcie was mulling over possibilities – OK, she was fantasizing about the reception her groundbreaking thesis would receive – when Jerry turned and held the phone out to her. 'He wants to speak with you.'

It was in a much better mood that she took it. 'So, you guys have a plan?'

'Something like. He and I are going to hack her emails.' He must have heard her gasp. 'I know, Dulcie. But, well, he's worried.'

Dulcie swallowed the comment she'd been about to make. In

truth, she simply shouldn't have asked. Chris's confession had brought up a thought, though.

'Chris, the police told me that there's been some identity theft – they think *I* might have been hacked.' She didn't want to ask. In truth, she wasn't sure what she would ask for.

Luckily, he did. 'Do you want me to check your systems, sweetie? I could do that.'

'Thanks, Chris.' She paused, not sure she wanted to know. 'You know all my passwords, right?'

'I'm not sure, but I'm willing to bet they all refer to a certain silver-hued feline.' She could hear the smile in his voice. 'Besides, Dulcie, I set up your security and, well, I'm guessing you haven't changed your passwords.'

'I haven't,' she confessed. Typing in 'MRGREY' each morning started her day off on such a good note. 'I guess I was supposed to.'

'Want me to do that for you, while I'm fooling around? We could update everything. Make them all "Esmé" or "Ms Esmé".'

It was a reasonable suggestion. A smart one, even, but it hit Dulcie like a slap. 'Oh, I don't know, Chris. I don't know if I'll be able to remember I changed them, and then it'll slow me down and I'll get all sorts of error messages.'

'OK, sweetie. I'll leave them.' He knew she was lying. The nice part was he didn't seem to care. 'Dinner tonight?'

'I'll even cook.' They both knew that meant pasta, but that was OK. If Dulcie had learned anything from her friends' relationship, it was that sometimes predictability was a good thing.

TWENTY-FIVE

Jerry had the grace to look slightly abashed as he made his farewell.

'Chris is going to help me,' he said with a shrug. They had moved into the sunny part of the plaza, and he shaded his eyes with his hand.

'I hope it all works out.' She was happy enough not to be able to look him in the eyes. Hacking Trista's accounts was a major breach of her privacy, and she couldn't condone it. Then again, she did understand it – a little. Jerry was honestly worried. And Trista had been asking a lot of all her friends. Dulcie just didn't want to know any more than she had to. 'Good luck.'

Watching him lope off toward the computer lab, Dulcie realized she hadn't yet decided how to order her day. That essay – that was key – and Dulcie could feel the weight of the blue-bound volume in her bag, its presence summoning her to read. She turned to follow Jerry into the Yard, enjoying the shade of an ancient beech tree. She slowed, watching the play of dappled shadow on the lawn. The day was turning hot, and it was pleasant to think how cool the depths of Widener would be. How inviting.

Rather like Trista's secret hideaway. The thought came unbidden, and for once Dulcie didn't think Mr Grey had any part in it. Her spectral pet would want her to get back to work, wouldn't he? Then again, he might want her to remove any unnecessary distractions first. Distractions that could seriously derail her career. Dulcie looked again at the lacing of shadows. There was little breeze, and the slight movement of their edges only rippled slightly against the grass. A shape appeared and faded. A passing cloud, most likely.

It was pointless. Dulcie knew from experience that even if Mr Grey appeared directly, he would be unlikely to advise her one way or another. He was always urging her to make her own decisions. To learn to cope on her own. The pang she had felt earlier returned, this time congealing in her throat like a stale dumpling. She swallowed and stepped out into the sun.

The blue ticket was the more pressing issue, she told herself. She needed to settle its mystery first, if she could. The decision calmed her, and she glanced back at the shadow with a warm glow of gratitude. Maybe she was learning, but it never hurt to have a little feline comfort.

That didn't help her with the next step, though. Without Trista around, where exactly could she turn for help uncovering the truth of the blue ticket?

From where she was standing, Dulcie could see the Widener steps. The sensible thing would be to go in – and go directly to the Mildon collection. After all, the blue tag in her bag was only the carbon. The rare book depository would undoubtedly have the original on file.

Then again, what if she ran into Coffin? The man scared her. Plus, he was looking for someone to blame. Dulcie liked to think of herself as a rational person, but every instinct in her body warned her off making herself vulnerable to the Mildon curator.

Thorpe! While physically less imposing than the large, mustachioed Coffin (physically less imposing than Esmé, Dulcie couldn't help adding), Martin Thorpe was her thesis adviser. He might not be able to protect her, but it was his job to advise her. And he probably knew more about the university bureaucracy than anyone else she could easily call.

If only he would step up for her . . . but Gustav Coffin had clearly gotten to the balding scholar. 'I'm sorry, Miss Schwartz. I really have no special insight into this matter.' She had reached him as she crossed the Yard, but when she explained her predicament, he had started stammering into the phone. 'If you have – if you *think* you have – something that, uh, might put you in the Mildon, well, um . . . ah . . .'

'I should go check the main register, right?' His fear should have been contagious. After all, he was faculty. Tenure track, even, with a departmental position. Strangely, it had the opposite effect. Maybe it was because a breeze had picked up, blowing Dulcie's hair into her face as she listened to his excuses and ruffling against her skin like cat fur brushing by. Maybe it was because she was already so close to the library – and so eager to just get this over with. Whatever the reason, as he dithered, she gained resolve. 'Never mind, Mr Thorpe. I've got it.'

Flashing her ID to the guard, she stopped herself from taking her usual path – into the stacks, three floors down – and pressed the elevator button marked with an 'M'. The Mildon was reachable through the stacks – its caged-off south-west corner could be seen from the more plebeian side of the underground labyrinth. But because of its rarities – or because of the VIP nature of its donors – it had its own entrance as well, one floor further down, and Dulcie stepped out of the car to see a gleaming white counter top, framed by an equally white and shining doorway.

'Poseurs,' Dulcie muttered under her breath. She was over-reacting, she knew that. The white surface was a lot prettier than the workaday metal grating and shelves that made up the majority of the stacks, but then, the Mildon collection probably garnered a larger share of donations than anything else here as well. Inside

these walls was a 'bad quarto', one of the earliest copies of
Shakespeare's *Macbeth*; a fragment of papyrus, even if it only
listed the contents of a shipment of grain; and, until recently, the
Dunster Codex. That it also held *The Wetherly Ghost* was probably of less importance to those big shots who usually used this
pristine entrance. That thought gave Dulcie a little more courage
as she walked up to the open counter, cleared her throat, and
called loudly. 'Hello?' She licked her lips. It was the air conditioning, certainly, that had made her mouth suddenly so dry.
'Anyone?'

'Coming!' A rustle from somewhere inside the brightly lit
collection followed the voice. 'One moment!'

She waited, curious as to what kind of dragon would be
guarding this hoard of treasures, and was surprised to see a little
man, barely her height, with glasses as large as his face. 'May
I help you?' The little mouse spoke with a voice both soft and
warm.

'Oh, thank you!' Dulcie jumped a bit in surprise. 'I was
thinking, maybe Professor Coffin would be here.'

'Did you have an appointment?' The eyes, unnaturally large
behind those huge lenses, scrunched up in concern.

'No, I just thought . . .' Dulcie felt herself smiling. This gate-
keeper was much less threatening than she'd expected. 'I was
afraid I'd have to speak to him.'

'Not here much.' The oversized glasses turned away, toward
a pile of papers that evidently required neatening. 'Only for
appointments. And to escort visiting dignitaries, donors, and the
like, of course.'

'Of course.' Dulcie found herself agreeing. This was going to
be so much easier than she had feared. 'Perhaps you can help
me, though?'

The glasses turned back. The eyes, Dulcie noticed, were brown.
They blinked, and she realized they were waiting.

'I found a blue tag, and I—' She paused. She hadn't really
thought how to present all of this. 'I don't have any recollection
of when I was last here. I was wondering . . .'

'Of course, hand it over.' The small person reached out, and
Dulcie was mildly disappointed to see a pale palm, rather than
a paw. 'I can check it against the register.'

'You can do that?' She put her bag on the counter and began

to dig through it. This was what she'd hoped for, of course. She hadn't expected it to be so simple.

'As long as I can make out the number.' Of course. That mysterious '5' hadn't been a date, it had been a register number.

She found the stub. 'It's a bit smudged,' she said, handing it over.

'Nuh,' the mouse man muttered to himself and then turned and scurried away. Dulcie longed to follow him, despite the unavoidable feeling that he had, in fact, darted down some minuscule hole in the library floor. She leaned over the counter. The tidy entrance seemed to open up to a regular warren of space, and she craned her neck, hoping to catch sight of where the little man had gone.

To the left, she recognized the reading area, where scholars would sit and wait for their requests to be delivered. She could make out the cup of pencils, but none of them seemed to be in use. Beyond, she saw a hallway, all in the same gleaming white as the entrance. Two doors, closed, were visible, and Dulcie seemed to remember – or maybe she just suspected – that there were more in the warren-like space. To her right, rows of bookcases – again of the nicer material – filled a large room. Beyond that, she thought she could see the chain-link wall, the fence that caged off the Mildon from the general stacks.

Directly in front of her were two closed doors, these taking on a decidedly more formal look. Although small nickel plates seemed to identify the row of locked doors, these were too small for her to make out what they said. One of them, she guessed, might have housed the Dunster Codex, a thought that led her to wonder about security procedures.

On a whim, she examined the counter before her. Almost undetectable hinges attached to one side. Yes – she worked it out – one panel would lift, allowing access. She slid her hands beneath it and tried. Nothing. Of course, there was probably a release button or switch on the inside of the counter. She pulled herself up on to the white surface and leaned over the back to have a peek.

'Excuse me? Miss?'

Dulcie looked up. From the stacks area on the right, a woman was approaching. The young blonde who looked like Trista. 'Oof?' Lying on her belly, it was the best she could manage.

'Oh!' The blonde stopped in her tracks. 'Oh!'

'Wait!' Dulcie slid back and called out, but the blonde had slipped into one of the two closed doors. 'Miss?'

'Excuse me?' The other door opened, and the mouse-like receptionist stepped out. 'Sorry, that took longer than I expected.'

'Oh, that's fine.' Dulcie craned her head to see if the thin blonde would reappear. 'I just saw one of your colleagues? A slim woman – undergrad, maybe?'

'One of our work-studies, probably. At any rate, I've found the listing.' He hoisted a large black leather register up to the edge of the counter, all the while keeping his finger in one page. Dulcie wanted to follow up, to ask about the girl, but hesitated. Maybe it was better if she didn't draw any attention to her near-trespass.

Instead, she helped pull the heavy volume up and waited while the mousy clerk opened it. The pages on the right were visibly doubled, each white page backed by one in blue. To the left, only the white pages were left. The tiny man was looking one page back, his finger tracing a line in the middle of the page.

'Says here that this ticket was issued a week ago, Friday.' He blinked down at the page, then back up at her. 'Here.'

With no small effort, he flipped the book around so she could read it. She looked to where he pointed: ticket number 5837 had been issued the previous Friday.

She shook her head. She'd been writing all that day. That had been the good day, when she had finally gotten down to work and hadn't stopped till Chris had come home. She remembered him clearing his throat. She'd looked up, blinking. He'd been standing in front of the window. Outside, it had been almost dark.

It didn't make sense. She looked back at the ledger. Yes, the date was the same: FRIDAY, MAY 22. And on the next line she read her own name: DULCINEA SCHWARTZ. The handwriting in the ledger was quite clear, written in big block letters. But she'd been home that day, all day. Writing. At least, as best she remembered.

'Could someone else have filled this out?' Visions of alternative universes were beginning to take hold.

'We *do* check ID.' The little mouse sniffed. 'And see this? This is our content-request notation.' The mouse-like man was still talking. He pointed to a set of initials, over in the corner of the ticket: *DC*. 'This is proof that someone in-house wrote this up. The content-notation is our private system. Most of our scholars aren't even aware that we keep track, because it doesn't come through on the stub, but it's our in-house system. That's how we know what work was requested.'

'What work?' Nothing was making sense. Dulcie hadn't been in the Mildon the week before. Not on Friday.

'Why, the Dunster Codex, of course.'

TWENTY-SIX

D ulcie did not know how she got out of there. One moment, she was staring, her eyes as wide as the Mildon staffer's glasses, the next she was in her carrel, staring at the wall. She remembered stuttering out a question, and the collection staffer repeating himself, his look of confusion exaggerated by those glasses. It didn't make sense, any of it. And when she asked the mousy staffer to double-check her copy of the blue ticket, he'd only blinked at it and handed it back to her.

'That's the blue ticket,' he'd said. 'The number is correct, as is the name.'

'But . . .' Dulcie had been at a loss for words. 'That's not possible.'

'We've checked it.' He'd tapped the edge of the binder with his fingertips. 'This is the source.'

Somehow, Dulcie gotten away from there, her mind racing. Was it possible that she had been dreaming – sleepwalking into the Mildon? No, her dreams might be vivid, but surely that was impossible. Besides, the Mildon had limited hours, and she wasn't likely to have wandered down here in a daze at midday.

Maybe it wasn't her. The fat detective's warning sprang to her mind, and Dulcie reached for her wallet. No, her university ID was in its usual place. In fact, she'd used it to get into the library – just as she did every day. Could there have been some other way of stealing her identity?

A quick glance around revealed nobody else and, feeling truly guilty now, Dulcie pulled out her phone. Yes, even down here, she could get a signal. She turned it on and dialed Chris.

'Hey, sweetie, I'm waiting for Jerry. What's up?' He sounded so normal that Dulcie started, cupping the phone to keep the sound contained.

'Chris,' she whispered. 'Can you hear me? I'm having a kind of emergency.'

'Where are you? Are you OK? I'm coming to get you.' With each successive question, his voice rose in volume and urgency.

'No, no, no,' she shushed him. 'Nothing like that. I'm safe. For now.' How to explain . . . 'I'm in the library.'

'Oh!' He got it and waited.

'Look, Chris, did you get a chance to look at my account yet?' It was too much to hope for, really.

'Actually, I just finished.' He sounded rather proud of himself. 'I just ran a check to see who had been using your login, where it's been used, the usual.'

'And?' Dulcie held her breath. Identity theft was the logical solution. If he could provide some sort of proof . . .

'Nothing. I mean, nothing that I wouldn't expect.' She felt the breath go out of her as her boyfriend explained. 'All the logons are from your laptop – nothing from any remotes. They all fit with places you usually go. There are no huge purchases or foreign sites, nothing like that. Though there is one to PetPsychic.Com.'

'I was just looking.' She felt her face color.

'I figured.' He chuckled. When she didn't, he sounded concerned. 'Dulcie, really, I'd understand if you did contact someone. Though, honestly, I think in our special case, with Mr Grey and all . . .'

'No, it's not that, Chris, honest.' Her eyes closed now, she could picture his sweet face. Would he believe her? 'It's that I was hoping I was hacked. You see, I think I'm being set up. My name is on the books as having gone into the Mildon Collection last week. To see the Dunster Codex. And I didn't. I haven't. Someone is framing me for the theft.'

'Dulce, that's horrible!' Chris's outrage warmed her. But just then, she felt a hand on her shoulder.

'No cellphone use.' The guard looked down at her as if she were a stranger. 'You'll have to come with me.'

'Gotta go,' Dulcie said as the stern-looking guard waited to escort her out.

TWENTY-SEVEN

'Oh, Dulcie.' Mona's voice was soft, but her round face sagged with sorrow as she looked over at her friend. 'How could you?'

'It was an emergency?' Dulcie heard the uncertainty in her own voice and watched her librarian friend shake her head. 'Kind of?'

'I just hope they go lightly on you.' The large librarian looked over her shoulder at the small office that the guard had entered several minutes before. 'I mean, if you lose your privileges . . .'

Dulcie winced. If she lost her library privileges, she might as well give up on her thesis. She looked toward the office. Through a small glass window, she could see the back of the guard's head bobbing up and down. Apparently, he was talking to someone. She could only hope it wasn't Coffin or anybody else connected to the Mildon collection. If anyone there looked at the evidence piling up, she'd be lucky to get a job at an auction house. She'd be lucky to get a job at Lala's.

'I just wouldn't have thought it of you.' Mona looked so sad, it made Dulcie feel worse. But before Dulcie could even attempt to explain, the head inside the window turned, and the door opened.

'Well, we spoke with your department head,' the guard said, shaking his head. Dulcie felt herself shrink further. Thorpe wasn't a bad man. She thought he even liked her, but he wasn't one to stand up to authority – for anyone. 'And he was shocked,' the guard continued. 'Shocked by your behavior.'

She waited for the death blow.

'But he said you were a good student, only under a lot of pressure.' The guard didn't look convinced. Dulcie herself could barely believe what she was hearing. 'So, after consulting with the head of services, we've decided not to follow through on this officially.'

She opened her mouth to thank him, when he held up a hand. 'Officially. Unofficially, I'm keeping my eye on you.'

She closed her mouth and nodded to show she understood.

'OK, you're free to go.' He turned to head back to his post. 'Remember,' he called over his shoulder. 'You've been warned.'

Dulcie looked over at Mona, but her large friend, usually so boisterous and outgoing, had turned away.

She thought about going back to her carrel then. 'Back on the horse,' she muttered to herself. She even walked toward the elevator and punched its button. Only just then two undergrads walked by, and one of them started giggling. She was laughing at something private, no doubt. Perhaps they were sharing summer plans, but at that moment, Dulcie felt like she had a scarlet letter on her, a big 'P' for phone, perhaps. And as she backed up into a corner, she realized that there would be little chance of concentration here today. No, her best shot at getting any work done at all would be to go home. Maybe Chris would have found something out. Maybe Esmé would be a comforting presence, for once, or at the very least, not all bitey.

The kitten, however, was not in evidence when Dulcie got home. Nor was Chris, though at least he had written a note:

Gather you got nabbed, he'd written. *Hope it isn't a big deal. Had a thought about your ID – tell you later.*

She smiled at it. Now that at least one particular storm cloud seemed to have passed, she could relax a little. If her hands ever stopped shaking, that is. But the fact that she hadn't lost her library privileges – or worse – and that her high-tech sweetie might be able to help her figure out how her name ended up on that ticket was encouraging. If only she could find the kitten.

'Esmé?' she called and was greeted by a resounding thump before the little cat came into the room. 'Where were you, kitten?'

The cat turned her green eyes up at her person and blinked before leaning in to rub against Dulcie's shins.

'OK, keep your secrets.' Her mood lifting by the moment, Dulcie reached down for the young cat. 'You're getting quite round, aren't you?'

At this, Esmé let out a small peep, and Dulcie couldn't help laughing. 'You and me both, Esmé.'

Maybe it had been the note from Chris, or maybe it was the comforting softness of the cat. Maybe there was something lingering in the atmosphere, a sense of deep contentment rumbling like a purr, but something had changed. Dulcie felt like herself again, which was to say, she felt like studying. And so with Esmé in one arm, she reached for her bag with the other, taking them both with her to the living room. Depositing the cat on the sofa beside her, she took out the big blue-bound volume. Finally, she was going to get something done.

TWENTY-EIGHT

As much as Dulcie wanted to work, Esmé seemed to want her not to. Although the little cat had been happy to sit beside her, the moment Dulcie reached for the bound volume, the kitten went into play mode.

'No, Esmé. Bad—' She thought of her own recent reprimand. 'Bad *behavior*!' She gently unhooked the tiny claws and held the white paws for a moment to emphasize her words. 'No!'

But thirty seconds later, the little tuxedo was at it again, this time pouncing on the open page.

'No.' Dulcie scooped up the cat, who reached for the pages as her person set her aside, almost succeeding in grabbing on. 'This is a *library* book, Esmé. Doesn't that mean anything to you?'

'Meh.' The face that turned up toward hers looked earnest, those round green eyes opened wide. But the moment Dulcie set the cat down, patting her black back to encourage her to sit, she was back again, this time diving at the cover to slam it closed.

'You'd almost think you don't want me to get any work done.' Dulcie paused. She was being silly. 'It's because I've been out so much, isn't it? Nobody plays with you any more.'

In response, the little cat flipped on to her back, exposing a fluffy white belly.

'Oh, no, I'm not falling for that one.' Dulcie smiled down at the downy fur, ignoring the one white bootie that reached up for her. 'I have no desire to have my hand scratched up.'

She had no desire to move, either, especially when her pet was being so cute. Instead, she ripped a page out of her notepad and balled it up, making as much noise as she could with the crinkling, crisp paper.

'Come on, Esmé.' She waved the impromptu ball. 'Go for it!'

But whatever playful urge the cat had been experiencing seemed to have passed. The ball skittered across the floor, but the cat remained, watching her person.

'Suit yourself.' Dulcie couldn't help but feel a little insulted. 'But I've got to get to work.'

A piteous mew followed her as she carried the blue volume back into the kitchen. 'Sorry, Esmé.' Dulcie hardened her heart. 'You had your chance.'

The kitchen had its own problems. For starters, the bright sunlight of earlier in the day seemed to be fading, and Dulcie looked up into gathering clouds. Even when she switched on the overhead, she found it difficult to get settled, as the fluorescent blinked and buzzed. And the kitchen chair, with its stiff back, was just a little too tall for her to get comfortable in. Only the thought of the library – in particular, of facing that guard – made her stick with it, fetching a pillow from the sofa where Esmé was still doing her best impersonation of a cute and harmless kitten.

With no table of contents to consult, Dulcie had to rely on her memory to find the essay. That took her another twenty minutes, by which point the sky had darkened, and she could hear the rumblings of an approaching storm. She found it – 'On Reading' – just as the first loud crack sounded, and for a moment she paused. Esmé didn't have much experience with thunderstorms, and she got up to check on the young animal.

'Esmé, are you OK?' She peered into the living room, but the sofa was empty. Only when she got down on hands and knees was she able to spy the white chin of the little face, deep beneath the sofa. 'It's OK, kitty. It's just a storm.'

It was funny. The little cat had never been skittish. Then again, the winter storms she had lived through thus far had been relatively quiet, heavy snow dampening even the loudest wind. The thunder rumbled again, and Esmé's mouth opened in a small, plaintive cry.

'I can't make it stop, Esmé. I'm sorry.' Dulcie looked back at the kitchen, at her open book, and immediately felt like a heel. What kind of person was she, abandoning an animal in distress? Esmé mewed again, and Dulcie made up her mind. Bringing the book back into the living room, she sat down on the floor to read.

'*Of reading*,' the essay began, '*we must take the utmost care.*'

That didn't sound like her author, but the next few lines were promising. Dulcie read further, and there it was – on the second page. Pay dirt! '*The education of young ladies, of virtue undimm'd, must be of concern to all who live in a generous and civilized society . . .*' Dulcie thumbed through her notes to check, but she barely needed to. This was almost exactly the same speech Hermetria, the heroine of *The Ravages*, made to Demetria, her duplicitous companion, when Demetria had tried to convince her that reading was '*improper for one of gentle birth*', or some such nonsense. Esmé mewed again, and Dulcie reached one hand under the sofa to comfort her without looking up. She couldn't stop now.

'*The question of such education, indeed its very focus of purpose, must be one of the central issues of the day . . .*' Another peal of thunder interrupted her as the little cat's cries grew more piteous, and Dulcie stopped. 'Are you OK?'

'Meh!'

Dulcie reached under the sofa and pulled the cat out. No, she didn't seem to have sustained any injury in the last few minutes. Her eyes were clear, her nose wet and cool. 'Is this just nerves, Esmé?'

The little cat said nothing, and Dulcie put her down. With an almost-human sigh of resignation, the tuxedo began to groom. And Dulcie went back to her book.

'*The female mind, long suppos'd to be as inferior as t'other strengths of her fair sex, has been kept from the greater efforts. Only the bravest of reforming souls dares to put forth the call for more. To teach the gently-rear'd to read is a great thing—*'

Yes! This was exactly what she'd been looking for!

'*—but to push philosophy of the mind, or to expose such gentle spirits to politics is the work of fools. Headstrong and wrong-minded, such efforts risk endangering all the traits that we hold dear.*'

Dulcie stopped, her thoughts muddled by the rumbling outside. This wasn't making sense. She had been reading too fast. The sudden darkness and humidity had confused her. She forced herself to go back to the top of the page. '*The female mind . . .*' She read on. '*All the traits that we hold dear.*' She looked up. It couldn't be. Was the author of *The Ravages* actually condemning education for girls?

She read the next line. '*Such exercises are sure to damage not only such fragile sensibilities but also endanger those very virtues which are so cherish'd, the very center of the feminine worth.*'

It made no sense. Then it hit her: Gothic authors loved convoluted sentences. In their novels, every other one would double back, filled with multiple meanings. There had to be a double negative in here somewhere, something that would show that the author meant the opposite of what Dulcie had at first thought.

She relaxed, even as the rain started in earnest, and reread the page, getting up only to close the windows a bit before reading it again. But even a fourth review didn't show any about-face. Still, there could be a surprise to come, couldn't there? Dulcie finished the essay and found herself growing cold. The phrases were filled with hate, their arguments foretelling the rise of women: '*Brazen and bad-tempered, these bookish wrens . . . Wretched half-men unsuited for their place . . .*' There was no last-minute save, no redeeming turnaround.

Dulcie swallowed hard, finding her mouth suddenly dry. If this were true, then everything she believed about the author – about *The Ravages of Umbria* itself – was wrong. Her thesis, all the work she'd done, had been going in the wrong direction. She heard the thunder, distant now, and couldn't help but think what it portended. She had been the headstrong one. What was the phrase? '*Headstrong and wrong-minded.*'

Thorpe had been right about her. She'd barged ahead with a half-formed idea, disregarding two centuries of evidence to the contrary. Why had she thought that she, Dulcie Schwartz, could find something new after two hundred years? Why had she thought that this minor work, by a minor author, was really a diamond in the rough? It had been hubris of the worst sort. Headstrong and wrong-minded.

She slumped against the sofa as the last of the rain died away, and not even Esmé's soft fur, as the little cat rubbed against her in sympathy, could make her feel any better.

TWENTY-NINE

C hris found her there when he got home, the cat asleep in her lap. She didn't respond when he came in and barely looked up when he turned on the light.

'Dulcie, are you OK?' Chris dropped his soaking jacket on the floor and knelt beside her. 'What's wrong?'

'It's over,' Dulcie murmured, blinking. 'My thesis, everything.'

'Those bastards.' Chris sat back. 'All because of a cell phone call? I'll go talk to them. I'll tell them it was an emergency. We'll get Suze to file a suit—'

Dulcie was shaking her head. 'No, no, not because of the phone,' she finally said. 'Thorpe stood up for me. Maybe they only meant to scare me anyway, but it doesn't matter.' She slid the opened book toward Chris. 'Thorpe was right. They all were.'

He picked up the book. 'What am I reading?'

'My author. She isn't who I thought she was.' Dulcie shifted the sleeping cat, who woke and tried to hang on. But she used paws, rather than claws, and ignoring the little tuxedo's efforts, Dulcie stood. With a sigh that sounded like a sob, she turned and dragged her feet into the bedroom.

'Wait, Dulce.' He followed her. 'I'm sure it's not that bad.' But she shut the door in his face, leaving him standing there. 'Dulcie? Honey?'

'Please, Chris.' The voice was muffled, as if she were already face down on the bed. 'I just need to be alone.'

'OK.' Chris looked down at his feet, unaware that Esmé was watching him. Mindlessly, he picked up his wet jacket and slung it over his shoulders. 'I'm going to go get us some dinner, then. I'll be back. And Dulcie?' He leaned his cheek against the door. 'I love you, sweetie. I'm sure . . . well, I'm sure it will work out.'

There was no response, none he could hear anyway. So with a last attempt – 'I'll be back in twenty minutes, Dulcie' – he took up his keys and headed back out.

After he left, darkness once again took over the small apartment. Somewhere outside, a street light had come on, and the fresh breeze – a remnant of the storm – tossed the budding limb of a tree. As its shadow played against the wall, one branch gradually became clearer, grey rather than black, and arched like a giant cat. It was to this that the kitten turned, her own stark bicolor coat fading in the dusk.

'*I tried.*' The little cat looked up at the shadow. '*I did everything I could to keep her from reading it.*'

'*Trying to hide things won't work, little one.*' The voice could have been the rustling of the leaves or the wind. '*They always dig things up, it's how they function.*'

Esmé sat, her head down. If Dulcie had seen her looking so dejected, she'd have scooped her up in her arms. But Dulcie was in the other room, steeped in her own misery, and Chris had gone out in search of the only comfort he could imagine might work.

'*Don't worry, little one.*' The soft voice came back, and the little cat looked up again in hope. '*You didn't do anything bad. You're still learning, little one. And so is she.*'

THIRTY

Ice cream helped, as Chris had hoped. And he gladly ignored the congealing Chinese food as he watched his girlfriend responding to the solace of butter-crunch swirl.

'Did you try the chocolate mint chip?' He held out his pint to her, eager to encourage her apparent recovery.

'Thanks.' She smiled at him, and even though it was a weak, sad smile, he felt his heart fill. 'I'd better not.'

'Come on,' he urged. 'You didn't have any dinner.'

'No, really.' She got off the bed. 'You should heat that up and have some, though. You have to work.'

He followed her back into the living room, where she'd opened her laptop. 'What about you, Dulce?' He was still timid about asking any more.

'I'm going to start looking for a job,' she replied. She was typing something, and Chris saw her hit return with a flourish. 'See if those auction houses are still hiring. I mean, I think my academic career is over.'

'Wait, Dulcie, what are you talking about?' He sat on the edge of the desk and put his hand on the laptop. 'Look at me, Dulcie. Tell me what's going on.'

'Chris, do you ever feel like everything in the universe is trying to give you a message?' She reached up to close the computer, taking his hand as she did it. 'Maybe this is for the best. Maybe this will help us stay together even.'

'Dulcie . . .'

She nodded and began to explain. 'You know about the whole Dunster Codex thing, about my name in the ledger, and that I got in trouble at the library. This is worse.' By the time she had gone through it all, they'd migrated to the kitchen, where Chris zapped the Chinese in the microwave. He coaxed her into a chair and placed the bowls down in front of them.

'This doesn't mean you have to give up your thesis, Dulcie.' He began to eat. 'It's just one essay.'

She poked at a mushroom and shook her head. 'You don't understand.'

'I know, but there has to be some explanation.' He put his chopsticks down as Esmé began to twine around his ankles. 'No, Esmé. This is spicy.' She responded by leaping into his lap, and as he reached to remove the soft, warm creature, a thought struck him. 'You know, Dulcie, I'm going to ask Jerry to cover for me tonight. He owes me after this morning – and I think we could use a night together, a normal night.'

She smiled, a wan smile. 'That would be nice.' He knew she wasn't convinced.

As they washed up, he tried to change the subject. 'You know, I never got to finish telling you my thoughts on the whole identity theft thing.'

'Hmm?' She seemed more interested in a chip in a bowl than in what he was saying, but he felt the kitten at his ankles again and continued.

'I'm wondering if we were looking in the wrong direction.' Nothing. 'I mean, I kept searching after we talked, and I really don't think any of your accounts were hacked. I'm also reasonably sure that nothing higher up the food chain happened. You know, I like to think that if there had been some online interference, I'd have found at least a trace of it.'

She put the bowl away. 'I'm sure you would have.'

'Dulcie, listen.' He reached for her hands. 'Maybe we're

looking at this the wrong way. Maybe someone has stolen your identity, but in a low-tech way. You know, old-fashioned.'

He thought that would do it. That he'd provided the spark of an idea that would lift her up. But she had been through too much. She shook her head sadly. 'You're trying, Chris, and I appreciate it. But I checked. I have my university ID. It's in my bag.'

'But—'

'And besides, Chris, why would anyone? I'm just another broke student, researching a book nobody cares about in a field that has no value. My ID isn't worth anything to anybody.'

For a moment, there was silence. Chris seemed about to choke out a few words, but even he gave up. Instead, he leaned in to fold her in his arms. Within moments, Esmé had squeezed between them, mewing for attention. As Dulcie turned to look down at her, the little cat stood on her hind quarters, reaching up with white mittened paws.

'Oh, kitty.' She picked the cat up and held her close, burying her face in the soft fur.

Chris held his breath. The young cat had never really showed a fondness for cuddling, preferring instead to play. And considering her predilection for biting, well, Chris hardly dared to move.

But instead of the expected tears, he soon heard a much more welcome sound. Dulcie was humming – to herself, to the cat – and the white paws, extended over Dulcie's shoulders, were kneading in pleasure, the pink toe pads grasping and flexing.

'What a little love cat,' she said, when she finally looked up.

'Yeah.' It was all he could think of to say.

'And you know what?'

Chris shook his head.

'I don't think she spoke to me, not exactly. But when she leaped into my arms, I got something from her.'

Chris waited, hoping.

'I got, "Don't give up, Dulcie."' She was beaming now. '"Don't give up." And she's right, Chris. I can't just sit back and let myself be railroaded. I've got to figure out what's going on. I mean, I'm a trained researcher. That's got to count for something, doesn't it?'

'Yes, it does.' Chris felt the tension drain away as the kitten nuzzled Dulcie's neck.

THIRTY-ONE

'First, we've got to look at what we know. We may not be able to figure everything out from there, but we should at least be able to plan our next step.'

Dulcie was leaning over the kitchen table, which now held a yellow legal pad. The cat had accepted the move and now sat at one end of the table, opposite Chris, as the three looked at the rough diagram Dulcie was drawing.

'This is what we know for sure.' She started numbering. 'Topic one: Roland Galveston. Section A: he's missing. Probably still alive –' she paused – 'we hope, but definitely not answering his phone. Section B: the English department thinks he is here under false pretenses.' She wrote *Identity?* under Roland's name and underlined it.

'What do you know about this guy?' Chris leaned over and retrieved a pen that Esmé had started to bat.

'Not much,' Dulcie admitted, tapping the paper. 'Victorian, like Trista. But I don't know what his thesis was on – *is* on,' she corrected herself. 'Or about his students or anything.' *Research/work*, she wrote, adding several question marks.

'We'll come back to that. Topic two: the Dunster Codex is missing.' She gave the purloined text its own Roman numeral.

Chris interrupted. 'Shouldn't Trista be second?'

Dulcie chewed on the end of her pen. 'I don't know. We know she was shaken up about something, and we know that she's disappeared, but that's it.' She looked up at her boyfriend. 'I know I should be worried about her, but for some reason, I'm not.'

'No?' He looked more skeptical. Then again, he'd spent the morning trying to help out Trista's panicked boyfriend.

'Maybe I'm just annoyed with her. Maybe I'll kick myself later. Right now, there's too much doubt about what was happening. I guess I just wouldn't be surprised to find out she'd gone to ground, you know? Still, something's going on. So, for Jerry's sake, anyway.' She crossed out *The Dunster Codex* and

wrote in Trista's name. Underneath, she noted: *Under suspicion?
Questioned?* And then, in all caps: *MISSING?*

'The Dunster Codex is third, then.' She wrote that down, with
one notation – *Missing* – and paused. 'Why would anyone take
that?'

Chris looked perplexed. 'Isn't it, like, the crown jewel of the
rare book library?'

She nodded. 'Yeah, but why steal it? Its value is scholarly, not
monetary. I mean, someone couldn't just sell it on the open
market.'

'You don't know,' her boyfriend opined. 'There are some crazy
rich people out there.'

She nodded. 'Our curator is one of them. I remember the fuss
when the Codex was acquired. You'd have thought it was his
first-born child or something.'

'But he wouldn't—' Chris left the sentence open. 'No, that's
too crazy.'

'Not entirely, Chris. If the Codex had been somewhere else
and it had been stolen, then I would look at Gustav Coffin.'

'Well, that's something, isn't it?' His pale face brightened
somewhat.

Dulcie shook her head. 'No, he already acts like the Mildon
is his personal collection. If it had gone missing from some other
college that would be a possibility. I swear, he'd have stolen it
if he couldn't have bought it.'

'I guess that's why he suspects all the grad students then.'

'Unless it's just because we're the low people on the totem
pole.' She stared at her outline. Something wasn't sitting right,
but she couldn't put her finger on it. Finally, she jotted *Blue
ticket*. 'OK, what else?'

'The identity theft issue.' Chris almost didn't want to remind
her. 'Or, at least, the idea that detective – the fat guy? – warned
you about it. That's got to figure into everything.'

'Maybe, maybe not.' She gnawed on the pen some more. She
looked at her list. 'I don't know, Chris. When we talk about these
things, they all seem so disconnected – OK, maybe not the rare
book and Roland going missing. But the other stuff? Trista,
murder, my name on that ledger? I'm seeing the same things
over and over – someone or something has gone missing.
Someone or something has been mistaken for someone else. But

I'm not seeing how any of them fit together.' She circled the words *Blue ticket* and underlined them. 'Except to frame me.'

'Maybe they don't, Dulcie.' He paused, afraid to even say it. 'Maybe we should just focus on your problem. On clearing your name, sweetie.'

She shook her head. 'No, Chris. I'm not seeing it, but it's all connected. I just can't quite see how.' She stopped. 'Am I sounding like Lucy?'

'A little,' he said shyly. 'But wait, let me take a look.' He turned the paper slightly toward him. They both sat in silence for a moment staring at it. Even Esmé seemed mesmerized. Then Chris pulled a mechanical pencil out of his pocket and began to draw.

'In applied sciences, we're often trying to find patterns. See how things fit together.' He drew a line between *Blue ticket* and *Identity theft*. 'Identify the unifying system, if you will. Sometimes, to do that, you have to try looking at all your information in a different light.'

He drew some more lines as she watched. 'For example, if we apply a kind of roughshod version of game theory,' he said. 'We'd be looking at trade-offs. Who would do what to optimize the situation.' He drew some lines and tilted the pad back so Dulcie could follow. 'For instance, we can assume that you did *not* steal the Dunster Codex.'

She squeezed his leg under the table, but didn't comment.

'So, Dulcie-to-blue ticket has to be someone else's play, right?'

'Well, that would fit in with the identity theft, except that I haven't been hacked in any way. You've checked out my online stuff, and I have my ID cards.'

He was still staring at the lines. 'Who else would benefit? Who has established the conditions for optimization?'

'Well, somebody stole the Codex – and someone is setting me up for it.'

He tapped one of the lines. 'Roland looks likeliest, doesn't he? Steals the thing, disappears, and somehow arranges to blame you.' He nodded. 'I like him for it.'

She shook her head. 'Nope. According to your rules, it doesn't make sense. He doesn't "optimize" anything. He's the obvious suspect. Plus, he's lost out on getting his degree. He was *this* close. Why would he do that for a one-time score?'

'If it were worth millions?'

She shook her head sadly. 'Thousands,' she said, breaking it to him. 'And only to a certain small group of collectors.'

Her boyfriend visibly deflated. 'That's the trouble with the theory. We have what we call imperfect information,' Chris concluded sadly. 'I'm sorry. I guess that doesn't help at all.'

Beside them on the table, Esmé started to wash. Each wet tongue stroke slicked down a small area of fur, flatter and shinier than its neighbor until her pink tongue came through again, adding another damp patch to the overall black of her back. 'No, it's a good idea,' said Dulcie, absent-mindedly. Watching the cat was making her think of something. The question was: what? 'What do you call it when patterns repeat? Fractions, or something?'

He smiled. 'Almost. Fractals – the larger patterns are reproduced even in the smallest parts.'

'That's it, Chris.' Dulcie was staring at the paper. 'We've got a bunch of parts. We just need to figure out the larger patterns.'

'Unless—' He stopped himself.

Dulcie looked up. So did the kitten. 'What?'

'Unless these are not connected at all.' He put the pencil down and lifted his hands in surrender. 'Maybe these are just random occurrences.'

'That's chaos, right?'

'That's one word for it,' he said as Esmé pounced, sending the pencil flying.

THIRTY-TWO

*S*he woke to the pounding of hooves, the carriage horses in their haste striking sparks 'gainst the frozen ground. The noise hadn't woken her, though, dragged under by an exhaustion as thick as the fog that had shadow'd her early steps. 'Twas the hand, the touch of the stranger beside her, reaching rudely beneath her woolen cape. Searching for her purse, or to accost her person. Perhaps, she dared not think, to uncover the secret she held so close. Clutching the hem of her cape, she tore *it from that noxious hand and turn'd away. None knew her here, none ever could. She had made her journey in darkness, without her name. She would not tear that veil of secrecy. She would not call out now.*

Their attempts at outlining the problem should have been discouraging; their conclusions had been so . . . inconclusive. But Dulcie woke energized. Maybe it was having Chris there. Maybe it was simply that she had hit bottom the day before, between the library and that essay. Whatever the reason, she bounced out of bed before the alarm went off, full of ideas.

'Shh, Esmé, let's not wake him.' The cat looked similarly wide awake, and Dulcie felt a pang of regret as she tiptoed by her to the bathroom. 'I can't play now. I'm sorry.'

The cat was still watching when she emerged and dressed, jumping up on the desk as she scrawled a note. *Going to talk to Thorpe. Touch base later*, it said. Theories were all well and good, but Dulcie hadn't gotten this far by applying abstract rules to her research.

'Start with what you know,' she whispered to the cat as she reached for her sweater. 'Then take it from there.'

The little cat watched as she left, jumping up to the window to follow her progress down the sidewalk.

'*She's so brave,*' Esmé said, her quiet voice just carrying to the grey shadow who had appeared at her side. '*And so trusting.*'

'*It's her great strength, little one. And her great weakness.*'

'*But, what if she doesn't see—*'

Just then, Chris walked into the kitchen, Dulcie's note in his hand. He joined Esmé at the window, in time to see Dulcie's curls disappear beneath the new green leaves of a maple.

'Good luck, sweetie,' he murmured, under his breath, his hand on the smooth black back of the cat, and then went off to shower.

'*Mr Grey!*' The little tuxedo cat looked around, once she was alone. '*This is scary. What can I do to help?*'

'*What we always do, little one.*' The voice seemed to resonate out of no one place. '*We keep the home safe. She'll need that, once she returns.*'

Three blocks away, Dulcie heard none of this, although a certain satisfied warmth kept a bounce in her step. It must have been having Chris around – and getting a good night's sleep – she decided, which made today's course of action so obvious. Thorpe might not always respect her, but he trusted her. His actions yesterday, speaking up for her after the cellphone mishap, proved that beyond a shadow of a doubt. She'd go to him and explain about the blue ticket, that there was no way she could have been in the Mildon the previous Friday. And she'd ask him to – well, not to intercede for her with Coffin, that would be asking too much of the skittish, balding man – but to advise her. That was, after all, his job.

And then? Her steps grew a little heavier as she considered the other topic she ought to bring up with Thorpe. That essay, the one from the blue volume . . . . If she accepted the identification, and she had no reason to doubt it, then she had to acquiesce to the obvious conclusion. The author of *The Ravages of Umbria* was a fair-weather feminist. For whatever reason, she'd changed her tone here in the New World.

Unless – Dulcie picked up speed again – the dream had meant something. A woman, pursued, traveling under cover – under a false name, maybe. Even though the morning was bright and sunny, Dulcie shivered, pulling her sweater around her. She felt that cold, the bone-jolting rhythm of the carriage ride. The woman in her dream had been exhausted, frozen, and scared. Dulcie flashed back to how she had felt the night before, when everything seemed allied against her. Was that all her dreams were? Gothic re-castings of her own daytime woes?

No. She stopped short. Her dreams had led her in the right direction before. They were linked to her author, to her studies. And the woman in her dream had been defiant. Had been traveling on, despite fatigue and cold and fear. Dulcie felt her spirit. The woman in the carriage, whoever she had been, was not the kind to recant her forward views, no matter what she faced. She might use subterfuge, she might hide, but she would not give in. Dulcie remembered the stranger's hand. She could feel how the dream woman had grabbed her cloak and roughly turned away, protecting herself and – *and what?*

Although she stood on a sunny Cambridge sidewalk, Dulcie tried to place herself back on that frozen road. The woman had been hiding something in her cloak. Jewels or coins, most likely; a woman traveling alone, especially in the early 1800s, would need to be able to pay and pay well, if she expected to be left unmolested. Still, somehow Dulcie didn't think that was all.

'Why send me this dream if it's just about her avoiding being robbed?' Dulcie asked a squirrel. The grey beast had paused, halfway down a tree trunk. He didn't respond, but he didn't flee either, remaining in place as the distracted human started to walk again, wandering past his tree in a daze. 'Was that scene – the groping hand – tied in with the essay in the blue volume? Part of her disguise? Was—'

Dulcie stepped off the curb into a space between two vans, not seeing the Zipcar that had come careening around the far corner, its driver unaccustomed to the narrow Cambridge streets.

Behind her, the squirrel lifted one white paw, reaching out as if to stop Dulcie as she passed between the vans, invisible from the road. The car wove, as the driver reached for a map. The squirrel screamed.

And Dulcie's phone rang, bringing her to a halt.

'Lucy?' She turned back toward the sidewalk, unaware of the squirrel, which was now panting with relief. 'What's wrong?'

Nine a.m. Cambridge time meant six in the commune. And her mother, Dulcie knew, was always more of a daughter of Luna than a sun worshiper.

'You do have the gift! I knew it.' Her mother's voice, crowing with pride, caused Dulcie to roll her eyes. The squirrel scurried away. 'It's no surprise.'

'I'm not psychic, Lucy.' Dulcie started off again, a little more aware of her surroundings. 'I'm simply stating the obvious. It is early for you to be phoning me. Therefore, by deductive reasoning . . .'

'Oh, Dulcie,' her mother interrupted her. 'Let's not argue. That will only make this harder to tell you.'

Dulcie bit her lip. Her mother never liked to call with bad news. Usually, it was up to Dulcie to find out what bills were overdue.

'You still there, honey?' Lucy, now that Dulcie thought about it, sounded anxious.

'I'm here, Mom.' Dulcie rarely used that word. Lucy had actively discouraged it when she was young, and Dulcie had chosen her mother's given name over Squash Blossom, her totem at the time. 'You can talk to me.'

The big sigh that followed, echoing all the way from the Oregon forest, actually served to relax Dulcie. If her mother could go for the drama, whatever was bothering her wasn't too bad.

'Did you have a vision?' Dulcie ventured. Though these had died down in recent years, Dulcie had heard her fill of them, most of them sounding suspiciously like the result of empty-nest syndrome. 'Again?'

'You say that like they're common.' Lucy had evidently regained her composure, so Dulcie waited. 'But, yes, I did. And, Dulcie, it was horrible, just horrible.'

Dulcie looked around. She was about ten blocks – maybe as many minutes – from the Square. There had to be a way to hurry her mother along. 'Did it have a message?' She tried the obvious. 'Was there a message you needed to impart to me?'

'As a matter of fact, there was.' Lucy paused, but before Dulcie could prompt her again, she came back. 'But it wasn't just the message, Dulcie. It was what I *saw*.'

'Oh?' Dulcie was passing the big psych tower now and had to walk more carefully. Pale and distracted undergrads were queuing up at the entrance, while others leafed through books. Dulcie checked her watch. The last exams of the semester were about to start.

'To start with, you were on a journey. Some kind of terrifying, desperate journey.'

'Really?' If it had been anyone else on the line, Dulcie would have interrupted to relate her own dream. Right now, she only wanted her mother to finish. She made her way through the crowd.

'You were being carried away – that was key, away. Like you were being kidnapped. And there was a tower: it looked just like the Rider deck's card for the tower. And so when I woke up, I did a reading for you—'

'Wait a minute. Lucy?' Dulcie paused as the worried under-grads milled about her. Right now, she envied them their focus. If she wasn't careful, this call could go on all morning. 'Was that it for the dream? That I was being carried away? Because if that's all there was . . .' She hesitated. How does an only child, on the brink of adulthood, break it to her mother that she is, in fact, leaving?

'No, Dulcie, there was more. It's just hard to say.'

Dulcie waited, looking around for the deliverance she knew would not come.

'It was—'

'Hang on!' Past a small clique of smokers, heads bent together, she'd seen blonde hair – a particular shade, almost white, cut in layers. 'Lucy? Just a minute.' She put the phone down as she leaped up, waving wildly in the air. 'Trista! Trista!'

Her mother was still talking. Dulcie could hear her voice as she pushed by the smokers. 'Trista!'

The head was retreating, caught up in a sea of brunettes. 'Tris!' Dulcie called again, silently cursing her lack of height – and her friend's tendency to wear earbuds. 'Damn.' She had lost her. 'Sorry, Lucy,' she said, speaking once more into the phone. 'What were you saying?'

'I was saying that it was dark, Dulcie. There was a heavy darkness covering you.'

There she was. The blonde, away from the crowd and turning toward Dulcie. Maybe coincidence, or maybe she had heard Dulcie's call – heard the urgency if not the name. Only, now that she'd turned, Dulcie could see it wasn't Trista. Younger, maybe a little more waiflike in her thinness, it was the undergrad who Dulcie had mistaken for her friend once before.

'It was blood, Dulcie.' Her mother's voice reached her, tinny and far away. 'You were covered in blood.'

In that moment, the blonde saw Dulcie. They locked eyes, and Dulcie tried to smile. But with a look of horror, the younger girl turned and ran away.

THIRTY-THREE

'Lucy, I believe you.' Dulcie was upset. Not at her mother's dream, but at the strange interaction. 'I promise. And you can tell me about my reading later. Tonight. I'll call you. And, yes, I'll be careful. Really, I have to go.'

It could be anything, she thought. Maybe she – Dulcie – looked like someone the girl knew and wanted to avoid. Maybe she had a thing about grad students. Or Goths. Still, the timing – seeing that look of horror just as her mother related her nightmare – had left Dulcie spooked.

'It's this week,' she said to herself as she turned the corner. 'What else could go wrong?' Then it hit her: she had forgotten to call ahead. Martin Thorpe might not seem to have much of a life, but it would have been a courtesy to request an appointment with the man who had so much control over her fate. Still, nine fifteen on a Friday, where else was he likely to be?

'Hi, Dulcie!' Nancy, the departmental secretary, sounded as chipper as always, her warm greeting going a long way to salve Dulcie's frayed nerves. 'I just put a fresh pot on.'

Dulcie found herself smiling back at the plump brunette. Thorpe might be the acting head of the department, but Nancy was its warm heart. 'Thanks, Nancy.' She dropped her bag on a chair and headed for the coffee-maker. 'Is Thorpe around?'

Nancy shook her head. 'You just missed him.' She sounded as sad as she ever could. 'He's been all caught up in this Codex business.'

'Great.' The coffee tasted the same as always, ever so slightly burned. It was Dulcie's taste buds that had changed. She put her mug down. 'Is he coming back?'

'I hope so.' The secretary lowered her voice. 'Professor Coffin came by just a few minutes ago. He just missed him, too. Only, he has an appointment.'

'He's up there now?' Dulcie looked up the narrow steps, but Nancy was shaking her head.

'Back conference room,' she said, her voice still soft. 'I didn't think, what with everything going on, Mr Thorpe would want someone alone in his office.'

'Smart.' Nancy clearly had more spine than her boss, Dulcie thought as she reached for her bag. The thought was inspiring, or perhaps the caffeine kicked in then, because she paused and reconsidered. Thorpe wasn't available, and when he did return, odds were that he'd be tied up with the bigwig now sitting in the back of the building. Maybe she should follow the secretary's lead and confront Coffin directly.

Dulcie pictured the large man. Somehow, she couldn't see him relaxing in any of the worn Harvard chairs, and she wondered if he'd taken advantage of the back door to let himself out on to the small porch. It was turning into a lovely day, and the porch, under the shade of an ancient, if somewhat shabby, oak, was a comfortable place to sit. It was also – she was thinking – her territory. If she ever wanted to approach the fearsome curator, this would be the place to do it.

'Do you think he'd mind if I joined him?' she asked, and Nancy looked up, silent for once. 'I just have a few quick questions.'

'Oh, Dulcie, I don't know.' Her broad brow wrinkled. 'Be careful. He's – he's not a nice man.'

'I know.' It helped to have someone else acknowledge it. But she was Dulcinea Schwartz, doctoral candidate. She was not going to be held back by fear of some overblown librarian.

Taking another sip of her coffee for courage, she headed down the hallway. At this hour, the building was silent, and the gentle clicking of Nancy's typing followed her all the way to the back.

The door was closed, and she knocked softly. 'Professor Coffin?' There was no answer, and she knocked again. 'Professor?'

If the curator had in fact stepped out on to the porch, he probably wouldn't hear her. Dulcie considered for a moment. She could go around the back, climb the steps by the big oak.

No, that was what she would do if she were afraid, sneaking around like that. Besides, she was short enough already. If he were up on the porch and she approached from the ground, she'd feel like she was approaching a king. She knocked one more time.

'Professor Coffin? It's Dulcie Schwartz. Could I speak to you for a moment?'

Nothing. She pushed open the door and stepped into the room, right into the puddle of blood.

THIRTY-FOUR

It was like a nightmare. A particularly vivid nightmare. And instead of a storm or a horse-drawn carriage, there was blood, a large pool of blood. And Dulcie was not, at that moment, a brave heroine, determined to continue her voyage. She was a goldfish on the counter. A breathless voice, gasping. Trying to scream.

'Help,' she whispered, the words barely squeaking from her throat. 'Help? Help?'

'Are you all right, dear?' The words like a lifeline reached her. Nancy.

Dulcie turned. 'Help?'

She had no clear recollection of what happened after that. Something in her face – or maybe its complete lack of any color – sent the secretary running, and the next thing Dulcie knew for sure, she was sitting in Nancy's office, a blanket wrapped around her shoulders. It hadn't been cold that morning, not that she could remember, but her teeth wouldn't stop chattering, and she pulled the blanket closer. The movement sparked a memory, a hand, but just then Nancy's face appeared, hovering like a worried moon. 'Drink this, dear.'

Dulcie reached for the mug, but Nancy held on to it, steadying her. She smelled tea and tasted honey.

'You need something in your system besides coffee. You've had a shock.'

'His face. It was his face.' Dulcie knew, in some vague way, that she wasn't making sense. But if the uniformed policewoman standing beside Nancy insisted on asking her questions, she could only try to say what was on her mind. 'It was . . . upside down.'

The young black cop turned back, toward a colleague who had just appeared. Dulcie could hear them talking softly, but the words weren't registering. All she could think about was what she had seen: Professor Coffin, lying spreadeagled, white-faced in a spreading dark pool. The young cop stepped away.

'So, Ms Schwartz, how are we doing?' She looked up as a large man took the chair next to hers. The nose, the craggy face . . . It was Detective Rogovoy. 'You need anything? Want to lie down? You've had quite a shock.'

'No, I'm OK.' She shivered and pulled the blanket tighter. 'It's just that . . . finding him . . . . I keep seeing it. Him.'

'Completely understandable, Ms Schwartz. And I promise, we'll let you go as soon as we get a statement. Nancy here has already spoken to your boyfriend.' He clicked the button on a ballpoint. 'But first, if we could just get your story.'

'It's not a *story*.' Dulcie didn't know where the tears came from, but suddenly her eyes were full. 'It was horrible.'

'I know, Ms Schwartz. I know.' The big detective reached out and awkwardly patted her on the shoulder. Rather to her surprise, she felt a bit better. 'I mean, I have a few questions here that you could help me with.'

She sniffed and nodded. 'I can do that.'

'Good. Now, Nancy here has already told us how she sent you down the hall to that back room. Can you take it from there?'

'I *can* and I *will* . . .' Instinct and training kicked in – Dulcie started to clean up the detective's slightly mangled diction – when what he'd said suddenly registered. Nancy hadn't sent her down the hall. In fact, the departmental secretary had tried to warn her off bothering the professor. That construction – at least if Rogovoy had gotten it right – sounded a little like the kindly secretary was covering for her.

'Wait, Detective Rogovoy?' She looked up at him. He looked friendly today, but still . . . 'Am I a suspect?'

'Now, now.' He did pet her this time, his hand thumping down on her shoulder. A dog person, obviously. 'Let's just answer the questions, shall we?'

'No, please.' She sat up straighter, and his hand fell back to his side. 'I'd like to know. Are you considering me as a suspect?'

The big mouth opened, then shut. Dulcie watched with interest. It wasn't like Rogovoy could deny that Professor Coffin had been murdered. People just didn't fall backward and bleed all over the conference room floor like that.

'He fell backwards,' she said. The thoughts came together suddenly. 'That's why I kept seeing his face as upside down. He must have been looking at the back door – the door to the porch.'

Once again, her treacherous memory replayed the scene. She had opened the door and seen something – something that she couldn't quite parse. She'd stepped in, trying to make sense of the scene. That's when she'd realized she'd been stepping in something – stepping in blood. And her eyes had traveled from her feet across the floor to where Gustav Coffin had lain sprawled on his back. How had she known he was dead?

'There was a big stain,' she remembered. 'A big stain in the middle of his belly. That must have been where all the blood came from. Someone must have shot him or – no, Nancy would have heard. Someone must have stabbed him with something. And the way he was lying, looking toward the back door? Someone must have come in from the porch. Maybe they'd been talking – or fighting. Or, no, he'd heard a noise. Turned, only to be surprised—'

'Ms Schwartz, please.' The broad hand was raised again and, seeing it, Dulcie stopped. 'Please. It is my job to figure out the chain of events. What we would really like you to do, how you could really help us, is to just talk us through what happened. You walked down the hallway and opened the door. You saw – what you saw. But did you see anything else? Anyone else? And did you hear anything? Maybe before you opened the door? If not a shot, then voices, maybe? Maybe you thought somebody said to come in?'

'No.' She shook her head, suddenly very, very tired. 'Everything was quiet. There was nobody there. Just me – and the late Professor Coffin.'

THIRTY-FIVE

'She saw it, Chris. Lucy saw it.'

By the time the detective had finally let her go, Chris was waiting with a cab. It had been all Nancy could do to hold him back, she'd said as she rewrapped the blanket around Dulcie and generally clucked her into the taxi. Dulcie had been grateful, but once home, she had thrown off the extra covering to pace around the kitchen. 'She saw me covered in blood. But there was more – a journey, only not voluntary. Like I was being kidnapped or carried away or something.'

'Dulcie, please.' Chris turned from the oven, a mug of cocoa in hand. 'Here, sweetie, drink this.'

'It's nearly June,' she said, taking it anyway. 'Oh, good.'

'Now, let's go sit.' He guided her into the living room and on to the sofa, where Esmé, who appeared to have been waiting, jumped into her lap. 'Dulcie—'

'Don't you start, too, Chris Sorenson.' She put the mug down and absent-mindedly began to stroke the cat. 'I know, my mother's usually as loony as they get. Or, well, lonely, anyway. But her dream and my dream have both touched on too many of the same themes recently. She even saw a carriage, a closed carriage.'

'I know, a journey. Against your will.' Chris reached for the mug and pushed it back into Dulcie's hand. She sipped, almost without thinking, and he continued. 'But, well, that's not that uncommon a metaphor. Especially at this time of year. I mean, think of it this way: your best friend is graduating. Another friend is about to defend her thesis—'

'Oh my god, Trista!' The cocoa slopped over the side as Dulcie put the mug down roughly. Esmé looked up in surprise. 'Has Jerry heard anything?'

Chris shook his head. 'No, nothing. He's climbing the walls. If she doesn't show up before tomorrow, he can report her as missing, but I don't know how he'll last that long. I assume you haven't heard anything?'

'Me? No. I thought I saw her, but . . .' She paused. Had she even checked her phone this morning? After the call from Lucy, she'd turned it off. Maybe there was a message.

The phone took forever to boot up, or at least it seemed that way to Dulcie.

Chris stroked the cat, who seemed to have picked up on his agitation, and Chris let loose with a soft, 'Yes!' when the voice-mail icon appeared.

'Hang on.' Dulcie thumbed in the numbers. Two missed calls, both from an unrecognized number. 'Neither of these are Trista,' she said. 'I don't know who this is.' Dulcie turned toward her boyfriend, worry etching her face. 'Let me try her again.' She punched in the familiar digits, all the while wondering at herself.

Her friend was missing, and she hadn't been trying to reach her? Hadn't been worried? Hadn't been thinking of her?

'You've been busy.' Chris might as well have read her mind, and he draped an arm around her and the cat both as they heard the call go straight to Trista's voicemail. 'Hey, maybe she tried you on a different phone. Maybe she left a message?' Chris looked like he wanted to reassure her, if he could.

'You're right!' Dulcie disconnected while Trista's recorded voice was still talking and hit the buttons for her own messages as Esmé settled on her hand.

'Hi, uh, Dulcie?' The male voice wasn't familiar. Dulcie looked at Chris and shrugged. 'You called? I'm sorry it's taken me so long to get back to you. But if you want to, well, we can talk or get together or something.'

The pause that followed lasted so long, Dulcie thought the caller had disconnected. She worked her hand out from under Esmé, but just as she was about to hang up, he came back. 'Oh, Dulcie? Sorry. This is, well, you know me as Roland. Roland Galveston.'

THIRTY-SIX

'Dulcie, please tell me you're not serious.' Chris was hovering as Dulcie put on a clean sneaker and laced it up. 'It isn't safe. He could be the one – he has a motive.'

'I know, but . . .' She hesitated, unable to explain her instinct. 'I just don't see it. For starters, he's a little guy. A grad student like us.'

Chris looked unconvinced.

'Besides, we're meeting at the Bagelry.' She retrieved the other sneaker from Esmé, who had pinned its lace to the ground. 'It's very public. Very open.'

He didn't seem any happier. 'At least let me go with you. I could follow you. Be your tail.'

She shook her head. Chris was too tall to attempt stealth. 'If he sees you, he might bolt. Besides, don't you have a tutoring session at noon?'

'You could wait.'

He looked so miserable, she almost relented. Despite the horror of the morning, she just couldn't see jolly Roland Galveston as a murderer. There was no sense trying to convince Chris of that, though. Instead, she gave him a hug. 'I don't want to risk losing him.' She finished her shoes and stood, determined. 'He suggested we meet soon. For all we know, he's leaving town this afternoon.'

'Maybe he has to,' Chris muttered. 'Just promise me one thing,' he said, a little more loudly, as he helped her back into her sweater. 'Just don't get into a car with him.'

'I promise.' She gave him a kiss and headed toward the door. 'And the next time you see me, I should have some answers. And a dozen bagels.'

With a jaunty wave she was out the door. It was only as the door closed behind her that she felt a momentary tingle of anxiety. Maybe it was the sound of the latch catching – ca-LICK – or maybe it was the sight of the shoes she had left on the mat, sticky and brown at their edges.

'It doesn't matter now,' she told herself and marched down to the street.

The Bagelry had been her idea. Roland – or whatever she was supposed to call him – had wanted a place that was public, but not mobbed by students. That left out Lala's and the Greenhouse, but as Dulcie walked toward the T, she congratulated herself on the choice. Only about a half mile past the university – one subway stop – the little bagel shop had multiple advantages. Situated on a corner, two of its walls were windows, which had calmed the worst of Chris's anxieties. And although the little storefront had several tables, few people actually sat and ate there. Besides, after the trauma of the morning, Dulcie was famished. A fat lox sandwich, rich with cream cheese and red onion, would remove the last of her jitters about meeting her missing colleague.

It wasn't that she wasn't still shaken. In fact, as she descended into the Central Square T stop, someone had jostled her, a young man rushing past, and a scream – or something very close – had caused her throat to close up. She'd had to grab the escalator rail tightly to keep from falling down. Then she'd seen him run into the arms of a woman, the happy couple embracing. The woman had just gotten off an inbound train, and she'd squealed in happiness as they'd embraced. Only then had Dulcie been able to continue to her own train, and her breathing still hadn't quite settled back to normal.

That sight had made her think of Chris, though. And of Esmé, who had stood up to push her wet nose into Dulcie's hand as she neared the door – an old trick of Mr Grey's that she and Suze had named 'the autopet'. And while she still felt a little dislocated in time – Chris had called it, simply, 'shock' – she knew that she would feel better doing something, rather than sitting around. Besides, she was curious. And Roland – or whatever his name was – might know something about Trista.

Still, it was with an odd jumble of emotions that she peered through the glass door at the colleague formerly known as Roland Galveston. Slumped over one of the little tables, he looked smaller than she remembered. Less jaunty. He was staring at a cardboard coffee cup and hadn't seen her, and for a moment she thought about retreating. Going home. She certainly had enough reason to take it easy, and the man waiting for her just might be a murderer. She should probably have reported his phone call to the police – or at least the department.

She hesitated and stepped backward – into a woman in a pink jogging outfit. ''Scuse!' the woman yelled, earbuds blasting tinny music as she reached for the door.

Roland looked up, and in that moment, Dulcie knew she would go in. There was nothing about her colleague that was at all threatening. His face was lined with fatigue, but he attempted a smile as he raised his hand in a half-hearted wave, and she followed the jogger in.

'Dulcie. Thanks.' He stood to greet her. Automatically, she took a step away, then stopped herself. Her colleague looked so normal . . .

'Hi.' She wasn't sure what name to use. 'Um, I'm going to get something to eat, OK?'

'Yeah, sure.' He'd felt her momentary withdrawal, she could tell by the way his face fell. But he sat back down as she went up to the counter to order.

'Nova, please.' But before she could specify a poppy-seed bagel, Dulcie was struck by an odd thought. Maybe she shouldn't be questioning Roland directly. After all, he had been caught lying. She didn't see him as a killer, but she couldn't be sure she should trust him. Maybe . . .

'Miss?' The counter guy was waiting, a waxed paper covered with smoked fish in his hand.

'Poppy seed, low-fat cream cheese, onions,' she recited automatically. Maybe she should try a more subversive tactic. Something like Hermetria, the heroine of *The Ravages,* would use. 'Oh, and bean sprouts?'

While she waited for her lunch to be assembled, Dulcie tried to think of a plan. In *The Ravages*, Hermetria had been deceived by her companion Demetria, who was secretly plotting to steal what remained of her fortune – and drive her mad, to boot. Of course, Hermetria uncovered Demetria's duplicity through sheer smarts. But she also, Dulcie remembered, got Demetria to reveal herself by pretending to be deceived just a little bit longer than she was.

'Seven ninety-five.'

Shocked out of her reverie, Dulcie handed over a ten. No wonder this place wasn't a student hang-out. Still, as she took her change and her sandwich, she mused that it would be worth it. If only she could carry out a Hermetria-like deception long enough to learn something useful.

'So.' She sat down opposite Roland. He looked miserable.

Dulcie took a bite of her sandwich. As a stalling technique, it was delicious.

'I guess you know,' Roland said finally. 'About my name.'

Mouth still full, Dulcie nodded.

'It's really Rodney, but I've always been called Rollie. Really.'

She nodded again to encourage him. Her technique seemed to be working.

'Rodney Gaithersburg, and I did go to Vanderbilt. Only, I lost my grants and had to start working to pay the rent and, well, with one thing and another . . .'

Despite herself, Dulcie sympathized. She'd also, by this point, swallowed. 'So, when Trista found out the truth . . .' It was, she knew from crime novels, what would be called a leading question.

He nodded, face still glum. 'Yeah, she was pretty disappointed in me.' The gamble had paid off. 'She really felt bad, because she'd been trying to do me a solid.'

'Oh?' Dulcie took another bite. The theory, she knew, was to offer as little as possible. Besides, she was hungry.

'The Rattigan Prize? When she was notified, as a qualification, they asked her to recommend other scholars. I can't imagine that was fun to do, but it was great of her to think of me. Only, someone raised a question about my degree, and she made a few calls and . . .' He shrugged.

She swallowed. Time to push further. 'She wasn't the one to tell Coffin, though.' Her statement hung there, and for a second she wondered if she'd made a mistake. 'Was she?'

'Coffin? No.' He looked distracted, and she tried to think of a way to get him to talk. While thinking, she took another bite.

It worked. 'I'm not sure how he found out exactly. I think he may have known for a while. There was some talk about an expert from Vanderbilt – someone who wanted to look at the Dunster Codex, actually – and Coffin held him off. Took him to some academic conference in Maui, even. When I found out – when he told me – I was really grateful. I mean, grateful and scared. The man had a hold over me, and, well, I always knew that he was going to want something in return.'

The Dunster Codex. They were all connected. Dulcie scrambled to come up with another prompt. 'The Codex. You worked in the library, right?'

'Paper conservation.' A fast flash of emotion, something Dulcie couldn't read, crossed his face. 'Documents. It's what I'm good at, right? Actually, Dulcie, there was a letter I thought you'd like to see. It came in with *The Wetherly Ghost*, but it was in bad shape for so long that we've only just now gotten it so it's legible again.'

He was trying to distract her. 'Let's stick to Coffin, OK?'

'OK.' His momentary good humor disappeared. 'Anyway, once he knew, it was just a matter of time.'

'He had the power to ruin you. To destroy everything you'd done.'

Even his nod looked discouraged. Dulcie pressed her advantage. 'And you are a scholar. Even without an undergraduate degree, you know your stuff. Trista wouldn't have recommended you if she didn't respect you.'

'Trista's the best.' He sounded like he meant it. He also sounded unaccountably sad, and Dulcie felt her stomach clench.

'What happened to Trista, Rol— Rollie?'

'What do you mean?' He looked up at her, so clearly confused that Dulcie found herself breathing again. 'I mean, I can't imagine she'll ever talk to me again. But, what? Did she say something?'

'No, never mind.' She'd follow that puzzle up later. 'Let's get back to Coffin.' He looked away, and Dulcie decided to up the pressure. Girding herself, she tried to put on her best TV detective voice. To imagine the scene: 'He knows the truth,' she said. 'Hell, he's even protected you. But he's not an easy man to deal with. Not one you want to owe anything to.'

Rollie looked at her, and Dulcie wondered if she'd overdone it.

'You can't know – you weren't there.'

Dulcie's mouth went dry. This was no longer a game of make-believe. 'I was, Rollie.' She swallowed, hoping that would help the nausea. 'After.'

'I'm sorry.' He was staring at the table now, shaking his head slowly. 'There was no other way. I mean, he was after me, and – and I thought it wouldn't hurt.'

'Wouldn't hurt? You stabbed him! Stabbed him in the belly so that he bled out all over the conference room!' She was standing now. Shouting. 'You killed him, and you thought it wouldn't hurt?'

'What the—? Dulcie, what are you talking about?' Rollie was standing now, too. Over behind the counter, the sandwich guy looked mildly interested. 'Professor Coffin? He's dead?'

'You didn't know?'

He shook his head, his mouth hanging open.

'You didn't—?' She didn't know how to ask, suddenly. The man who had collapsed in his chair in front of her looked pale and stunned. Ready to faint. The world was turning. Nothing was making sense. She sat down as well, and for a moment, they both just stared, blinking.

'I didn't kill him,' Rollie said, finally, as the color began to return to his face. 'I didn't kill anyone, Dulcie. You've got to believe me. What happened was horrible, wrong, but not— All I meant was: I gave in. I did what he wanted.' Rollie had lowered his voice, but he was speaking with such urgency that even through the fog, Dulcie heard every word. 'He wanted me to do something for him. Something he couldn't do himself.' He paused to swallow, then looked up to meet Dulcie's gaze. 'He wanted me to fake some documents for him, Dulcie. Professor Coffin was blackmailing me.'

THIRTY-SEVEN

'**H**e was – what?' Dulcie knew she'd been in shock earlier. She hadn't realized it had affected her hearing. 'Rollie, what are you saying?'

But her forlorn companion had questions of his own. 'Someone killed Professor Coffin? And you thought – you thought—' He pushed his chair back with a loud scrape and ran off to the little café's restroom. Even before the door stopped swinging, the sound of retching began.

Dulcie, on the other hand, found her appetite returning. Her ruse had worked. She'd elicited a confession. Problem was: that confession raised more questions than it answered. Finishing off the bagel and lox, she licked her fingers with satisfaction and tried to digest the new information. Trista had known that 'Roland Galveston' was a fake. And Coffin had, too, for some time before Wednesday's announcement. Now Trista was missing and Coffin was dead – Dulcie quickly moved beyond that thought – and something even stranger was going on. She looked up as her former colleague emerged from the bathroom, his face pale and shiny.

'Are you OK?' He might be a fraud. He had certainly done illegal things. Right now, however, Dulcie just saw a sick young man – one whom she did not believe could have committed murder. 'Do you want some water?'

'Had some, thanks.' He sank into his chair. 'I'm sorry. That was just a shock.'

She watched him, wondering if he was going to say more.

'But, I mean, I can understand why you – well, why you thought maybe . . . But no. I did what he wanted, but I thought he'd turned me in anyway. I knew he'd blame it all on me, so I split. I packed up my office – everything that mattered to me – and took off. I didn't think, well . . . you know.' He looked up. 'What happened?'

She told him in the barest detail possible, not wanting to relive that awful discovery. Still, she saw him turn alternately red and then pale again at her story, but he stayed in his seat.

'You found him?' he asked, when she had finished. 'This morning?'

'Yeah.' Her own voice had grown soft.

'Wow.' He grimaced, and Dulcie made a decision. She wasn't psychic, no matter what Lucy said. But she did trust her instincts. Rollie had gotten caught up in something, something bad, but he wasn't a bad person.

Before she said anything else, though, she had one more question. 'Rollie, tell me, why did you call me today? Why did you wait so long?'

'It's only been, what, two days?' He scratched his head.

'Three.' She counted backwards. 'I called you on Tuesday.'

'You're right. I'm sorry, I should have called you right away.'

That wasn't really what she meant. She'd been thinking that if her ersatz classmate had decided to disappear, she wanted to know why he had surfaced. For now, though, she'd let him run with it.

'I mean, I didn't want to get you in any more trouble. I figured once I was blown, it would all become clear.' He was getting some color back. Confessing seemed to be good for him.

Dulcie, however, was only growing more confused. 'Trouble – *me*? Wait.' She latched on to the one thing she knew something about. 'You knew you were going to be exposed?'

'Yeah, some guys came around. Acted like cops, but they weren't. They were way scarier. Maybe FBI; maybe, I don't know, something worse. I don't know what was going on with Coffin. I didn't know if he didn't like my work, or had just decided I was too dangerous to have around. But he must have told them something. They had a lot of questions, and they were throwing around the wildest accusations.'

Trista. This sounded like her visitors. 'Did you talk to Trista about this?'

'Excuse me.' They both looked up. The counter guy was hovering, holding a wet rag in his hand. 'You guys done?' They looked around. The café was empty.

'Don't you have bagels to bake or something?' Dulcie did her best to sound authoritative – and like someone who might actually buy another overpriced sandwich. 'Cream cheese to churn?'

In response, he pointed to a sign: *NO LOITERING*, it said. Below it, smaller letters read: *Be courteous. Twenty minutes per table, please.*

'Courteous, indeed.' It was the best she could muster. They both stood, and she reached for Rollie's arm. 'Wait, I've got more questions.'

He nodded. 'I could use some air, anyway.'

The sun was hot, reflecting off the Mass Ave sidewalk as if it were a mirror, and Rollie led them down a shady side street. For a moment, Dulcie felt a pang of fear. She'd believed him when he'd said he hadn't killed Coffin. Still . . . as they continued walking, it was enough to make her hesitate before her next question.

'Over here.' He gestured to a weeping willow, and she froze. He didn't seem to notice and went to sit on the top of a low garden wall. Taking a deep breath, she joined him – keeping a little distance between them. 'You wanted to know more, right?' He broke the silence. 'About, well, what I did?'

She nodded. 'You said "trouble". You got me in trouble?'

'Yeah, I'm sorry.' He kicked at the dirt. 'Really. You see, when Coffin first told me he wanted me to fake someone's ID, he told me to fake Trista's. I think he knew we were friends – knew we knew each other, anyway. But . . .' He kicked the dirt again.

Dulcie didn't need to examine the stones for what followed. 'But because you were friends, you didn't want to get her in trouble. Me, on the other hand . . .'

'I know, I'm sorry. I didn't think it would come to anything, really. I mean, you're a straight shooter and . . . and . . .'

'I wasn't your friend.' She let that one stew for a while, before curiosity got the better of her. 'How'd you do it?'

He shrugged. 'It was easy. I work in documents, remember?'

'Yeah, but, the university ID number, all of that?'

'You know how you leave your bag when you go into the Mildon?'

She nodded.

'Coffin started having his staff Xerox the IDs. He said it was for extra security. Nobody was supposed to say anything about it.'

'That's illegal.' She heard how silly that sounded. 'I mean, all of it is, but copying our IDs?'

Rollie shrugged, and Dulcie followed the thought further.

'But, wait, if he had copies of lots of ID cards, why did he want you to fake Trista's?'

'I don't know.' Rollie shook his head sadly. 'Maybe because we were friends. Maybe it was his way of punishing me further. He even had me slip something into her bag . . .'

'Wait.' As much as she didn't want to interrupt Rollie, something was pushing at the edge of Dulcie's consciousness. 'If Coffin wanted fake IDs, that meant he was looking for a fall guy – fall person. He set me up, with your help. Professor Coffin must have staged the theft of the Dunster Codex.'

'The what?'

She looked at him with disbelief. 'Don't tell me you haven't heard about that, either.'

'No, what happened?'

She closed her eyes and thought back. Coffin had told them all about the theft at the meeting on Wednesday morning. According to Trista, the cops – or whoever they were – who had questioned her about 'Roland Galveston' had come by Tuesday night. Dulcie herself had called Rollie later that night, and he had already disappeared. It was possible.

She filled him in, watching his face as she talked. He looked shocked, but she had to be sure. 'That wasn't why you bolted?'

'No, it was those guys.' He shook his head slowly. 'They were scary.'

There was something else, something he wasn't telling her, but right now Dulcie's head felt full to bursting. She stood up. 'I've got to think about this, Rollie. I mean, my name was used. I'm now a suspect – they think I stole the most valuable manuscript in the Mildon collection.'

'Second, after the *Wetherly*.'

'To Hades with *The Wetherly Ghost*.' She was fed up. 'I don't care if Paine read it every night to go to sleep. I don't even believe that story.'

'You would if you could read that letter—'

'And, and—' She was about to tell Rollie off, only pausing to see if she could find an appropriately biting aphorism. In that moment, she saw she needed him. His testimony could clear her name. Could she march him down to the university police? 'Look, Rollie. You've got to make this right. You've got to confess.'

'I know, Dulcie. I know. I did drop a dime to the police, to put people on the alert about, well, the fake IDs. I mean, I wasn't specific. I didn't want Coffin coming after me, but—'

He stopped, staring. His eyes were fixed on a point beyond Dulcie, back at the corner from which they had come. She turned. There stood a young woman. A blonde, waifish, whose the studs caught the light. The student who looked like Trista. She had stopped as well and seemed to be staring back.

The sound made Dulcie turn, but it was already too late. Rollie Gaithersburg – aka Roland Galveston – had taken off. Despite his sickly appearance, he was making good time, already disappearing down the street.

THIRTY-EIGHT

For half a second, Dulcie thought about running after the fleeing Rollie. In that time, he turned a corner and disappeared. She turned back to the blonde.

'Hey, miss? Excuse me?' But she was gone, too, running toward the main street with a speed Dulcie was simply not up to matching. 'What the . . .'

Before she could even try to make sense of the odd behavior of those around her, her phone rang. She started after the blonde, planning on ignoring the insistent tone, when the realization hit her – it had to be Chris. He'd been so worried. She stopped where she was and dug in her bag.

'Hi, honey! I'm alive and unharmed!' She meant it to sound jaunty, but the silence that greeted her was momentarily disorienting.

'Um, Ms Schwartz?'

Dulcie looked at the phone. No, it wasn't Chris calling.

'This is Cara, from English Ten?'

How embarrassing. 'Sorry, Cara, I thought you were someone else. Look, I can't talk right now.' She looked up. The Trista lookalike had disappeared as well. Dulcie was a teacher, not a track star.

'Never mind,' she said with a sigh, turning her attention back to her caller. 'So, Cara, how may I help you?' Class had ended more than two weeks ago, and Dulcie had to struggle to remember the quiet girl who always came in late. 'Is this about your final grade?'

'Oh, no. You were more than fair.'

Dulcie felt a wash of relief. She hated disappointing students. Almost as much as she hated arguing with them.

'I wanted to ask you about summer classes. I think I'm going to enroll, get a head start, and there's a course on the literature of the afterlife?'

'The Dante.' Dulcie nodded. Not her take on the afterlife, but a good course nonetheless. 'The instructor is wonderful, but it's a really compact course. Have you read *The Inferno* before?'

'Well, yes, I mean, in translation, but . . .'

As they talked, Dulcie started back toward the Square. Despite her frustration with how lunch had ended, as she walked she found herself relaxing. It felt good to have a normal conversation, a teacher-student interaction, particularly since this student was not asking for anything more than advice. Almost, Dulcie regretted not trying for a section in one of the summer literature courses. Teaching one of those would be more casual, and she could use the money.

'Well, thanks, Ms Schwartz. You've been really helpful.'

Dulcie could barely remember what advice she'd given the girl, finally. Something about how rereading, about how it could be useful to get a fresh take on something you thought you knew.

Of course, revisiting an author could also take you the other way. Like, when you read something new by an old favorite and discovered that not only was everything you imagined wrong, but also that the person you'd been focusing on for years was a disappointment.

Dulcie felt her feet becoming heavier, until she finally stopped on the corner of Linnaean, where a bus stop offered a bit of shade from the midday sun. What was she doing, anyway? Her life was a mess. If Rollie wouldn't come forward to confess, her reputation was shot. Her thesis was in shambles. Her cat liked to bite . . .

She sat down on the bench. Her cat. She'd said that to herself, and she'd meant Esmé. No wonder Mr Grey didn't visit any more. No wonder he'd chosen Chris over her. Only a year, and she'd already replaced him in her heart. It was all too much. Sitting at a bus stop on a busy Cambridge street, she put her head in her hands and let the tears come.

'Miss?' The voice came from too far away. 'Miss, are you all right?'

She looked up. A tiny figure, barely taller than the seated Dulcie, was leaning over, a concerned look in her wrinkled face. 'Excuse me?'

'I asked if you were all right.' Two dark eyes blinked behind thick glasses, reminding Dulcie of something. The red lipstick, applied like spackle, was distracting however. 'I thought, perhaps, you might need some help.'

Dulcie smiled, despite herself. The idea of this tiny woman, eighty if she was a day, coming to her rescue brought home the reality of her situation. She stood up and dried her eyes. 'I'm fine, thanks.'

The dark eyes blinked, their concern unabated.

'Really, I've just had a difficult day. I guess it all got to me.'

'Well, I can understand that.' The woman reached for two shopping bags that she must have put down when she approached Dulcie. 'Mercury is retrograde, and that's especially hard for Leos like you. Remember –' she hoisted the bags and turned, addressing Dulcie over her rounded shoulder – 'Mercury is the messenger. When he goes retrograde, it doesn't only mean that you may be misunderstood. You may be misunderstanding others as well.'

Before Dulcie could respond, a bus pulled up, brakes squealing. A flood of passengers poured out, and when they cleared, the old woman was nowhere in sight. Dulcie strained to see if she'd gotten on the bus, but it was too packed to reveal one tiny figure. She found herself alone as the bus drove off. Alone, but strangely comforted.

'Mr Grey, did you send her?' She looked up at the cloudless sky. 'Did you?' A faint breeze blew, thrusting a leaf against her ankle before it skittered away. Dulcie watched it with a feeling of awe.

Still, the old woman could have just been a local crazy.

There was one way of checking. 'Hi, Lucy, it's me.' It didn't pay to be grammatically correct with her mother. 'Just checking in.'

She owed her mother a call, anyway. For all her scoffing, her mother's dream – er, vision – had actually come true.

'Dulcie! What a surprise.'

So she wasn't too psychic, then. Or too worried. Dulcie chose to ignore that thought. 'Yup, I wanted to tell you. Your vision? All that blood? It came true.' Hearing her own words, Dulcie hastened to add. 'But I'm fine. Everything's all right.' That part wasn't necessarily factual – not for Professor Coffin, anyway – but it should serve to reassure a worried parent.

'I know that, dear.' Assuming that the parent had been worried. 'As soon as I'd had my yerba maté and thought some more about your reading, I saw that I'd misinterpreted everything.'

'Oh?' Dulcie was in a mood to be amused.

'Why, yes. I should have recognized the blood from the start. Especially when I turned over the ace of wands. It was the blood of childbirth. Of new discovery.'

Dulcie opened her mouth. No words came out.

Lucy didn't seem to notice. 'You're on the edge of a great breakthrough, my dear. That's why you were covered in it in my dream.'

'I'm on the edge of something, anyway.' Dulcie decided not to tell her mother about the more realistic manifestation of her vision. Why upset her?

'Of course, birth can be painful.' Her mother wasn't even listening. 'I remember when I had you, despite the blessed smoke your father kept blowing . . .'

'Mom,' Dulcie interrupted. Her mood was fragile enough. 'Is Mercury retrograde?'

'Why, let me check.'

Dulcie was a little surprised that her mother didn't know offhand, but she waited.

'Why, yes, dear. It has been since Tuesday.' Her mother sounded unaccountably pleased by the discovery. 'No wonder I've been fighting with Moonglow. You're so smart. You must have sensed it.'

THIRTY-NINE

I t wasn't even one, and Dulcie felt exhausted. Conversations with her mother could do that to her, she thought, and then corrected herself. Finding a dead body could do that to her. She looked at her phone, now silent in her hand. She should call Chris, let him know that she was OK. He'd still be with his tutees, however. She should at least wait till half past. And if he wasn't going to be home . . . By habit, she headed toward the basement office she shared with Lloyd. Maybe seated at her desk, with her notes around her, she could find a way to get back into her thesis – a way to incorporate that horrid new essay. At the very least, she should see if any of her other students had come by. She should never have blown off office hours without posting an alternate time.

'It's not like they've got any pressing work,' she said to nobody in particular. The trees leading up to Memorial Hall were in full leaf now, and a grey squirrel had paused to watch her pass. 'I'm the one who has to finish the grading.'

The squirrel looked at her expectantly, and Dulcie paused. Something about his manner, the sharp stare of his black beady eyes, made her feel he had a message for her. A warning, even. But he only chattered in an agitated manner. 'What?' she answered, unable to get anything more from the beast. 'So I like cats? Deal with it.'

That was it. Cats. Almost like a waking dream, a memory came to her: Mr Grey, outside and on the hunt. She saw him lurking, his plume of a tail lashing once, twice, and then a third time in his agitation. Then she saw him crouch and creep forward, a grey squirrel just like this one in his sights. Her beloved cat had made his way forward, placing himself between the small rodent and the only nearby tree. With a thrill of fear, Dulcie found herself holding her breath – and then, Mr Grey had lunged. Only, the grey predator had overextended himself. Even before he leaped, the squirrel seemed to know he was coming. With a quick feint to the right, the squirrel had sped left, ducking down to run *under* the giant cat's outstretched claws. Dulcie remembered laughing with joy as the terrified squirrel had scurried up the tree. 'I'm sorry, Mr Grey!' She had scooped him up. 'It's better this way. I promise.'

'Now, what brought that on?' She found herself laughing out loud as she entered the building. It had never happened; she was almost sure about that. Mr Grey had been a house cat, not a hunter. 'Must have been a dream,' she decided. The squirrel's chatter faded behind her.

Squirrels! She was still chuckling as she descended the stairs. Only when two shadows emerged from a doorway did she stop, a chill suddenly running down her back.

'Um, hello?' She took one step backward, then another. 'May I help you?'

Usually, this hallway was buzzing with activity. But it was spring, a Friday afternoon, and she could hear her own footsteps clearly on the old tile.

'Hello.' The first man stepped toward her. He was wearing a suit and smiling.

To anyone else, Dulcie thought, he would have looked respectable. As Lucy's daughter, however, she had an ingrained distrust of white shirts and ties. Especially loud ties.

'Please don't worry, miss. We've already checked in with security.'

She opened her mouth – and hesitated. There was a guard, upstairs. Not that he ever noticed much.

'Actually, miss.' The other man stepped into the light. Another dark suit. Where ever they had bought them, neither had been properly sized. Fashion might not be Dulcie's forte, but she was reasonably sure jackets were not supposed to bunch up like that. 'We *are* security,' the second man was saying. 'We're with a special detachment of the university police.'

He pulled out a billfold that contained a badge, as did his partner. Advancing carefully, Dulcie took it. 'Officer Read,' she read out loud. 'Community-university liaison?'

'Uh huh, and I'm Harris,' the first man said, holding out his badge.

Feeling a little silly about her hesitation, Dulcie waved it away. Rogovoy had said that the insurance company was pushing for an investigation, and she suspected he had relegated it to the back burner. It made sense that some extras had been called in. 'I'm sorry.' She found herself breathing more normally. 'I should have been expecting some kind of follow-up. It's just been a crazy day. How may I help you?'

'We have some questions,' the second one – Read – said. 'Is there a place we can talk?'

'Sure.' She'd assumed they'd come to her office looking for her. Then again, perhaps they were just being polite. She unlocked the door and led them in to the tiny, book-filled room she and Lloyd shared. 'Please come in.'

She turned to switch on the overhead as the two men crowded in. Rather to her dismay, Harris strode over to Lloyd's desk, pulled out his rolling chair, and sat down heavily without pausing to ask permission. Read, who in the light she could see was the slightly smaller of the two, headed toward hers, but she scooted around the big, metal desk and claimed it first, leaving him with the rickety, but perfectly adequate wooden chair usually occupied by visiting students. That was probably immature of her, she realized a moment later. After all, they were both taller than she was and more formally dressed. But when she thought about rising, about offering the officer the better chair, she just couldn't. Besides, Read seemed comfortable. He even tipped the chair back and put his feet up on her desk.

'So?' She tried to smile as she moved a stack of books away from his feet. 'I'm all yours.'

'Thank you.' Read, across from her, smiled, revealing oversized canines. They didn't make him look particularly friendly. Then again, she'd thought Rogovoy was an ogre when she first met him. 'We appreciate your time.'

'No problem.' Dulcie tried to relax. She'd managed to salvage her day. Put the horror of the morning behind her. Just the thought of what she had seen – the blood, the still body – began to bring it all back. She shook her head. 'But I don't think I know anything that will help.'

'Sure you do,' Read said, his jovial tone startling her out of her reverie.

'What we want to know is about the Professor.' The voice of the other man – Harris – was deeper, as befitted his size. 'How well did you know him? What was your relationship?'

'What?' Dulcie swung around to look at him. This wasn't about library usage. 'I don't know what you're talking about.'

'We think you do.' Harris was leaning forward. He was, she noticed with a sinking feeling, quite large. 'And we think you should tell us.'

'I told everything to Detective Rogovoy this morning.'

Harris turned to exchange a look with Read.

'I assume you've spoken with him?' Dulcie asked cautiously.

'Yeah, Rogovoy.' Read tossed the name out like a bone. 'We talked with him, too.'

Something was wrong, terribly wrong. Too late, Dulcie remembered how Trista had been visited by two men who claimed to be police. Rollie, too. Somehow, she felt they had moved beyond merely trying to scare people. She braced herself against her desk.

'I don't think I want to talk to you.' She stood and put her hand on the back of her chair. 'It's all on file. I've got to go.'

Harris acted first, lurching out from behind Lloyd's desk. But Dulcie was ready for him. She shoved her own chair at him, rolling it hard into his belly, and then pushed at the books on her desk. They hit Read's feet, and he tipped over backward with a yelp. Harris roared and lunged for her, shoving the chair out of the way. But she'd bought herself a few seconds – and her size served her well. Grabbing her bag, Dulcie ducked under his outstretched arm and bolted down the hall. She'd left her office wide open, but she didn't care. Mr Grey had warned her, and she raced up the stairs, as fast as any small animal in fear for its life.

FORTY

The guard, of course, was absent from his post. Absent or ... No, Dulcie didn't want to think of what else could have happened to the jovial senior who usually sat behind the desk at the top of the stairs. He was half deaf and no taller than she was, and Dulcie had long suspected the job was something like tenure for the old man, providing a place for him to sit until retirement. He wouldn't have stood a chance against those two. The image of Professor Coffin as she'd last seen him – bloody and still – flashed through her mind again, causing her to pause for a moment. To grab at the wall. Better not to think of it. Of him. Better to just keep moving.

But where? As she pushed out the big door and found herself in the improbably sunny grounds by the Science Center, Dulcie paused again, breathing heavily from her panicked bolt, and looked around. Home was twenty minutes away. The university police, ten. A quick glance behind her showed nobody on the steps, nobody in pursuit, but Dulcie couldn't relax. Even if she had escaped, her safety was temporary. They thought she knew something. Besides, they had terrified two of her classmates – one of whom was missing.

Trista. So brash and sure of herself, her friend was not easily scared. Had they come back to question her again? Had she called their bluff about being cops? Dulcie didn't want to think about it. She did, however, pull out her phone as she set off again, breath ragged in her throat. She was heading into the Yard. There would be people there. Students packing up, parents. Alumni gathering. In the relative safety of the crowd, she could think for a minute. She could make a plan.

As her phone powered up, she saw that she had a message.

'Dulcie, are you OK?' It was Chris. 'Please call. I'm leaving my phone on.' She checked the time: he had called only a few minutes ago. Tutorials were supposed to be cellphone free, but she hit redial.

'Dulcie!' He sounded overjoyed to hear her voice. 'Hang on a minute, guys. I've got to take this call.'

He was still meeting with his students. Of course, he would be for another half hour. Dulcie tried to keep it short.

'Hi, Chris. I'm OK. Really. But I think I need to tell the authorities. Those guys are dangerous. I mean, I think they might be involved with Coffin and they kept asking me what I knew and, well, it was just instinct, but—'

'Wait! Dulcie? Who are you talking about? What guys? Are they with Galveston?'

She hadn't filled him in. 'This is something different, Chris. Rollie – I mean, Galveston's scared, too. The same two guys came after him, I think. There were two guys, two men in suits. They called themselves Harris and Read, but if those are their real names, then I'm Mrs Malaprop. Anyway, they were in my office and I got away. I'm in the Yard now. I don't know whether to go to the police or the departmental offices. I mean, this is all tied up with the Dunster Codex somehow—'

'Dulcie, Dulcie, please! Hang on.'

Dulcie paused; he was shouting.

'Dulcie, please. Get somewhere safe – somewhere with people – and then call me back. Right away. Please.'

'If you're sure it's OK . . .'

'Dulcie!' She agreed and hung up. Maybe it was hearing her boyfriend's voice, maybe it was being outside, surrounded by milling students and their families, but she felt a little more relaxed now. Less scared, but – as she thought about it – angrier. It was time to call a halt to this nonsense.

'Detective Rogovoy, please.' Dulcie had started walking again, craning her head to see if anyone was following her. She wasn't going to be foolish about this. 'Tell him Dulcie Schwartz is calling.'

While she waited, she kept walking, striding along the paths that criss-crossed the shaded Yard. Turning left on one, she realized, without much surprise, that she was heading toward Widener. Well, it was her safe place. And she didn't have to go in. She could wait with the guard. If the detective wanted her to, she could head up to the police headquarters from there. Maybe he'd want to send a car to pick her up. The important thing was that she stay in the open.

'Ms Schwartz?' Whoever had answered the phone was back. 'I'm afraid Detective Rogovoy isn't available right now.'

She stopped in her tracks. The detective wasn't available?

The voice was still talking: '—will speak with you.'

'Excuse me?' She turned around again, hoping to catch sight of the burly detective on one of the paths.

'I said that Detective Rogovoy left very specific instructions in case you called.' The speaker sounded young, and Dulcie wondered if the police department used work-study students. 'He said if you had any questions or concerns, or thought you might have any new insights to share, he would like you to come in.' Or interns. He could be an intern. 'He said to tell you that Detective Sanchez has been briefed on the case and, um, on your history, it says here. He said you should come in and talk to her.'

'He did, did he?' It wasn't rational, she knew that, but she couldn't help the feeling that she was being pawned off on a junior staffer. 'He told her my history?'

'That's what it says.' The voice sounded sheepish now. 'I'm just quoting.'

'I bet.' Dulcie thought for a moment before replying. 'Well, would you get a message to Detective Rogovoy, please? Would you tell him I *do* have new information, but I also have my own work to do. He can reach me at this number. When he's available.'

She snapped her phone shut with a satisfying click. So much for trusting in the police to be there for her. It didn't matter. Widener stood right in front of her. Her intellectual home, the library was the ultimate safe haven. She looked in through the glass doors at the uniformed guard, standing to attention. It wasn't the same man as the day before, she was happy to see. But she was reasonably sure that anyone posted here would be able-bodied. He certainly wouldn't be deaf.

She climbed the last few steps, batting away a twinge of guilt, as if it were an annoying fly. Before the day was over, she'd talk to Rogovoy. Probably when he got back from lunch. But everything had gotten so complicated, she didn't want to have to explain it all, especially not to some subordinate who wouldn't know all the players and probably had been deputized to keep her calm. Until the big detective could make time for her, she'd be safe in the library. Maybe she could even find out a little bit more of what was going on.

She was about to enter when another thought hit her. That girl – the one who looked like Trista – she worked in the Mildon. Dulcie could stop by and get her name, maybe her phone number. She had been hesitant to ask more about the girl before, back when she thought that she was still being framed for the Dunster Codex theft. Now, thanks to Rollie, she at least had a rough idea of what was going on. And the fact that Rollie had been spooked by the young blonde was added proof that the girl was somehow involved.

Rollie wasn't a bad sort, Dulcie thought. He'd surface again to clear her name. Wouldn't he?

Turning her back on the big glass doors, she scrolled down till she found 'Roland Galveston' in her contacts. She felt for him, she really did. The financial pressure on students was intense. And if Rollie had already been outed as a fraud, he had nothing more to lose – well, not much more to lose. All he had to do was explain how he had been pressured to copy Dulcie's ID.

She hit 'call'. Maybe she'd start by asking him about that letter he'd told her he'd helped restore. That was a friendlier note, and she'd never followed up on it. 'Rollie?'

Three rising tones greeted her, followed by a message she knew too well. 'The number you have reached is not in service . . .'

Damn! She clicked off, trying not to panic. This didn't mean that her one-time colleague had gone to ground. Lucy had had her phone turned off many times, and Dulcie had just been thinking of the financial pressure on her colleague. He wouldn't have bolted, would he? Not when she needed him to clear her name by explaining how Professor Coffin—

Professor Coffin, who had just been murdered. Dulcie had felt instinctively that Rollie was incapable of such a crime. That didn't mean the cops would agree. And now that she had filled him in on the news – of the theft and the murder – Rollie had enough sense to see that he'd be the prime suspect. If, that is, he could be tracked.

Well – she turned back toward the library entrance – she would simply have to prove her innocence some other way. Finding that skinny little blonde would be a start. With a new determination, she pushed open the door and strode in.

FORTY-ONE

I t was nothing, Dulcie told herself as the guard seemed to take an unusually long time to examine her ID. A new guard. Normal precautions. She'd already turned off her phone. There wouldn't be any kind of a watch list with her on it, would there?

Only once he waved her in did she realize she'd been holding her breath. Safely in the elevator, she took out her card to examine it. Photo, check. Name and student number . . . For a moment, she was seized by a horrible thought. What if *this* were a fake? Maybe her real ID had been the one taken. She flicked the card back and forth under the elevator's fluorescents. The holographic 'Veritas' seal reflected back and disappeared again. It looked real enough, but Dulcie made a note to talk to Thorpe anyway. She didn't know what would happen to the investigation now that Professor Coffin was dead. She did know she didn't want to be caught short.

The elevator stopped on the third lower level, and Dulcie had to stop herself from getting out. She'd pressed this button automatically, but she wasn't going to her carrel this afternoon. Even if she didn't have other matters more pressing, she didn't necessarily want to go back to work. Call it thesis fatigue, even brain freeze. Ever since reading that essay, Dulcie had simply lost all taste for *The Ravages of Umbria.*

The automatic doors slid closed to descend another floor, and Dulcie allowed herself a moment of reverie. *The Ravages* had been so much of her life. She'd lived through that book, found excitement first in the wild adventures of Hermetria as she battled to save her castle, her inheritance – and then her life. And as Dulcie had gotten more involved in the work, she had been caught up in the drama of its creation as well. The anonymous author, a woman of brains and spunk. Fearless, or so it had seemed, and willing to face down the authorities with her near-revolutionary fervor. No wonder she'd had to flee England. A country at war with Napoleon didn't want to consider social upheaval. The New World must have seemed so much more inviting, and with peace between her homeland and the new republic, travel was finally possible.

Except, well, would that have made her new home less welcoming? With the fledgling United States once more allied with England, would that have meant the conservative forces here would also be on the rise? Could she have been in danger here, as well?

A loud bark caused her to open her eyes. A stooped man, clad in tweed, was waiting. She was blocking the elevator door. 'Sorry,' she apologized under her breath, and stepped out.

'Women,' she clearly heard him mutter as he took her place

and the doors closed. Maybe things had not changed all that much.

Knowing how her identity had been compromised, Dulcie approached the front desk of the Mildon with trepidation. Whatever she did, she wouldn't leave her bag there, but it was hard not knowing who had been in on the curator's plot. Of course, it might all be moot, she realized as she approached the white counter marking the entrance. Nobody seemed to be on duty at all, and she pressed the buzzer set there for the purpose, only to see the small mouse-like attendant emerge from behind a closed door. 'Yes, yes, I'm coming.' He pushed his glasses up on his nose as he scurried forward and peered up at Dulcie. 'Oh, it's you again.'

Dulcie blinked at the unexpected rudeness. 'Yes, I'm back.' She paused, then let her curiosity get the better of her. 'Are you surprised?'

'Well, we'd heard there were some problems.' He waved one pale hand. 'Never mind, never mind. Here to serve. How may I help you?'

He seemed earnest enough and certainly confident in his self-righteousness. Dulcie wondered briefly if he had been one of the people photocopying IDs – and, if so, if he had been told it was part of a legitimate security proceeding. That wasn't what she'd come to ask about, though.

'I'm actually trying to get in touch with one of your employees.' Dulcie remembered, with that, what the little man had said at her last visit. 'She may be a work-study student. Slim, blonde hair cut kind of short. Pierced nose.' She might as well be describing her missing friend. All she lacked was a name.

It wasn't necessary. 'I can't give out personal information—'

She stopped him with a raised hand. 'I wouldn't ask you to.' She added a fake smile. 'I'd just like to leave a note for her, if that's OK?'

'Well, it may be. I won't make any promises.' He snorted, a tiny mouse-like snort, but he reached under the counter and came up with a notepad and pencil. 'Here.'

Dulcie took up the pencil and thought for a moment. She didn't want to scare the girl away. She also didn't want to write anything that might incriminate her. Dulcie's days of trusting library employees were over.

Please call, she finally wrote, trying to make her usually cramped handwriting as legible as possible. *It's important we talk.* She followed that with her cell number and signed it: *Dulcie Schwartz.*

She folded the notepaper in half, but she had no illusions of privacy as she handed it, along with the pencil, back to the clerk. All she could do was hope it was delivered – and that the girl would at least be curious enough to call. Aware that the little man was staring at her, she thanked him and walked away, back to the elevator.

There, she paused. Where should she go from here? The idea of going back to work seemed too dreary and, really, considering the day she'd had, she thought she could afford to take the afternoon off. But since she was here . . . She paused to consider. Weren't the conservation offices somewhere down here, too? Maybe she could see where Rollie had worked. Find out more about how he had faked her ID.

'Not any more,' the clerk at the circulation desk told her, once she had given up and surfaced to ask. 'Used to be everything was down on Level Two. Now they have their own labs – special equipment and everything – over in the Holder. There's a tunnel, of course, but . . .'

He didn't have to finish. The heightened security that had been installed following the library renovations of a few years ago clearly hadn't been enough to protect the Dunster Codex. It did, however, make the clerk's life much more complicated.

Not to mention her own: Dulcie caught herself up short. The other guard – the one from the day before – was on duty now, waiting to go through the student bags. It was silly, she knew that, but she just didn't want to face him and so turned, to walk the long hall toward the back exit. As she did, she wondered about those tunnels. It was probably still possible for someone with the proper access to move unhindered among the university libraries. Could someone have spirited the Codex out that way – shuttling it from library to library until it finally made its way through some less well-protected door? It was possible. This hall, for example, was rather dark and often deserted, at least until the guard's station – a little booth right by the door.

Which, Dulcie realized, she was approaching. At least it was a different guard. Out of habit, she reached down to open her bag as she walked. Two catches and a zipper could be tricky, but she had the bag open and ready to hand over when she realized another person had gotten there first.

'Taking off early, I see.' The guard was talking to someone on the other side of the booth. 'Have a great weekend. Next?'

Dulcie was coming forward, her eyes on her own opened bag, when a shadow descended, causing her to look up. The woman in front of her was in the doorway, blocking the sun, but as she emerged into light, Dulcie recognized the Trista lookalike.

'Wait! Please!' Dulcie started to surge past, only to have a wooden barrier crash down to block her way.

'Bag, miss.' The guard was looking at her, his face stern. 'Your bag?'

'Here!' She threw the bag on the counter and ducked under the trestle as pencils went flying.

'Miss!' The guard sounded alarmed. 'Miss! Please!'

But this time, she wasn't going to lose her. The girl must have gotten the note. Why else leave early? Why else— There! She saw the slim figure turning toward Mass Ave. Dulcie took after her.

'Miss!' the voice called from inside the guard booth. Never mind, she'd get her bag later. She started off at a run, only to find herself grabbed from behind. She kicked – hard. A male grunt behind her let her know she'd connected. But it was too little, too late. She felt herself being hoisted in the air.

FORTY-TWO

'Put me down!' she yelled, pushing at the arms that held her in a bear hug.

'Whoa, there,' the bear holding her said as he lowered her to the ground. 'And here she is, perfectly safe and sound.' She wheeled around to find Detective Rogovoy, an expression of supreme annoyance standing in stark contrast to his relatively jovial tone. Beside him stood Chris, looking paler and more worried than she'd ever seen.

'What?' She couldn't believe they'd stopped her. Couldn't believe her quarry was getting away. 'Why did you stop me?'

'You disappeared.' Chris choked out the words. 'I tried to call. We both did. There was no answer. And after what you said . . .'

Dulcie could have slapped herself. She had meant to call Chris back as soon as she got somewhere safe. But her preoccupation with Rollie and the blonde had distracted her, and then being in Widener had made her feel so secure that she'd forgotten.

'We were worried, Dulcie. We both were.' Her boyfriend came forward to embrace her, and she let him fold her in his arms, his old shirt soft against her face. Beside him, Rogovoy glowered. 'We thought they'd gotten you.'

'I'm sorry, Chris. I wasn't thinking.' She looked up at him, into eyes wide with fear. 'There's just been so much going on.'

'I know,' he said into her curls as he buried his lips in them.

'I don't,' said a gruff voice beside them. Dulcie looked up. Rogovoy was not only peeved, he was sweating. 'Some of us are paid to protect the university population, and when we get urgent calls and then can't reach the people who made those calls, we become concerned.'

'I am sorry,' Dulcie apologized again, this time facing the fat man. 'I wanted to talk to you, to tell you what happened. I didn't want to have to explain everything again . . .'

'Never mind.' He waved one big hand as if he were swatting away a fly, and Dulcie was struck by the impression that the detective was slightly embarrassed. 'Got me out of the office. Now, your friend here told me something about these two impostors. Why don't we go sit somewhere, and you can tell me the whole story from the beginning.'

With a small sigh of regret for her aborted pursuit, Dulcie led the two men back into the library. The guard didn't dare say anything, not with Rogovoy in attendance, but she felt his icy glare on her as she retrieved her bag.

'Thanks so much.' She tried to put her heart into it. 'I'm sorry to have blown past you like that.'

The guard refused to melt, but he did hand over a pencil. 'This is yours, too.'

'She's helping with an official investigation,' Rogovoy, right behind her, said, flashing his badge. Dulcie made a mental note to be extra nice to the detective as she led them up to the library's spacious reading room.

'Pretty nice.' Rogovoy looked up at the arched ceiling. 'So this is where you work?'

'Beautiful, isn't it? But not really,' Dulcie confessed. 'I have a carrel down on Level Three, but it's pretty tiny and, well, conversation is discouraged in the stacks.'

'This isn't exactly South Station,' he said in response, following her to a table in the corner. The reading room was nearly deserted, their nearest neighbor snoring gently behind the day's paper. Dulcie figured they could talk in here, as long as they did it quietly. At least with Rogovoy as a companion, she wouldn't get into any more trouble.

'So, Chris told you about the two men?' Dulcie was glad to be telling someone official about them, even if the memory left her shaky. 'They were waiting for me by my office.'

'The beginning, please.' Rogovoy held up one of those big paws. 'Start from when, after everything you'd been through in the morning, you went to meet Roland Galveston.'

Dulcie turned toward Chris, a spark of anger flaring. Rollie was a colleague, and he was, she was sure, no threat. Chris met her gaze, though, and slowly shook his head. No, she had no right to be angry at him – or to hold anything back. Starting with the phone call, she told the detective everything. Everything except the encounter with the strange old lady and her waking dream about the squirrel. Chris would understand those. Rogovoy never would.

When Dulcie finally got up to seeing the young blonde fleeing, she was hit by a thought. 'Chris, have you heard anything? Has Jerry?'

Another shake of his head. 'I called him when I didn't hear back from you. I didn't really ask.' He bit his lip, and a wave of sorrow swept over her. How could she have made this dear man worry so? 'But he would've said—'

'Trista Dunlop, right?' Rogovoy cut in. 'Yeah, your friend called again about her.'

'Are you still going to make him wait until tomorrow?' Dulcie turned back toward the detective. 'I mean, I'm sure that those two goons were the same ones who went to talk to her.'

'Yeah, I'm going to look into that.' Rogovoy's voice sounded flat, but Dulcie had the feeling he was angry. 'I've got some ideas about them.'

But if Dulcie was hoping he would share them, she was to be disappointed. Once he had her statement, he stood to leave.

'What do you want me to do next?' She stood, too, ready for her marching orders.

'You, Ms Schwartz?' He looked from her to her boyfriend and back. 'Hey, it's a Friday afternoon. Why don't you two knock off early? Go get a beer.'

'But isn't there something you want us to do? After all, I've seen all the major players.'

'You've seen enough for one day, Ms Schwartz.' He turned to Chris. 'Is she always like this?'

Chris smiled, his first real smile of the afternoon. 'Pretty much.'

'Huh,' he said, shaking his head as he walked away.

'He's not all that bad,' said Chris, after the oversized detective had left.

'No, he's all right.' She watched him trundle off.

'When he called, when he said who he was, I was so scared.' Chris made a sound halfway between a hiccup and a cough, and Dulcie turned just in time to take him in her arms. Tucked away in the corner, nobody bothered them, and soon Chris was wiping his face and trying gamely to smile again. 'I'm sorry. I just got worried.'

'It's me who should apologize, Chris. Really.' She took her boyfriend's hands in her own. 'I wasn't thinking, and I caused you pain. I'm sorry.' She paused, trying to think of how to make it up to him. 'Would you like to get a beer somewhere?'

That did it. 'You *hate* beer, Dulcie,' he said with a laugh. 'And, to be honest, I should go back to work. I haven't really gotten anything done. Besides, I should've known you were all right.'

She waited, curious.

'Mr Grey would have warned me, don't you think?'

With a kiss – and a promise to touch base around dinner time – he left, leaving Dulcie alone in the cavernous room.

FORTY-THREE

Rogovoy had gotten one thing right, Dulcie thought as she turned another page. She'd been through too much today to get any work done.

Dulcie had gone back to her carrel after Chris left, determined to salvage some of the day, if not her thesis. She'd even made herself reread that noxious essay. Now she was going back to the earlier pieces by her author, trying to understand how she had been so misled.

If only she could have been wrong. Dulcie turned page after page, hoping she had been mistaken. Hoping she had misremembered some crucial phrase, or had gotten two similar styles confused. After all, the flowery prose of the late 1790s could all start to sound alike to a contemporary reader.

But, no, there were too many specific touchstones. Certain phrases jumped out at her, as if to scold her for her arrogance.

'*The education of young ladies, of virtue undimm'd, must be of concern to all . . .*'

'*The bookish mind, far from challenging the finer qualities, shall enhance them . . .*'

'*Learning shall be the setting for her jewel'd countenance . . .*'

All those phrases were taken nearly verbatim from her author's earlier writings. The first two came from *The Ravages* intact. In fact, they had been central to Dulcie's initial thesis – that the novel was not simply a fun distraction, but a pointed political argument hidden in a thrilling adventure. Only, now they were used to make the opposite points – that learning was dangerous for a young lady. That education was at odds with feminine ideals. It was almost like the author was purposefully dismissing the earlier works, turning her own words against herself. The question was: why?

Dulcie shook her head and closed the book. She had some serious rethinking to do. Chris was right; she wouldn't abandon her degree, not when she had gotten this far. But it would no longer be a labor of love. It would be a job, the thing she had to finish in order to proceed with her career.

Sitting there, her hand on the collection's blue cover, she thought of Trista. Where was her friend? Was she safe? Right now, Dulcie found it all too easy to believe that the pressures of finishing the degree might have caused her friend to snap. It was preferable to thinking that those two goons had come back. That she was lying hurt somewhere. Or worse.

She stood up. Rogovoy hadn't said much, but she trusted him. He knew about those horrible men now, and he'd be on their trail. But he was wrong when he had said there was nothing else she could do. Trista was her friend, and Dulcie still possessed some specialized knowledge that the large detective had lacked. Dulcie wasn't getting anything done in the library. That didn't mean she couldn't try to track down her friend.

After being extra courteous to the guard, Dulcie retraced her own steps out the back entrance. She'd been heading to the right – after the blonde girl – when Rogovoy had grabbed her. The elusive undergraduate still seemed like her best shot at figuring what was going on. Rollie knew her, clearly, and Dulcie was pretty sure that the girl had recognized Dulcie, too. Else why did she leave so precipitously? And the resemblance between her and Dulcie's missing friend was uncanny.

It wasn't much, but it was the best she could think of. At least it was better than beating herself up about another lost woman, two hundred years' gone.

Dulcie started walking, trying to figure out where the girl could have been heading. At the same time, she pulled out her phone. Trista's voicemail was now full, no surprise considering the number of messages Dulcie figured she and Jerry had put on it. And when she tried Jerry's cell that answered with a message also.

Maybe the universe was trying to tell her something. She clicked through to her own unplayed voicemail. Sure enough, multiple messages from Chris and from Detective Rogovoy confirmed their concern – and her own inattentiveness – and Dulcie silently promised to make up for her carelessness toward her boyfriend. He had been truly scared. Besides, she wasn't sure he had been right, that Mr Grey would have appeared to warn him, had she been in real danger. She thought of the vision she had been given of the great grey cat and the squirrel – a warning disguised as a memory. Her spectral pet had been there for her then, showing her how she could save herself. In the past, he had even intervened directly, throwing his ethereal self into the mix. Why would he have gotten Chris involved at all?

Silly question, she realized. *She* had brought the lanky young man into their lives. She should be happy the feline spirit connected with him. After all, she didn't mind sharing Esmé.

Esmé. That kitten was a handful, but Dulcie had begun to recognize the inevitable. The little cat had her own personality. She had such personality, in fact, that when Dulcie heard a young woman's voice, she started. Esmé had never sounded quite like that.

But, no, the voice was coming from her phone. A more recent message, from – she checked – an unknown number. Quickly, Dulcie hit 'replay' and, this time, paid attention.

'Hi, I'm sorry,' the message began, with no preamble. 'I shouldn't have run, but the library and everything – it's just gotten so complicated. Look, I'm walking toward the Commons now. You know that statue of Lincoln? I'll go there. I'll hang out as long as I can. Just don't bring that cop, OK?'

That was it. Not that Dulcie needed any more. The voice was female, and it sounded scared.

FORTY-FOUR

The Cambridge Common used to be the grazing ground for the city's first inhabitants. Back when the settlement was called 'New Town', the common must have been all grass, Dulcie figured. Now, a scattering of trees shaded one end of what had become a city park. At the far end, a baseball diamond and an open field hosted what seemed to be overlapping games. But the bronze and marble edifice she was heading for stood somewhere in between, half in the lengthening shadows of the trees, but far enough back from the street to have a sense of privacy.

Dulcie hadn't paused once she'd heard the call. It had come

in more than ten minutes earlier, and if the blonde – and it had to be her – lost her nerve, Dulcie didn't know if she'd get another chance.

Phone in hand, she half walked, half trotted back across the Yard, pausing only to dial Chris's number. 'Hi, sweetie. Guess what?' She tried for nonchalance, even as her breathing became ragged. 'That girl – the Trista lookalike? – she called,' Dulcie said to his voicemail. 'I'm meeting her on the Common.' She owed him that much.

Rogovoy would probably want a call, too, she figured. But by the time she hung up from Chris, she was at Mass Ave, and the light was blinking. Racing across, she had no time to look at her phone. Besides, she told herself, it would probably all amount to nothing. She was meeting a young student, another woman, in a public place. If she got something from it, well, maybe it would help repair her reputation. Dulcie didn't like the idea that she wanted to impress Rogovoy. Still, the idea was poking around her consciousness as she race-walked into the park.

And saw . . . nobody. 'Just as well I didn't call,' said Dulcie, as much to herself as to the bronze Lincoln. 'That would have made me really seem like an amateur.'

She looked over at the statue, standing in the middle of the ungainly marble edifice. Was this really the best the city could do? Dulcie was hit by the suspicion that the memorialized president was supposed to be bigger. Only after this life-size statue was delivered, she decided, had the city fathers decided to make a grander showing, surrounding the figure with all these marble pillars. City mothers would have left well enough alone.

Considering his dour expression, Lincoln seemed to agree. For a split second, she thought he was turning toward her. Then she realized, no, she was seeing through the memorial's central arch. Someone was on the other side, almost hidden by the statue. Dulcie shook her head at her own foolishness. She'd forgotten how ornate the ridiculous monument was. As the shadows lengthened, it was easy to miss one slight figure on the other side.

'Halloo!' she shouted once and started to wave. She caught herself in time. This woman was scared; she would want Dulcie to be discreet. Luckily, Dulcie was still too near the busy street for her call to have been out of place. For all anyone knew, she was hailing a bus. Chastened, Dulcie started toward her at a quick but careful pace. Just another commuter cutting through the Common on her way home.

The statue, she realized, was larger than it looked, and it took her a good thirty seconds to get around to its other side. When she did, she was alone. Had her eyes played tricks on her? She peered back across the wrought-iron fence and through the encircling marble pillars. Lincoln was still there, but no slight female figure. Perhaps the girl had assumed Dulcie wasn't coming. Maybe she'd simply had a change of heart.

'Great,' Dulcie said to no one but the sparrows. 'She was the one lead I had.'

The sparrows didn't answer, but just as Dulcie was about to give up, she heard a soft flutter. Two mourning doves, spooked by something, had begun their whirring ascent. Dulcie turned to watch, wondering what had caused them to take flight, when she saw it – another movement, back in a thicket of maples. Their wide leaves had shadowed the little copse, a precursor of the dusk to come. Only yards from the road – maybe twenty feet from the statue – it was an oasis of darkness.

So the girl had stayed, retreating into the shadows. Did she not trust Dulcie? Or was someone else waiting for her, too? Slowly, all senses on alert, Dulcie walked toward the trees.

'Hello?' she called, more softly this time. In response, the slight figure stepped forward. It was the blonde, and she raised one hand in a tentative greeting as she took a step out of the shadows.

But before she could proceed further, another figure appeared, cutting her off. As Dulcie watched, the second person – a man – threw the slight girl against a tree. Dulcie froze, aghast, and reached for her phone.

'I don't *have* it,' the girl shouted, while Dulcie punched in numbers. 'I never did.'

Dulcie looked up to see the girl being grabbed, being shaken.

'Rogovoy.' The detective sounded tired, but Dulcie had no time to explain.

'Detective, it's Dulcie. I'm in the Common. There's something happening. Please come quickly.' She snapped the phone shut before the cop could tell her to leave it to him and crept forward, determined to intercede if she could.

'—don't know what you're talking about.' The man was going on about something. 'You're talking nonsense.'

Could this be a domestic dispute? A private matter? Dulcie toyed with the phone, and with the idea of calling Rogovoy back, then decided against it. Whatever was going on, it didn't call for a large man to grab a woman by the arm and shake her.

'Hey, stop it!' Dulcie stepped forward. Rogovoy had to be on his way, but she couldn't just stand here and watch this. 'You – over there – cut it out!'

The girl turned, pulling away from the man, and stepped into a gap between the trees. Her face, suddenly in the sunlight, looked so much like Trista's that Dulcie gasped. Her gasp turned to a small cry as the man reached forward to grab his victim – and Dulcie recognized him as one of the two who had interrogated her. Harris. The bigger one.

'Dulcinea Schwartz.' The sound of her name made her jump, but the voice was coming from deep in the copse. As she watched, Harris and the girl turned. It was Read, coming forward with an evil smirk that made Dulcie remember those oversized, fang-like teeth. And what he said made Dulcie's head spin.

'When will you quit talking nonsense and save yourself? We don't care about some old rag. We want our money, Schwartz. And we know where you live.'

Dulcie stood frozen to the spot. Read wasn't talking to her. He was talking to the blonde girl, and Dulcie watched, mouth gaping, as he advanced toward her, a large knife in his hand.

FORTY-FIVE

'At least you helped her get away.' Chris was trying to cheer her up, Dulcie knew that. But all she could conjure was a faint smile as she squeezed his hand. They were sitting in the back of a university police cruiser, one of two that had shown up, sirens wailing, causing the two men to flee in one direction – and the young blonde in another. 'You might have saved her life.'

'Maybe.' Dulcie couldn't get that last scene out of her mind.

She had been so sure she was about to witness something horrible. Something that somehow or other involved her. 'I just don't understand it, any of it,' she said as she kept replaying it. 'He called her by my name, and I don't even know who she is.'

'Jessica Wachovsky.' Rogovoy climbed into the front seat. 'She's a junior. I've sent someone to her room, though who knows if she'll be going back there.' He looked up from his notes. 'I have been looking into this, you know.'

'And I appreciate it.' Dulcie tried to summon more enthusiasm. 'If your guys hadn't shown up then . . .'

'You could have called earlier, you know. Like when she first got in touch.' Rogovoy had already taken her statement, but had asked her to stay while he spoke with the two uniformed cops who had been first on that scene. He'd already sent one car racing up Garden Street, following the direction the two men had taken. The other cop was now talking to some passers-by, probably trying to pick up a trail. 'Lucky for us, you found time to call your boyfriend and he had the common sense to contact us.'

'It wasn't luck.' She ducked her head. 'I just didn't want to be crying wolf.'

'Huh.' The detective had a laugh that sounded like a cough. 'Ms Schwartz, I don't think Little Red Riding Hood had anything on you.'

Beside her, Chris opened his mouth to complain, but Dulcie squeezed his hand. The detective might have his parables confused, but he did have a point.

'OK, then.' The detective closed his pad. 'I'm going to ask Officer Denny to drive you two home. Where I hope you will have a very quiet evening.' From the emphasis he put on the last three words, Dulcie knew this was more than a suggestion.

'It has been a day, Dulce.' Chris pulled her close, and she allowed herself to collapse against him.

'Were you able to get any work done?' She looked up at him.

He shrugged. 'I was kind of useless during the tutorial and then, well, my concentration hasn't been the best.' He touched her cheek. 'You've kind of shaken me up, you know?'

'I know. I'm sorry.' She leaned against his hand, thinking. When she looked up again, she sounded determined. 'You should go back to work tonight.'

He raised his eyebrows, but didn't say anything.

'You took last night off. Jerry is probably a wreck, right? And I'll be home. I'll be OK. In fact, I'll feel better about everything if I know that I'm not destroying your entire schedule.'

'If you're sure . . .'

'I am.' She settled into his arms. 'But you can go out for dumplings first. I think this week merits another round.'

During the ride home, Chris filled her in on Jerry's dilemma. Thanks to Rogovoy's urging, he said, the police had been willing finally to take a report about Trista's disappearance. But because Trista was an adult, it didn't sound like they could *do* anything, besides keep an eye out.

'One more day,' Chris told her. 'So, yeah, he is climbing the walls.'

She digested this in silence and found her eyes closing.

'Come on, dream girl,' she heard Chris say and realized the cruiser had pulled up in front of the apartment. 'I'd carry you if I could.'

'I'm awake.' Dulcie sat up with a start, in time to hear the cop in the front seat chuckle. She thanked him anyway and let Chris help her out.

'I can't believe I conked out like that,' she said as they climbed the stairs.

He gave her a look. 'Dulcie, if this wasn't the longest day of your life, I wouldn't want to see what is.'

She nodded. 'That reminds me, I should call Lucy. She was hoping we'd be out for the solstice.'

'Maybe you should give yourself the night off?' He unlocked the door. 'Deal with your mother tomorrow?'

'Maybe.' As she stepped in, she felt something smash into her ankles. Esmé, who must have made a running start, was butting her head against Dulcie and purring like an engine. 'After all, it seems like someone else has put in a claim on me.'

She scooped the purring cat up and buried her face in the warm, soft fur. Up close, the purr came in waves, rising and falling like a ship far out to sea. 'You're a wonderful creature, do you know that?'

In response, Esmé threw her paws around Dulcie's hand and bit her.

'Ow! Bad—' She stopped herself and kept petting the small

cat even as she placed her back on the floor. 'I'm sorry. I left you alone all day, didn't I?'

'Why don't you two make up?' Chris called from the closet, where he was donning a light jacket. 'And I'll go get us some dinner. And Dulcie?'

She looked up.

'Please make sure you lock the door behind me.'

'*As if we'd let anyone get to her.*' The voice, like the memory of a dream, was lost in the closing of the door.

'Mr Grey?' She paused, mid-pet, and scanned the hall. Nothing. Nothing except one small cat, who looked up and bit her once again, before scampering away.

FORTY-SIX

B y rights, she should have been asleep before Chris left for work. The stress of the day, the warm Chinese buns filling her belly. The presence of Esmé, once again purring by her side. But even though Chris had tucked her in before he left, Dulcie found herself wide awake and wondering.

'Maybe it was that nap I had in the cop car,' she remarked to her feline companion. 'Is that how it works for you guys?'

Esmé said nothing, only tucking her nose into her tail as Dulcie got out of bed and walked over to her desk. It took her laptop only a moment to boot up. In that moment, she remembered Rogovoy's warning. He and Jerry had seemed appalled that she hadn't changed her passwords, even though Chris had given her system a clean bill of health. In fact, from what Rollie had told her over lunch, a much lower-tech form of identity theft had been to blame. Lunch – she thought of the bagel and lox. Had that all been today?

The weight of the day seemed to collapse on to her. No wonder she'd been so famished when Chris had finally returned, two bags full of goodies in his arms. Then again, maybe it was that second helping of spicy *moo shi* that was keeping her awake now.

Since she was . . . She typed in the girl's name and her class.

Two entries came up. The first had a photo, and it took Dulcie a moment to recognize the girl. An undated photo showed an Ultimate Frisbee team. J. Wachovsky was clearly identified, but the girl Dulcie saw looked worlds apart. Her hair was long instead of feathered short, drawn back in a pony tail. The only piercings Dulcie could see were two studs in her ears. This girl looked like a rough draft of Trista, or her younger sister.

She clicked on the second entry. It was a 'Work in Progress' feature, a regular in the student newspaper. '*Jessica Wachovsky, sophomore,*' it read. '*Learning to preserve fragile documents in the Prints and Paper Conservation program.*'

Dulcie was too tired to think it through. She'd eaten too much, and the Szechuan peppers were burning a hole in her belly. 'Is this just déjà vu, kitty?'

Esmé yawned and stretched, showing the pink cuticles of her extended claws. 'Am I just imagining things? Seeing connections?'

The cat rolled over, placing one of her paws on Dulcie's thigh before she stretched again. The little claws didn't need to do much to sink through Dulcie's nightshirt, and she gingerly removed Esmé's paw. 'Is this your way of claiming me, kitty? Is that it?'

That's when it hit her, and she turned toward the cat. 'Rollie worked in the paper lab. That's where he made the fake ID. And that's why those thugs were using my name.'

It was coming together so fast, Dulcie had to say it out loud. 'They wanted Rollie to steal Trista's ID because they had a Trista. A fake Trista – or someone who they could make look like her. But Rollie wouldn't, so he gave them my name and ID number to use with her photo. That's why the blue ticket had my name – and why Rollie planted it on Trista.'

She looked at the cat. 'Trista probably found it and couldn't make head or tails out of it. But those bullies thought Jessica was me. They didn't know about Rollie's switch – or about the fake ID.'

But if they didn't know, then what was going on? From what Rollie had told her, it seemed Professor Coffin had been involved with the theft. Rogovoy, she knew, was less likely to take the fugitive student's word for anything, especially once they confirmed that not only had his phone been disconnected, but also that his apartment had been emptied out of most of his clothes and toiletries – seemingly in a hurry. Now Coffin was dead, and Rollie was on the lam. Trista was missing, and this girl – this Jessica – was in danger. But why?

It was hopeless. Even if Rollie was to be trusted, he hadn't had a clue about why Coffin had needed a fake ID – or might have wanted to steal a book he already owned. And the girl herself had fled. Those two men – Harris and Read – had meant business. Dulcie thought of the knife with a shudder. Maybe memory and fatigue were coming into play, but in her memory it loomed both large and lethal.

'We want our money,' the smaller one, Read, had said. She thought of him as the mean one. The brains to Harris's brawn. And then it hit her. He'd said he knew the girl. He knew where she lived. But he didn't mean Jessica Wachovsky, or even Trista Dunlop.

He was hunting Dulcie. Dulcinea Schwartz. She could still hear his words. 'We know where you live.'

FORTY-SEVEN

'Yeah, you told us.' Rogovoy had to be off duty. It was after eleven. But he'd given her his cell number, and she'd called it, spooked. 'No, I'm glad you called. Shows you're developing some smarts of the other kind, too.'

Now that he was on the phone, she felt a little silly. Those two men were hunting for a little blonde, not for her. Still, the detective's next words were comforting.

'I've got a patrol going by your place. Talked to your boyfriend about it. He's a good kid, too.'

Dulcie wasn't entirely sure how she felt about being called a 'kid'. Lucy, she knew, would get all bent out of shape, start fuming about the paternalistic patriarchy and all that. Then again, she recalled with a pang, Lucy had rescinded her own warning. Even after she'd called to tell her mother about Coffin – about all the blood – Lucy had gone on about birth and new beginnings.

Rogovoy was still talking. 'We're looking into the paper lab, too. Whatever you call it. Seems to me that if two students are able to make fake IDs there, then security isn't what it's supposed to be.'

'I was wondering about that,' Dulcie broke in, another thought forming. 'I was thinking about the Dunster Codex and how someone snuck that out of the library. I mean, there would be records, right? If someone had taken it to have restoration work done or something?'

In response, she heard a low chuckle. 'Dulcie, Ms Schwartz, you are something. You don't have to solve every problem this university has tonight. Give it a rest, kid. Get some sleep.'

She tried, she really tried. But after tossing and turning so much that even the cat abandoned the bed, Dulcie followed suit. A quick peek out the window showed a quiet street. No cars, despite what the detective had said, and Dulcie forced herself not to think about that.

'I must have just missed them. Right, Esmé?'

The cat, who had started to wash, did not respond.

Dulcie paced around the apartment. One thirty, too late to call anyone. Even Lucy would likely be asleep, unless . . . She lifted the shade for another look at the sky. No, the moon was still waxing. Lucy would not be dancing at a circle tonight. And Chris, well, Chris thought she was sleeping. She should let him have one night of uninterrupted work after everything he'd been through.

On a whim, she opened her laptop again and entered a search for the Dunster Codex. Most of what this turned up, she already knew – or had learned since the announcement of the theft on Tuesday. The manuscript – more like loosely bound pages than a modern book – was a late medieval treasure, the recounting of a tax role that served to illuminate not only the population but also the social structure of a certain province in what would become East Anglia. The university had purchased it from a private collector, after a substantial fund-raising drive that had drawn heavily from the professor's former colleagues in the private sector. It had been Professor Coffin's latest and largest acquisition.

'His last, too,' Dulcie noted, skimming over the rest. She'd been surprised to see that the professor himself had been one of the donors, making a gift of some undisclosed amount that had supposedly been critical in obtaining the treasure. More fund-raising, she read, had since been commenced, largely for the purposes of conservation, since the ancient work – about a thousand years old – needed constant attention.

'That would explain it not being in its case,' she mused out loud. 'Poor Lloyd, scared by a ghost story.' She typed away at her keyboard, wondering what else she could turn up. 'I wonder if the restoration work was all done here,' Dulcie mused, tapping her keyboard gently. Lloyd might know, or Darien, their resident medievalist. But, no, this was a bureaucratic question – process and permissions. She opened her email program and typed in: MTHORPE.

Hi Mr T, she typed. *Would you be able to tell me the dates the Dunster Codex was being restored? I feel like it was in and out all spring. Also, did it ever go off campus?* She looked at her note. She had to give him a little more. *I've been talking to the university police about this, but I don't know if they understand how we work here.*

There, that should appeal to his departmental vanity. Besides, it made her sound involved – on the side of the angels. With a satisfied nod, she hit 'send'. Esmé landed on her laptop just as she closed it, so she picked her pet up and returned to bed.

FORTY-EIGHT

riting, writing, writing. She paused to push back an errant curl that had adhered to the dampness of her forehead, felt her eyelids start to close 'gainst the stifling heat. Close, too close, the befoul'd air choked her breath, threatening to steal the very life from out her chest. The heat, like the pestilence itself, closed upon her, the tainted air like curs'd spirits dragging her down. How she long'd to throw open the casements and to breathe anew, to free herself from this hidden room, this prison, this cage.

But, no. She fought against the panic, her heart beating like a caged dove against the bars. This had been her choice, her decision. Driven as she was by forces unforeseen, she had sought this sanctuary. Let them do their worst, steal her name, her very soul. Writing, she was writing. Soon she would emerge, her work complete, to reclaim that very Heritage that she so long'd to pass on . . .

Dulcie woke, gasping, in the dark. The cat, lying on her chest, looked up and blinked.

'Esmé, was that you?' She picked some fur from her mouth and wondered. Lucy had taught her all the old wives' tales – but only so she could debunk them.

'Cats don't "steal" anyone's breath,' she had said with exasperation. 'They simply like the warmth. Or the smell of milk on a baby's breath.'

Or perhaps, Dulcie thought now, looking into Esmé eyes, they do what they need to in order to wake a troubled sleeper. And after the horror of the day before, it was no wonder she'd had a nightmare. At least Professor Coffin hadn't made an appearance. She'd been so busy yesterday, the full impact hadn't registered. Now, however, it did. Closing her eyes, she saw him once again, laid out and still, the blood pooled around his body. Was this because of the Dunster Codex? Perhaps it was true that the thing was haunted or, perhaps, cursed.

She shivered, fully awake now, and checked the clock. No, Chris would not be home for hours yet. Climbing out of bed, she reached for her robe. The night had gotten cool, the hint of a sea breeze rattling the shade. She looked out in time to see a car cruise silently down the street. One of Rogovoy's, she told herself. Those two thugs had probably been bluffing. They were looking for a blonde, for someone who resembled Trista. And even if they did come by here, they didn't stand a chance.

It didn't help. In need of a distraction, Dulcie went to her computer and opened the file she had started the day before listing all the familiar quotes that had reappeared in that horrible essay.

'*The fettering of the feminine mind,*' she read. In her dream, the heroine – Hermetria, the author, whoever she was – wanted to throw off her fetters. To free herself. '*For fear of losing her ladylike graces.*' The woman in the dream hadn't been bothered by such things. Her strength had been that of a woman, a free woman. A writer setting out to reclaim her name.

Dulcie rubbed her forehead, feeling the beginnings of a headache coming on. *The Ravages of Umbria* had never been a hit with the critics. It had never even won the kind of grudging respect given the bigger Gothic novels, books like *The Castle of Otranto* or *Udolpho*. Had its author fought back against the negative reviews and naysayers? Maybe, Dulcie thought glumly, she had sought to win back their favor by writing something different. Something that catered to their traditional – no, misogynistic – tastes.

Her headache getting worse, Dulcie looked back longingly at the bed. Maybe she should have asked Chris to stay home again tonight. She could call him, but then he'd worry about her. No, better to pass the time – and take some aspirin.

Two minutes later, she was sitting by the computer again, a glass of water by her side. Maybe she would ping Suze, see if the soon to be lawyer was up working. Dulcie knew her old room-mate: all through exams, she'd kept up her hours at the legal clinic. There was no reason for her upcoming graduation to stop her now.

Hey room-mate, how are you? she typed. At her feet, she felt the soft brush of fur. Esmé had come over to keep her company.

You're up early. The answer came back immediately. *Bad dream?*

Dulcie smiled and reached down to pet the cat. Suze hadn't heard the half of it. Esmé pushed her wet nose into Dulcie's left hand. With her right, she typed: *Weird dream.*

Any more with your friend? The words were well meant, but Dulcie felt them like a blow. Suze knew Trista. They'd hung out. But Suze and Dulcie had drifted so far apart that Suze couldn't even remember Trista's name. Did she remember Esmé? Did the little cat remember her?

The little chime broke into her brooding. *Trista, I mean. Sorry.*

She's gone missing, Dulcie wrote back. She was as much to blame if they were drifting. She hadn't even told Suze the news. *It's been crazy. Theft from the Mildon. Professor Coffin murdered!*

Heard that. The reply pinged back. *Wonder who gets his donor list?*

Dulcie shook her head. Suze did not know that Dulcie had

found the body. She'd never have responded so casually if she had. But she had raised an interesting point. From what Dulcie had read, Coffin was among the most successful fund-raisers at the university. He would be missed.

You OK? Suze might not be up on the latest, but even across town, she could read Dulcie's silences. *Chris working?*

Yeah, I'm fine, she typed – and meant it. At her feet, the cat had begun to purr. *Miss you.* She meant that, too.

FORTY-NINE

A crack, and a rattle broke the night, the sound like a skeleton's fingers across ice. Dead things, cruel and grasping, sought entrance, drawn by the life within. The woman at the desk shivered and drew her cloak around her. Phantoms, phantoms all, bare branches against a window, the dried leaves of plants she did not know skittering across the panes. They could not reach her, she knew that. Friendless and alone, she toil'd on. Her last effort, her best, would be her only legacy, and she must labor on. True demons lurk'd, real ghouls, and her trust, too precious, could not be squandered now. Girding herself against those who would in verity suck her life's blood, she set to work, taking up the pen once more and steeling herself against the phantoms of the night.

When she woke again, Chris was by her side with Esmé tucked under his chin. It was a charming sight, the opposite of the lonely nightmare setting, and Dulcie lay there for a moment, basking in their warmth. When she did finally slide out of bed, she did so quietly, letting Chris sleep. The little cat, however, opened one eye and watched her as she dressed.

For Dulcie, even such quiet company was a balm. The dream had been disturbing, all this talk of real phantoms and ghosts – and its setting had shifted ahead by several months, from sweltering heat to bitter cold. But the May morning Dulcie woke to already felt balmy, the daylight that poked around the shade promising a better day ahead. Things were crazy. A man had been murdered. But the people she loved most were safe, and they loved her. Everything else was details.

She was taking her laptop into the kitchen when it hit her. Trista wasn't safe; not that she knew, anyway. She looked up at the clock. Too early to call Jerry; he kept the same hours as Chris. Today he could file an official missing persons report, at least. And, she reminded herself, after her encounters with those two thugs, the university police would take it seriously. Rogovoy had said they were already on the lookout for Trista. Now it was all about the waiting.

She opened her laptop, hoping to hang on to some of her waking optimism. A new day. A new start. It didn't help. Any way she approached it, her thesis was in the toilet. And her name was probably still mud, too, her only defense against possible charges having decamped and disconnected his phone. A small ping alerted her to an email, but if she hoped for a reprieve, she was disappointed: MTHORPE. She knew she'd emailed him with questions, but she couldn't shake the idea that he was contacting her now to let her know her grants had been revoked.

For a moment, Dulcie was tempted to flee. To pack a lunch and head for the Greyhound station. Not back to the commune – Lucy would just be another failed responsibility. Just . . . someplace different. New York, and one of those auction houses. Santa Fe. Chris would understand. He'd take care of Esmé. More and more, she was his cat, anyway.

The fantasy grabbed her. It would be so easy. She reached to close the computer, to start her new life – and felt something soft and warm push her back. Esmé had landed in her lap and stared up at her with grave intent.

'What is it, Esmé? Would you really miss me?'

In response, the cat thrust her head into Dulcie's hand, pushing her velvet ears against Dulcie's palm. She was just too irresistible, Dulcie decided, and she began stroking the cat. And then, since she was stuck there anyway, she opened the email.

Ms Schwartz, it began. *So glad you got in touch. Have been meaning to call. Heard last night from the university police that your identity card had been stolen and have started the process to remove you from disciplinary probation.*

That caught Dulcie up short. 'Disc pro' was the first step

toward expulsion. She had known she was a suspect, but not that she had already been judged guilty.

Call me to set up an appointment, the email closed. Well, that was an eye-opener. To top it off, Dulcie noticed, Thorpe had not answered any of her questions.

Despite the hour, she was able to reach him in the departmental office. From the sounds in the background, she guessed that he was trying to work the coffee maker. 'Only time it's quiet enough to get any work done,' he grumbled over the phone as the water ran. But when she asked about the Dunster Codex, he seemed as in the dark as she was.

'It's been in and out of the conservation center since it arrived,' he said. 'Hold on.' A clatter of crockery, and then he was back. 'A pity, really. So much money, and it arrived in such bad shape.'

'How much did it cost, exactly?' For all the gossip, she'd never heard an actual figure.

'Huh. Like they would tell me,' her adviser chuffed in a moment of frankness. 'Thousands? Millions, maybe.' He sipped, noisily, and Dulcie took the phone over to her own coffee pot. 'They used some complicated financing procedure. Private donors, loans – Professor Coffin was constantly on the move.'

She missed a bit as her own tap ran. Something about loans and endowments.

'Honestly, if he hadn't taken charge, I don't think the university would have pursued it,' Thorpe was saying by the time she had the coffee brewing. 'And when you think what else has become available in the past year alone. The Olmstead Dickens, for example. Three serialized novels in manuscript form. *Manuscript!*'

Dulcie had no response to that, not being particularly enamored of Dickens, and let him talk as she fetched both milk and sugar. Would the cops – the department – ever find out that Coffin had been behind the fake ID scam? That he might have been involved in the Codex theft? She tried to remember if she'd told Rogovoy. Not that it mattered much: the only source she would be able to cite would be the missing Rollie.

She was trying to think how to bring it up when her adviser asked about her own research, and she scrambled for an answer. 'I'm looking at some new material,' she said, milk in hand. That was honest. 'I'm not exactly sure how it all plays in.'

'New?' Thorpe almost laughed, causing her to spill.

'New to me,' she confessed, reaching for a paper towel. 'An essay that seems to belong to the canon.'

'Speaking of, you might want to take a look at something in the Mildon Collection.'

'The Mildon?' She swallowed hard. With the milk, the coffee wasn't that hot. It was more the thought of that subterranean trouble spot.

'Yes, there's a letter, recently restored. It pertains to that Lord Richmond book, *The Wetherly* something? But I gather it has some interesting discussion of the genre. Might be something you can work in. Lord Richmond, Thomas Paine, and all.'

Dulcie made what she hoped was an encouraging noise as she sipped. 'I think I've heard about that.' From Rollie – not that she wanted to cite that particular source. 'So, um, I still have access to the collection?'

'Of course.' Her adviser didn't miss a beat. 'You were only under investigation. Now, I gather, all the attention has been placed on one of the work-study students.'

'Jessica Wachovsky?' She thought of the slim undergrad as she'd last seen her, running across the Common.

'It's appalling, such a betrayal.' Thorpe sounded like he was talking to himself, but his outrage made his words carry. 'A personal betrayal.'

'What do you mean?' The girl had been involved, sure, but she'd wanted to confess.

'The job at the Mildon. She never would have had it without Professor Coffin's approval. The professor – excuse me, the late professor – personally hand-picked everybody who worked there.'

FIFTY

There were just too many coincidences. Dulcie stood by the kitchen window, mug in hand, and tried to make sense of them all. Professor Coffin had been in the center of something, that much was clear. Whatever it was, it had gotten him killed.

The logical approach, she knew, was to look at who had

survived. For starters, there was Rollie, who claimed he had been helped and then blackmailed by the late professor. Then Jessica, picked by the professor for a job – and maybe also as a model for a fake ID. Dulcie had been struck by the transformation she'd witnessed in the clippings. Somehow, it seemed unlikely that an innocent undergrad could have dreamed all this up – and gotten a professor killed as well. But she'd liked Rollie, trusted him even when he'd confessed to getting her in a jam. Rogovoy, she suspected, didn't. Then again, Rogovoy was a cop. It was his job to suspect everyone.

Dulcie couldn't see how, but it must all be tied up with the theft of the Dunster Codex. Had Trista been involved? Dulcie didn't want to think so, but at this point, everything was on the table.

And what about those two thugs, Harris and Read? Dulcie thought of Read as she'd last seen him, holding that cruel knife, and shivered. Could that have been the same weapon that had left the professor bleeding on the floor of the back conference room? It was all too likely. If only she could—

'Ow!' She jumped. Esmé scampered away, leaving Dulcie to examine several small red marks on her foot. 'You bit me. Bad—' No, the kitten only wanted to play. 'I'm sorry, Esmé,' Dulcie said, searching in vain for a cat toy to toss. 'You startled me.'

Besides, she thought as she balled up some aluminum foil, Rogovoy had asked her to leave it alone. Commanded her, actually. She'd been sitting in the cruiser, and he'd come over one final time, leaning over as if to give her his benediction.

'This is a police matter, Ms Schwartz,' he'd said instead, his deep voice gravelly and tired. 'The theft. The murder. This is what we do. Our job. We have resources that you do not. Please, do not complicate our job further by getting involved.' He'd paused, staring down at her. 'More involved, that is. Just – just go finish your thesis, OK?' He'd closed the door then and watched them drive off. Dulcie had seen him standing there until traffic had surrounded them.

'Are you trying to tell me the same thing?' Dulcie tossed the ball and watched as the white paws grabbed it out of the air. 'That I should simply mind my own business?' The black tail lashed as Dulcie feinted then tossed the foil again, and Esmé got down to the serious business of the hunt.

She was so busy with the kitten, Dulcie didn't hear the next ping from her laptop. And by the time Esmé had lost interest, stopping mid-volley for an impromptu bath, the computer had faded into sleep mode, the Mr Grey screen saver obscuring the message marked: '*Urgent. Please Read.*'

She wasn't thinking of her email at that point. It was almost nine. Chris, Rogovoy, even Thorpe had been telling her the same thing, more or less, and her dream had confirmed it. Shoving her laptop, some pencils, and a yellow legal pad into her bag, she headed toward the door. Esmé looked up, and she paused to pet the silky fur. But even as the young cat reached up with her white mitts to grab her hand, Dulcie detached herself. Horrible things might be happening outside. But Dulcie Schwartz had to get to work.

FIFTY-ONE

D espite Thorpe's assurances, Dulcie felt a shiver of anxiety. They wouldn't let her in. She'd gotten to the Mildon just at its Saturday opening time, and the mouse-like clerk had peered at her ID for what seemed like hours. Then he had turned his gaze on her, his eyes exaggerated and large behind the huge glasses. He must have heard that she was a suspect, Dulcie decided, and she kept her mouth shut. Finally, with a small huff, he checked her in, filling out the blue ticket and handing it to her.

'I'll need to take that.' He stared pointedly at Dulcie's bag. She hesitated. This, after all, was where the trouble had started.

He noticed. 'We – ah – have instituted new security proceedings.' It was the closest thing she would get to an apology, she suspected. Removing the pad, she handed the bag over. He placed it in a closet next to the entrance and then used a key from his key chain to lock the door, she noticed with gratitude. That done, he pressed the button that released the front counter and beckoned Dulcie to come in.

As she stepped inside, she looked around the small entrance-way. Set against the ceiling she could see the security gate, ready to come down in case of an emergency. Supposedly, there would be a barrier like this at every entrance – even at the chain-link wall to the far right, which separated the rarities from the more common confines of the Widener stacks.

Theoretically, these gates presented an extra layer of protection – an internal system above and beyond the guards at every entrance to the larger library. Their presence, though, only raised more questions. Why hadn't they been activated when the Dunster Codex had been stolen? Were they just as much for show as the charade of the 'blue tickets'? As secure as when visitors' bags were simply thrown underneath the front counter?

'Follow me, please.' Without looking back, he led her down to the left, to a small sitting area outfitted with a table, several chairs, and a cup of sharpened pencils. She knew the routine and pulled a pair of gloves from the box in the middle of the table, then sat and waited.

'*The Wetherly Ghost.*' He placed a large box in front of her and opened the hinged lid, using both gloved hands to carefully lift out a fraying, leather-bound book. 'And related correspondence.' The book was followed by an acid-free binder, which the clerk also placed on the table. 'Call me when you're done, please.' The courtesy was automatic, Dulcie decided as the mouse-like man marched off without waiting for a response.

Once he had retreated, she opened the book. It had been a while since she had looked at the *Wetherly*. At least a few months since she'd been in the Mildon at all, she thought with a twinge of bitterness. At least her name seemed to have been cleared; she owed Thorpe her thanks for that.

'*The howling Harpie, epitome of the friendless Female, grabbed at the poor Virgin's lustrous hair, jealous of the resplendent beauty having spoil'd her own good name in life and her chance of Heaven e'en in death.*'

Feh. Dulcie skipped the rest of the passage, a thinly veiled diatribe against women disguised as a horror story. The next chapter started no better.

'*The heathen Moor joined then with the Catholic Priest for an unholy Mass, unsanctified by blood or prayer . . .*'

She hadn't missed anything. As she leafed through the pages, she found more of the same. Sexism and racism, larded up with the clichés of horror and the supernatural that had given the genre such a bad name.

Thomas Paine, the author of *Common Sense*, had read this? He must have been desperate. She closed the book. This had been a complete waste of time, and she half stood, about to call for the clerk, when she remembered the letters. Rollie had said he'd worked on one of them and thought of her. Thought it would interest her. Then again, Rollie had said a lot of things, none of which he was around to defend. Still, she was here. She might as well check it out. With a sense of resignation, she pulled the folder toward her and opened it.

The letter must have been in lousy shape, she mused, removing the first page. Encased in some kind of clear protective covering, it looked as fragile as birch bark, its edges browned and ragged where they hadn't already crumbled into dust, and she laid it flat on the table before her, afraid to risk even moving it much.

'*Dear Friend,*' it began. '*Many thanks and my heartfelt Gratitude for this Diversion, which has helped to pass the Hours.*' Despite herself, Dulcie felt a slight tremor of excitement. Thomas Paine had written this, a thank-you note for the gift of a book. She wondered if he would comment on its quality, and read on.

'*Its Fantasies of Horrors and Ghouls, completed by the most Monstrous of Devils, a corrupt Religious, have served to divert me most ingeniously . . .*'

She read on as the Revolutionary thinker continued to praise the book, citing some of the passages that he seemed to have interpreted as political allegory. Well, that was his world; he essentially wrote propaganda. Reading on, she tried to figure out if he had actually enjoyed it, but the frayed page ended in the middle of a sentence, before she could really tell.

Carefully removing the next page from the file, she saw that she'd missed something. '*. . . peopled with Characters of such Life and Sense, 'twere as if they breath'd upon the page,*' she read. '*Expressing such Philosophy as any Man of Sense could champion, such a Woman serves as Beacon to her Gender and indeed to all our Race.*'

Dulcie stopped. Woman? *The Wetherly Ghost* had not been written by a woman. She went back to the book and checked. Yes, just like every attribution she had ever seen, this copy credited with Geoffrey Thomas, Lord Richmond, as the author. And

Thomas had been a known public figure, a man about town –
which probably had accounted for the book's success.

Paine must have been talking about a different book. A properly
revolutionary work, written by a woman. Could it be?

Trying desperately to contain her excitement, Dulcie read on.
'*Such works of Imagination spawn'd the Rancor of Philistines,
no doubt accounting for the Esteemed One's Exodus from
confining Shores . . .*' The page ended, and with trembling hands,
Dulcie reached for the next.

Again, she picked up in mid-sentence, some crucial lines lost
forever to decay. '. . . *lacking the support of a Radcliffe or her
sister She-Authors whose Conventions may amuse, this esteemed
Author lies vulnerable to malicious Minds that have sought to
counter that special Genius, turning her own Words against . . .*'
A stain – mold or ink, ages old – obscured much of the page.
At the bottom, Dulcie could just make out a few more words.
'. . . *a new Work eagerly await'd.*' And that was all.

It was slight. Fragments without a name. But for Dulcie, it
was enough. Her heart racing, she sat back, willing herself to be
reasonable. Everything she had read fit with what she knew of
The Ravages of Umbria and its author. The forward-looking
philosophy. The originality. Even the persecution that had caused
her author to flee.

'Malicious minds? Her own words?' This was more than criticism. More, even, than the threats that might have caused the
author to emigrate. Paine was in the United States when he wrote
that letter. Was it possible that the ageing diplomat had known
something of the contemporary backlash? Perhaps he was writing
his friend about an attempt to sabotage an author's reputation?

Dulcie had known something was wrong with that essay. Her
author's exact phrases had been lifted and twisted into something
very different. Something that would indeed 'defame that special
genius'.

She needed to be careful, though. Even if her instincts – and
Rollie's – were correct, this was only a first step. One letter was
not enough to go by – not when neither her author nor *The
Ravages* were named. Paine could have been talking about any
one of a dozen authors. Perhaps there were other letters, not yet
restored.

Dulcie stood and peeked down the hall. The mousy clerk might have some ideas. He was not at the front desk, though, and the place was so quiet that she wondered if he'd gone on a break. It seemed unlikely for such a conscientious little man, and she was about to turn, to try the other offices, when a noise disturbed her. At the hall's end, a large door opened. Through it stepped two figures she recognized all too well. Harris and Read, the thugs who had come to her office. The men she had seen in the park.

Dulcie stepped back, flattening herself against the wall. What were those brutes doing here? How had they gotten in? With slow, careful steps, she began to creep back down toward the reading room. She didn't think they had seen her. She could still escape.

She looked up as another door opened and the clerk stepped out. Raising her finger to her lips, she motioned him to be silent, but those oversized glasses never turned her way as he walked down the hall – toward the intruders. Peeking around the corner, she saw them look up in surprise and start to back away.

'Excuse me, excuse me,' the little man called down the hall after them. 'You can't be back there.'

Dulcie held her breath, afraid to intervene. For a moment, her spirits rose. They were retreating, rousted by the determined clerk. And sank again as the bespectacled librarian went after them. The smaller of the two – Read – had turned. He seemed to be talking to the clerk, and Dulcie hoped he had a good story. Maybe nobody would get hurt. Then she saw it. The knife. The little clerk stumbled backward, into the arms of the bigger suit – Harris. Ducking down, Dulcie watched as they dragged the little clerk into one of the side rooms.

That was it. Dulcie could no longer hide, could no longer hope the danger would pass by. She needed to get help. Leaving the relative safety of her hiding place, she tiptoed over to the front desk. With Rogovoy's number already programmed into her phone, she could summon him quickly. Maybe quickly enough. She pulled gently on the door of the closet, hoping for quiet, praying for speed. It didn't give. She pulled again, rattling it back and forth to no avail, and she remembered the new security procedures that had prompted the clerk to lock the door. Cursing the moments lost, she looked around for a landline. Precious seconds were ticking by. There had to be a phone. She would dial the emergency number and hope for a speedy response.

Then she saw it: a little red box with a handle. The fire alarm. Pulling it would sound an immediate alarm, as well as bring the authorities. It would also, she read, activate a 'non-water fire suppression system'. The phrase sparked a memory; the student handbook had had a section explaining it, detailing how the area would be sealed as inert gases – a mix of nitrogen and oxygen – were pumped in, replacing the air she was breathing now. The mix was supposed to act quickly, squelching any fire by starving it of oxygen. The question was: would it squelch Dulcie, the mousy clerk, and the two thugs, as well?

Her mind racing, Dulcie tried to think. What did she really know about the system? The handbook had called it 'safe', pointing out that the nitrogen was actually less dangerous than many elements of a fire. Student rumor, however, had called it 'the suffocation machine', pointing to the apparent speed with which it switched out atmospheres.

'Why do you think it works so well?' She couldn't remember who had asked, just the voice talking. 'What makes fires burn? Oxygen. What do we breathe?'

The gathered students had all answered as one: 'Oxygen.'

She glanced down the hall. The door remained closed. Then she heard it, a small cry – like an animal in pain. The clerk. She pulled the lever.

FIFTY-TWO

WAH! WAH! WAH! The bleating of the siren made Dulcie jump.

'PROCEED TO EVACUATE! PROCEED TO EVACUATE!' the loud recorded voice commanded, before urging her to: 'STAY CALM.' Somewhere above her head, a swirling light threw whirling shadows over the hallway, while the red emergency exit signs glowed. And the metal gates began – slowly – to descend.

'PROCEED TO EVACUATE!'

Dulcie looked around furiously. Should she run? What about

the clerk? Before she could decide, the hall door flew open. Read, still holding his knife, looked around. Saw her. Stared.

'You.' He pointed the knife and slowly smiled, revealing those animal teeth. 'Well, well.'

Even over the siren, Dulcie heard herself gasp. Unable to move, she stood there, mesmerized as the alarm light flashed and flickered over the open blade.

'Come on.' Harris, the larger suit, was pushing by his partner. 'We gotta go,' he said and turned toward the back hall.

Read didn't follow. He stepped instead toward Dulcie, who stood transfixed. The lights, the siren. The blade.

'Come *on!*' Harris yelled again, heading down the hall. 'The damned door is closing.' Cursing, Read turned and ran.

Dulcie knew she should follow or – better yet – head for the front exit and safety. Knew she should save herself. She was small enough, she could duck through what space remained as the emergency gates descended on their tracks.

Instead, she ran to the room the two men had just vacated. Crumpled in the corner, she found the clerk.

'Sir! Sir! Are you OK?' Dulcie was yelling over the mechanized warning. She ran to him and took his arm. 'Are you hurt?'

The little clerk looked up, his eyes curiously small without his glasses, and opened his mouth, his words drowned out by the bleating wail.

'Can you get up?' she yelled in his ears. In the flashing light, it was hard to tell, but she didn't think she saw any blood. 'Sir?'

'My glasses.' His voice came through in the pause between the alarms. He reached around her on the floor.

'Here.' She found the big brown horn-rims and watched as he fitted them to his nose. 'We have to go.' She looked back out the door. 'If we can.'

The clerk was kneeling now, giving Dulcie a clear view of his thinning, grey hair as he adjusted his glasses further. Then he stood and brushed off the front of his brown corduroy trousers.

'Sir?' The gases must have started. She waited to feel a constriction in her chest. To black out. Perhaps it was better to be fatalistic, like this little man, but she couldn't stop trying. 'May we—'

'Don't get your panties in a bunch, young lady.' The clerk

brushed off his shirtsleeves next, and then led her to the front hall. Taking a key chain out of his pocket, he unlocked a small cabinet, inserted another key, and turned it.

Suddenly, all was silent.

'You can do that?' Dulcie's ears were ringing, and she was yelling.

The clerk blinked up at her. 'Of course I can. I'm Thomas Griddlehaus, senior librarian staff clerk for the Mildon Rare Books Collection. And I believe you owe me an explanation.'

'I–I–I thought I was saving your life.' Instead of a library, Dulcie thought, she'd slipped down a rabbit hole to some alternative world. 'Those men. They were going to kill you.'

'Those men? They were common thieves. They seemed under the impression that we kept riches here. Common misperception, really, among the uneducated. I used to tell Gustav that the word "rare" was misleading.'

'Gustav?' Dulcie was still in shock. 'Professor Coffin?'

'Of course.' The clerk – Thomas – looked away, and Dulcie had the fleeting impression that the little man was slightly embarrassed. 'Not to say that he listened to me. I am, of course, merely a functionary, whereas he is – he was a great man. You know he made this possible.'

'The Mildon?' Dulcie's head was swimming. 'But doesn't it predate him?'

'Technically, of course.' He had unlocked another drawer and removed a phone. 'Excuse me, please.'

Dulcie didn't know what to think, and she stood there, watching and listening as he reported in to some authority that, yes, yes, the fire-suppression system had been activated, but no, there was no need to evacuate the entire building. When he hung up and proceeded down the hall, picking up a chair Dulcie had knocked over in her haste, Dulcie followed.

'Mr Griddlehaus?'

He turned back, as if surprised that she remained.

'What are you talking about?'

'Professor Coffin was a masterful diplomat of the mind, young lady. He was able to convince donors of the vital nature of such resources—'

'Yes, he raised money. I know.' The shock was wearing off, and Dulcie felt something like a temper. 'That's not what I mean.

Those men. They had a knife. They grabbed you. That's why I set off the alarm. I thought they were going to kill you. And you seem – you seem—'

'I'm sorry.' He looked down at the chair in his hands. When he looked up, Dulcie could see that he was blinking back tears. 'I'm not used to . . . this sort of thing. I'm afraid my default mode is to – is to—' He sniffed and then hiccuped, and Dulcie stepped forward to take him in her arms . . . but the voice behind her stopped her: gruff, loud, and familiar.

'Why am I not surprised? What am I going to do with you?'

She turned to see two firefighters, fully suited for a blaze, and the library guard, white-faced and trembling. In front of them all stood Detective Rogovoy, panting as if he'd led an uphill charge.

FIFTY-THREE

B y the time she had explained everything, Dulcie was exhausted. Rogovoy and his people had finally taken both her and Griddlehaus into the library's administrative wing, ostensibly to answer additional questions while the fire marshal checked out the systems. As he'd ushered them through a previously unseen, anonymous door, Griddlehaus had put up a fuss, unwilling to relinquish his attempts to monitor the policemen, not to mention the firefighters and all their equipment, in the Mildon.

'You had two killers in here, and you're worried about my ballpoint?' Rogovoy had finally barked at the nearsighted clerk. That had shut him up, and as the detective seated them in an over-bright passageway, he'd glanced again at Dulcie, obviously shaken. She'd given him a brave smile as they led him away to take his statement.

'He's had a rough morning,' Dulcie whispered to Rogovoy as a clerk wheeled a book cart by. 'Can't you go easy on him?'

Rogovoy made a face. 'Hey, maybe you should think about that, too, young lady.'

'Me?' Dulcie sat back, her own eyes suddenly smarting. 'I

thought I was doing the right thing. I mean, they had a knife. Knives. *He* had a knife.' Tripped up by her own grammar, Dulcie felt the tears start to come.

To her surprise, she felt a heavy paw on her back. 'There, there.' Rogovoy's voice was softer now. 'It's OK, kid. I didn't mean you'd done a bad thing.'

She looked up, blinking. 'But you said . . .?'

'I just meant, can't you keep out of trouble for one day?' His eyes, even hidden deep in that craggy face, looked concerned. 'It's Saturday. Why aren't you sleeping in with that nice boyfriend of yours?'

She stared at him. He didn't understand. 'Because I'm working on my thesis,' she said. 'They have a letter here – well, over in the Mildon collection, anyway. It was written by Thomas Paine, and it may touch on the author I'm writing about—'

Rogovoy interrupted her by raising his hand. 'I'm sure it's fascinating, Ms Schwartz.'

'It is. It could open up a whole new line of inquiry for me, and I was really grateful that I was allowed back in or I'd never have—' She stopped and looked up at him. 'How did they get in here?'

'Excuse me?' Rogovoy looked up from his notes, and she suspected he hadn't been listening.

'Those two men. The ones who attacked Mr Griddlehaus. How did they get in here? Into the library – into the Mildon Collection?'

'Same way as anyone else.' He shrugged. As if to emphasize his point, a stout young man pushed another book cart by. Although the two were seated at a table in an alcove – Dulcie suspected it was a lunch nook – the bustle around them was considerable. Especially for a Saturday morning.

'No. They didn't.' Dulcie wasn't convinced. 'I mean, they didn't come in through the Mildon's main entrance. I would have seen that. Besides, nobody buzzed them in. They were just *here*.'

'The tunnels, I guess.' Rogovoy didn't seem that concerned, but something was off. 'This place is like an anthill.'

'Probably the same way someone got the Dunster Codex out, huh?' She was watching his face.

A rock would have given more away. 'I don't think we should talk about that right now, Ms Schwartz. That's an ongoing case.'

'But they have to be related, don't they?' Dulcie started ticking

off the factors: Rollie, Jessica, the Codex, Professor Coffin . . .
A third cart went by, rattling on a loose wheel. 'And now this.'
Something still didn't add up. 'But, if they threatened the
professor into helping them, and the professor got his students
involved, why did they come back?'

'You're forgetting one other common factor who keeps
popping up.'

'A factor is not a "who",' Dulcie corrected him automatically.
She was still thinking out loud, oblivious to the people milling
around them. 'Why did they have to kill the professor? Why in
our back conference room?'

A large hand came down on hers, stilling it, and she looked
up into those deep-set eyes. 'You, Dulcie Schwartz,' Rogovoy
said, his face close enough that she could smell the coffee on
his breath. 'You're the common factor. You keep coming up, too.'

FIFTY-FOUR

'You don't—' Dulcie could barely get the words out. 'Surely,
you don't suspect me?' She looked around. Had that little
clerk – Griddlehaus – said something? Was this why
Rogovoy had separated them? 'I'm—' She paused, not sure how
to phrase it. 'I'm the heroine here.'

The face Rogovoy made was impossible to read, and when he
ducked his head down before answering, she feared the worst.
When he looked back up, however, he was smiling.

'Believe me, Ms Schwartz, if I could put you under house
arrest, I would.' He raised one meaty paw to block her protests.
'Not that we think you did anything wrong, really. But you do
have a habit of getting in the middle of things. Besides –' he
kept his big hand up – 'we still have a dangerous situation here.
Those two perps are still out there.'

'Oh.' Somehow she had managed to put that out of her mind.

'Tell you what.' Rogovoy hunched closer. 'I've got a solution
that will take care of everything, if you'll put up with me here.'
She nodded, and he continued. 'I'd like you to stay here, in the
library, with one of my guys, if that's OK.'

She shrugged, not sure exactly if she was being asked or informed.

'I don't think those jerks have gotten far. This is gonna be over pretty quick. But knowing that you're here, under our watch, would just make me a little easier, OK?'

Put that way, it sounded nicer. 'Sure.' She nodded this time, meaning it. 'Do you think I can get back into the Mildon?' She looked around the busy passageway. 'I mean, there's not much I can use here, and it's not particularly conducive to writing.'

For some reason, that seemed to amuse Rogovoy. 'Conducive.' He chuckled. 'I'll see what I can do.'

Five minutes later, he was back. 'It's gonna be a while before you can go back to the Mildon,' he said. 'But at least you can start with this.' He handed over her bag.

'Wow, I'd almost forgotten . . .' She opened the messenger flap. Laptop, pad . . . Everything seemed to be in place. Including her phone, which she pulled out and started to power up.

'Oh.' She looked around. 'I wonder if it's OK to make a call?'

'I'm sure.' Rogovoy sat down again, just as another cart rolled by. The one with the loose wheel.

'Detective, do you think there's someplace a little quieter I could use?'

'Calling your boyfriend, huh?' He smiled and pushed himself up. 'Yeah, sure. I'll find you a hidey-hole.'

She followed at a distance as he checked in with an older woman behind a desk. When he gestured, she came closer.

'Look, there's some unused offices down the end of that corridor. I've got to check in with my guys, so I'm gonna send Officer Salazar with you. Not to eavesdrop; I'll tell him to keep his distance. But just to make sure you're OK. OK?'

'OK.' She felt better already. Chris would probably be awake by now and worried that she hadn't called. Still, it didn't hurt to be careful. She jogged back to the table and grabbed her bag, hiking it on to her shoulder as Rogovoy motioned to a young cop down the hall.

'Stay out of trouble,' Rogovoy said to one or both of them. 'I'll be back for you soon.' She watched as he walked toward the Mildon.

'Miss?' The young cop looked serious. Having a nose like a hawk's beak didn't help.

'Sorry.' She tried smiling at him. 'Shall we?'

She had started to extend her arm – just in play – but he frowned, dark brows meeting over that beak, and she let her hand drop to her side.

He turned without another word and led her down the hall. Through a door to the right and then left into another passage, they left the busy sounds of library business behind, but he continued to stride ahead, dour and silent. He was doing her a favor, she knew that. A raptor like that, he'd probably rather be out chasing Harris and Read. Still, she was one of the public he was supposed to protect and serve, right? He stopped at a door and, turning, motioned for her to enter. Dulcie pulled in her tongue just in time.

FIFTY-FIVE

D ulcie wasn't sure whether to be relieved or disappointed. Not only had Chris not been worried about her, he had barely noticed she'd gone. She'd only gotten as far as saying that she was at the library and would be there for the near future when her ordinarily polite boyfriend interrupted.

'Sorry, sweetie, I only got up about a half hour ago. I figured that's where you'd gone. Though, to be honest, Esmé did seem a little agitated.' She could hear him crunching something. Cheerios, probably. Her own stomach rumbled in sympathy. It must be close to noon. 'But Mr Grey told her everything was fine. Something about you knowing about a false alarm.'

'He knew I pulled the alarm?' It should have been comforting, probably, that Mr Grey had been so confident. That her spectral pet had made the effort to reassure her current kitten and, by extension, her boyfriend. But Dulcie felt her hunger pangs replaced by a slight ache. It should have been reassuring, but it wasn't. Mr Grey hadn't been in touch with her. 'You heard him?'

'Only like a whisper, you know.' He crunched again. 'I didn't want to eavesdrop. Besides, I'm sort of dealing with another situation here.'

'Oh?' Dulcie wasn't really listening. It wasn't even that she hadn't gotten to tell him exactly what happened. It was that he hadn't asked.

'Yeah, I'm not sure if I should be concerned or what.' Another crunch. Very little short of mortal danger could put Chris off his food.

'Tell me.' Dulcie decided to forgive him. After all, he *had* been reassured of her well-being by no less an authority than Mr Grey.

'Well, it might be nothing.' Another crunch. 'Mr Grey would probably tell me I'm worrying needlessly.'

Try as she might, Dulcie couldn't avoid a stab of jealousy. 'Chris . . .'

'Sorry. It's Jerry.'

She waited while he swallowed.

'I think he might be in trouble.'

'Jerry?' Dulcie realized she had shouted when she saw the dour cop turn. She waved him off as she'd shoo a bird. 'Chris, what happened?'

'It's probably nothing—'

'*Chris!*' She cradled her hand over the phone.

'Sorry, sweetie. He called me. At least, I think he did. The phone rang, and I was asleep. It was early – like, eleven. Anyway, I picked it up, and I'm pretty sure it was Jerry, only the connection was really bad. I think he said something about Trista, and he sounded, well, agitated. Then we got cut off.'

'Didn't you call him back?' Dulcie was standing. The cop stared, those brows closing in again. She turned her back on him.

'Well, yeah, but my call went straight to voicemail, and I haven't been able to reach him since.'

First Trista, now Jerry. Dulcie didn't know what was going on, but it wasn't good. True to his words, however, Chris seemed to have recovered.

'So, what's up with you, sweetie? How's your morning going?'

'It's been kind of complicated.' Dulcie turned around. The young cop looked no more pleased with her company than she was with his. She needed to talk to Rogovoy. 'I'll tell you later, sweetie. Promise.'

With a nod to the stern cop, Dulcie signaled that she was ready to go. If he wouldn't talk, she'd use the time to think.

Jerry was both loyal and persistent. Smart, too, she reasoned as they turned back down the first hallway. He had reached Trista somehow. Or he'd found out something – and gotten himself in trouble as well. Rogovoy had met Jerry. He knew about the situation with Trista. She'd tell him what was going on.

Only, when they got back to the lunch alcove, nobody was there.

She broke down and asked one of the cart-wheeling clerks. 'Detective Rogovoy?'

'Sorry.' He shook his head.

She turned to the beaked cop. 'Do you know where he is?'

'He's on the job,' he said. She hadn't really expected more from him, but it was still disappointing.

'I'm going to go look for him.'

The young cop took a step, blocking her path. Standing there, he shook his head. 'My instructions are that you are to remain here.'

'Great,' Dulcie said to nobody in particular. She might not be a suspect, but she was a prisoner. At least she had other things to do. Returning to the table, she took a seat facing away from the cop and pulled her laptop out of her bag.

'There are no limits on my intellectual life,' she muttered, half hoping he could hear. 'Or my online communications.'

Not sure whether she'd complain to the dean or to the police liaison first, she opened her email. Maybe she'd just tell Chris what had been going on. As she waited for her email to download, she saw a couple of diverting possibilities: a call for journal entries. An invite to a party for Suze. And there, among all the unread emails, was one labeled: URGENT. PLEASE READ. It had come from a Qmail account – one of those free email services so beloved of spammers – and Dulcie was about to delete it unread when she saw the sender: JESSIW. She clicked to open it.

Dulcie, she read. *Whole story is not what you think – not at all. GC wasn't only victim. DC is a phantom. Please – save yourself!*

FIFTY-SIX

Her first instinct was disbelief. No, even though Dulcie had spent most of her academic career reading about ghosts and demons, she wasn't going to fall for this one. Even though her colleagues had been whispering about the Dunster Codex ever since it first went missing. Even though one man was dead and several other people were missing in connection with the medieval treasure, she wouldn't buy it.

How could she? Even Lucy, she thought, would think twice before believing that an ancient book was a ghost. She stopped herself. No, her mother would believe it. Would actually say that the book itself was not the phantom, but that an inanimate object could carry the spiritual projections of those who had owned it. Of those who had, perhaps, cursed it.

For a split second, Dulcie seriously considered the possibility that the missing book – the Dunster Codex – was in fact haunted. For a moment, she wavered, afraid. Perhaps she should let sleeping books lie, she thought. A haunting . . . a phantom. Maybe the book was cursed. Maybe her dreams – nightmares, really – had been warning her of just such an outcome. Maybe . . .

A brush, just a touch, on her shoulder made her turn with a start. That annoying cop – but, no, he was standing with his back toward her. Probably standing guard, Dulcie realized, on the direct order of his commanding officer. There were two dangerous criminals on the loose. They had seen her; she had thwarted them. She was legitimately in danger, even here in the bowels of the library. And here she had been, blaming the young cop for his rigorous attention to his duty.

Dulcie felt herself relaxing a little, grateful for her own personal eagle scout. Grateful, too, for the realization that made both her captivity and her relationship with her raptor-guard a little easier. But that touch – what had it been?

'*Dulcie, Dulcie.*'

She sat up straight. That voice. It had been so long.

'*And you thought I had abandoned you. Didn't you, little one?*'

'I worried,' she admitted under her breath, so softly that she wondered if he would hear.

She was answered with the soft brush of fur against her cheek. The affectionate head-butt of a beloved pet.

'I missed you, Mr Grey.'

'*And I, you, little one.*' The low rumble of a purr underscored the deep, soft voice. '*But you are doing well, Dulcie. You are learning – learning who to trust. What to trust . . .*' The purr subsumed the voice, and Dulcie strained to hear as the remainder of the sentence was absorbed in the rolling rumble. '*Ghosts . . .*'

'I'm sorry, Mr Grey, I missed that.' All her senses on alert, Dulcie craned forward, hoping for more. She was losing him.

'*You can trust your instincts, Dulcie. You've always known you can.*' That purr, a low vibration in the air. '*And ghosts, Dulcie, be wary what you believe of ghosts.*' The voice was fading now, as was the purr. '*Real ghosts are nothing to be afraid of . . . nothing more than the echo of love.*'

He was gone. But for the moment, Dulcie didn't mind. Mr Grey had visited her. He had come with affection and reassurance, and even if she didn't totally understand what his message meant, she got that she was doing the right thing. That in her heart, she would know what choices to make.

Besides, the great grey cat had given her something to think about. He was, she figured, the ultimate authority on things in the spirit world – more so even than Lucy. And if he said that ghosts were a manifestation of love, then she believed him. All of which cast doubt on that message.

The email! Why hadn't she thought of it? She flipped her laptop open and typed a quick reply: *Jessica – where are you? We need to talk.* She hit send. But less than a second later, a ping alerted her to a response. ADDRESS INVALID/USER UNKNOWN, it said. Jessica had used a disposable account and had already covered her tracks.

Well, that was frustrating. But, as Dulcie – a newly invigorated Dulcie – reminded herself, it was all information. Maybe it meant that Jessica couldn't be trusted. After all, if someone wanted to get her off a case, to keep her from asking questions, scaring her would be one way to do it. Perhaps Jessica had been around enough of the student scuttlebutt to know the rumors. Hades, maybe Jessica had been a source of the rumors? Maybe she and

Rollie had been working together to keep people from asking about the Dunster Codex.

But why? It was inevitable that the theft would be discovered. Dulcie remembered the way Professor Coffin had glowered at them all. The entire English department might as well be culpable, that look had said. His moustache had fairly bristled. No, Professor Coffin was not a man to be scared off by a ghost story.

Then again, Professor Coffin had been killed.

Dulcie paused. There had to be another way of looking at this. Something else was tickling the back of her mind. A memory or phrase that wouldn't be forgotten, like something she had dreamed—

Of course! Dulcie could have kicked herself. Her author – or, at least, the woman in her dreams – had talked of phantoms, of ghouls that sought to suck her blood or steal her life essence, or whatever. A flash of the professor lying in his own blood came to Dulcie, and she shook her head, willing it away. Those phantoms had been real to the woman in her dreams, enemies who sought to discredit her. To steal her life's essence – her work . . .

Could it be? Suddenly, everything Dulcie had suspected about that essay – everything she had been on the verge of proving – came back. If that essay were a fake, could it be, possibly, that the Dunster Codex was, too? A fake – a *phantom* – and that was why she was being warned off investigating?

But Professor Coffin would have known. *Must* have known. And if he had known, he wouldn't have reported the real rarity as stolen. Then again, if he had found out, that could be a motive . . . There was too much up in the air. Dulcie needed to find out more. She stood and approached the young cop.

'Excuse me.' She reached for his arm, but he was already holding his arm out. Holding her back as he looked down the hall. It was Rogovoy, flanked by two other officers in uniform. And he was smiling.

'Good news!' He waved Dulcie's guard away and directed himself to her. 'We got one of them. The bigger guy – the one you called Harris. He made it to South Station, and we caught him boarding a train for Providence. He's not talking – not yet – but we figure his partner can't be far behind. Oh, don't worry –' he raised his palms in surrender – 'we know they might have split up, too. The interesting thing is that this proves they're not local talent. But it's harder to leave town these days, and we're watching North

Station and the buses, too. If he has a car, it might be tougher. But, hey, weekend traffic? If he's on Ninety-Three, he'll be wishing he was in custody.'

'Oh, thank the Goddess.' Dulcie felt the last of the tension leaving her body. 'I mean, thank you, Detective Rogovoy. And I think I've figured something out, too.'

He wasn't listening. He was accepting congratulations from the young cop when another detective came up to join them. Rogovoy was giving them details – apparently a security officer had been instrumental and was up for commendation. Dulcie didn't want to wait. Slipping by the men, she headed toward that unmarked door. If she could only get Thorpe on the phone, she might be able to clear everything up – the Dunster Codex case, her thesis, and all.

FIFTY-SEVEN

Was it left or right? The empty hallway wasn't marked, and Dulcie regretted not paying closer attention earlier, when the beaked cop had escorted her down there. She'd been distracted then, and wasn't necessarily at her best now either – something Rogovoy had said was tickling at her brain. A left, definitely, she was almost sure as she turned down a long passage painted an industrial grey that reflected the flickering fluorescent lights. Were there two turnings?

It didn't matter, she told herself. All she needed really was a quiet place where she could make a few phone calls in privacy. She didn't want anyone hearing her outlandish theory until she had some proof. And she certainly didn't want another incident like the last one. She'd gotten off lightly, she knew. A second cell phone offense, even here in a maintenance tunnel, would be harder to explain.

The hall she was in turned right abruptly, and she followed it, her sense of direction shot. Up ahead, a door – labeled in black paint. She approached carefully, not wanting to be caught tres-passing. MILDON, the door said. Dulcie could have laughed. She'd been walking in circles, making a circuit of the outer part

of the left wing of the level. She'd come to the back entrance of
the Mildon, the tunnel entrance. Live and learn. She stepped back
to where the passage had turned. So much for finding a private
room, but if she backtracked a few yards, she'd probably have
enough privacy.

Dulcie turned one more corner and, leaning back against the
wall, pulled out her phone.

'Ms Schwartz? Where are you? You sound like you're calling
me from a sauna bath.' Martin Thorpe was still at the departmental
office, though he now sounded fully caffeinated.

For a moment, Dulcie regretted calling him. This theory,
however, would not wait. 'I'm sorry, Mr Thorpe, I'm calling
from—' She stopped herself. Better not to say. 'I don't want to
disturb anyone, so I've got my hand over the phone.' Turning to
face the wall, she sank down into a seated position. Between the
wall and her body, the call had to be at least slightly muffled.
'You know that new information I told you about?'

'Your thesis, yes. I gather you followed up on it?'

'Well, yes, I did.' For a moment, Dulcie was tempted to get
into it. But she didn't yet have enough evidence, and besides, as
hard as it was to admit, the *Ravages of Umbria* were not the top
priority right now. 'But that's not why I'm calling.'

'Are you in trouble again, Ms Schwartz? Because really, at
this point in your academic career, if you hope to *continue* said
academic career—'

'No, no, it's not that.' She had to get to the point. 'It's about
the Dunster Codex. I had an idea.'

'You had an idea.' They both paused, Dulcie trying to figure
out how to phrase her theory so that it would sound almost
plausible. 'Ms Schwartz, if you know or have heard something
about the Codex, then I really must direct you to the police. I
am not—'

'No, no. It's not about the theft or Professor Coffin's – about
Professor Coffin.' Somehow the word 'murder' was still difficult
to say. 'Or not directly. Mr Thorpe –' there was nothing to do
but put it on the table – 'have you ever considered the possibility
that the Dunster Codex isn't – well – isn't all that we think we
might be?'

'All that we think—?'

She didn't let him continue. 'I mean, think about it, Mr Thorpe.

Virtually nobody has seen it. None of us students, anyway. We only know about it through its reputation. In fact, it has rarely been in the library at all. Since it was purchased, it's spent most of its time in print and paper restoration, right? And now the folks who work there are under suspicion for all sorts of things – fake IDs and the like. And, well, isn't it possible that the Dunster Codex is the biggest fake of all?'

She didn't get into the ghost email. Mr Grey and the dream, with its mention of phantoms, would carry no weight with her adviser. Without them, her theory sounded thinner than gauze, but it was out there. On the table.

And just like that, Martin Thorpe knocked it off. 'Nonsense.' Her adviser snorted into the phone. 'What a nonsensical idea. The Dunster Codex? The pride of the Mildon Collection?'

He paused, and for a moment Dulcie almost thought she could hear him thinking. Yes, the Dunster Codex was the pride of the collection. One item built up by reputation to be . . . unassailable?

'Besides, we've gotten word about its whereabouts.' Thorpe sounded like himself again. Calm, collected. Insufferable. 'The ruffians responsible for this despicable act had enough sense to understand its value. It has shown up on the roster of Ackerland and Dolby, the premier auction house for antiquities. I was informed less than an hour ago. The university is sending a legal team to New York to discuss the Codex's recovery as we speak.'

'Oh.' Dulcie slumped forward, her head touching the wall. 'Well, that's good news, right?' If the Dunster Codex wasn't a fake, what did that mean? Maybe that email was only meant to scare her. Maybe the dreams only pertained to that one essay. Maybe they meant nothing at all.

Thorpe was still talking. 'Such wild flights of fancy might be understandable in a younger mind, but by this stage in your career, Ms Schwartz, discipline is key.' He paused, perhaps hearing the harshness in his tone. 'You've had a shock, I gather. It's understandable that you would want the crime to be other than what it was. Why don't we forget this call ever took place and focus instead on your research. You did find something, you said? Something *real*?'

'I found something,' she said, her voice – and spirits – flat. After this, he would never believe her theory. He would insist she take the essay at face value. Insist that her author had caved in to the prevailing philosophies about women and education. She would have to make her case. 'There's something in the Mildon collection,' she said, finally. 'I think . . . I don't know for sure, but it could important.'

'Very good, Ms Schwartz.' He wasn't listening. He was busy. 'Let's speak on Monday, when you can tell me more about your ongoing research.'

'Sure,' she managed to choke out. 'Thank you, Mr Thorpe.'

The painted wall felt cool against her forehead. She would stay here, she thought. It was quiet. So quiet that she heard the squeak of shoe leather on the concrete floor, only a moment before she felt the touch of cold steel at her throat.

FIFTY-EIGHT

'Get up.'

The voice was cold, as cold as the blade pressed against her throat, and Dulcie complied. As she did, she felt her curls being grabbed, her head yanked back. The knife began to dig in.

'No!' she choked out.

'Shut up.' The voice had become a hiss. 'Be a good girl and everything will be all right. You hear me?'

She nodded, the movement only making her more conscious of the blade.

'Good.' She felt a shift behind her. The knife-wielder pulled her hair as he looked around. 'You're my ticket out of here. You've got to know another way.'

'Another?' She whispered so softly she wasn't sure he'd heard, but then he pulled her back.

'Not through the paper lab. They've got that marked.' His breath was hot and damp on her ear, and she could smell his sweat.

She had to think. 'There's – there's the Mildon.' The collection would still be crawling with cops.

'Right.' He jerked her hair back. 'Like I'm going back there.'

She caught a glimpse of an unshaven face. A filthy suit. Of course, it was Read. The one they hadn't captured. 'Come on, girl. The professor said this place had miles of tunnels.'

The professor. That knife. This man had killed Professor Coffin. Dulcie felt the room start to spin.

'Oh no, you don't.' He pulled at her curls again, forcing her to stay upright. 'Don't get all girly on me.' He laughed. It wasn't a friendly laugh. 'The professor said you liked ghost stories. Scary stories, right? Think of this as your own little adventure.'

Coffin had talked about her? To this man? Despite herself, Dulcie found her curiosity piqued. 'How did you get in?' she whispered, trying to keep her voice even.

'I've got an ID, a key card, don't I?' She felt him moving again, craning to see down the long hall. 'He gave me my very own. Come on.'

He pushed her around in front of him and started to walk. Dulcie gasped, a reaction that had nothing to do with the movement of the blade against her neck. She had known Coffin was mixed up in something – but with these guys?

'Why?' The question slipped out.

'Money, you stupid girl.' He was walking her in front of him, one hand in her hair, one on the knife. 'He needed it. We provided it.'

They'd come to the turn, and he shoved her against the wall. She did not dare turn, but could feel him, straining around the corner. The seconds ticked by.

'Why?' As soon as the word was out, she winced. He would hurt her, she knew that – but she still had to know.

The man she knew as Read seemed to sense that, because he laughed again. 'Said the place was a treasure chest, didn't he? And we knew we'd end up owning it.'

Despite her best instincts, Dulcie heard herself sigh. If she could have, she would have shaken her head. 'He didn't mean like that.'

'What?' She felt spittle on her ear, and she clenched her eyes tight.

'The treasure – it's books. Knowledge.' She thought of the Paine letters. Of her thesis, and of all she'd hoped to prove.

'Bullshit.' He jerked her head back roughly. 'He said the place was a gold mine. He was sure planning on cashing in.'

'He did.' Dulcie's voice was barely a whisper. It all was becoming clear. She thought of the stories about Coffin. Of his jet-setting life, fêting the wealthy and powerful all the while building his own reputation as a scholar. An authority. All for the glory of the collection, supposedly, but in the meantime, letting him lead a life of luxury and prestige far beyond the normal reach of academe. 'He did cash in, in his way.'

'So where's my money?' A hiss like death.

'It's all gone.' Coffin must have filed for the insurance, she realized. Must have engineered the theft to pay off his debts. And Rogovoy had held that up. Had he suspected foul play? Did it matter now? A deep sadness flooded her. 'All gone.'

She closed her eyes again and felt herself relaxing. So this was how it would end. Read would get no satisfaction, and Rogovoy – watching the bridges and tunnels – would never guess they were so close. Well, Chris would look after Esmé, and Mr Grey would comfort them both. She would miss them. She would even miss Esmé's antics, the way she went wild when they played.

Another noise – a door, some footsteps – and Read slammed her against the wall so hard she squeaked. He let go of her hair then and grabbed her face, wrapping one hand over her mouth and nose. She gasped, tasting blood where he had pushed her lip against her tooth. The knife dug into her neck. She couldn't breathe.

Footsteps. Read leaned closer. He would kill her and make a break for it. She would suffocate while he waited. She was seeing stars – green stars – her knees were giving out.

'Oh no you don't.' He jerked her up, his hand pressing against her lips, sliding into her mouth. Choking her.

Green stars like eyes. Esmé. That hand. Dulcie bit down hard and felt the spurt of blood. Felt the knife jerk back by reflex as Read tried to free himself. She kicked – it wasn't enough. Then she heard it – a loud, dull thud! – and she was free.

Gasping for air, she spun around. He had a knife, but she had spirit. And he was lying on the floor. Next to him stood Thomas Griddlehaus, library clerk, panting, a leather-bound folio of Ben Jonson plays held between his hands.

FIFTY-NINE

'I believe I owed you a rescue.' The little man was blinking down at his victim. Read had been thrown off his feet by the clerk's swing, but the first cop on the scene kept him there, hands cuffed behind him. 'I was afraid I wasn't going to get the opportunity.'

They'd moved down the passage a bit. Griddlehaus had been urging her into the library, but Dulcie couldn't go any further and sat slumped against the wall. There was something satisfying in watching the police as they swarmed. Someone had put the knife in a bag, she noticed. Someone else was going through the pockets of Reed's ruined suit.

'This was the first item at hand.' He was looking down at the folio. Its binding had cracked. 'Well, it's all ruined, anyway.'

'What do you mean?' Breathing was still difficult, her throat hurt, and Dulcie welcomed the distraction.

'The collection. Everything.' He sat beside her, his eyes on the book. 'Our Codex.'

'I know,' she said gently. 'He made it all up, didn't he?'

Griddlehaus nodded and pushed his glasses up.

'Is that why the insurance inspection was held up? Did Rogovoy know?' She'd seen the panicked look the detective had given her as his men had secured Read. He wouldn't thank her for this.

'I don't know, not really.' Griddlehaus seemed to find the cover of the folio fascinating. 'I do know Professor Coffin was quite frustrated with the delays.'

'I bet,' Dulcie added. 'So how did you find out?'

'The auction house. New York.' Another sniff. 'I was on the phone with them discussing provenance. I got quite up on my high horse, you know. I was so sure it was stolen.'

'It was a fake, wasn't it?'

The little mouse shook his head. 'No, the Dunster Codex is real. It's too well documented for anyone to make up that much of a story. But we had never owned it. The professor put down earnest money and a letter of intent. Then the time ran out, and the seller was tired of waiting.'

'Huh.' Dulcie leaned back against the wall. So the Dunster Codex did exist, but the professor hadn't managed to buy it. Was that what had pushed him to borrow money from people like Harris and Read? Was it, as she'd first imagined, that he'd simply spent more than he'd saved, playing the role he'd imagined for himself? Maybe it didn't matter. The Dunster Codex was supposed to be the professor's crowning achievement, the ultimate acquisition. It had proven to be the phantom that had brought about his death.

'That's it for the collection.' Griddlehaus was barely audible. 'The Mildon. Our reputation is ruined.'

'What are you talking about?' Dulcie roused and turned toward the little man.

'This scandal? And then to find out the truth? We have no treasures.'

'Yes, you do.' Dulcie reached out and gently took the Jonson. 'You've got tons of important works. This Jonson, for instance. And *The Wetherly Ghost.*' She paused, an idea coming together. 'And I could be wrong, but I think I may be on the track of a lost masterpiece – a Gothic novel that was praised by none other than Thomas Paine himself.'

Just then, a clatter of footsteps and raised voices caused them both to start. Dulcie scrambled to her feet in time to see the amassed police turn as one. Then Rogovoy nodded and turned, letting the intruder pass. It was Chris.

'Dulcie! There you are. It's been crazy.' He looked around, as if suddenly seeing all the police activity. 'Oh man, what happened? Are you OK?'

And she was. 'It's a long story, Chris. A really long story.' She turned to the clerk. 'This is Thomas, Thomas Griddlemaus – *Griddlehaus.*' But Chris was pulling her away.

'Dulcie, it's Trista. She's been found.'

Dulcie gasped. Had Read—?

'She's OK. She's fine.' Chris had his hands on her shoulders. He was staring into her eyes, making sure she understood. 'She's been in Providence all along. She gave that lecture – the Kiplinger? – at Brown yesterday. That's what Jerry was trying to tell me when his cell cut out. She'd just taken off.

She was freaked, I guess, and decided she needed some time. She called him right after, and he went down to meet her last night. Jerry says she aced it. Brown is going to offer her a fellowship.'

The relief was physical, draining, and Dulcie collapsed against the wall.

'Sweetie, are you OK?'

'Yeah, I'm fine.' She looked up at him and tried to stand. When she stumbled, he caught her. 'I'm just famished.'

'Want to go out? Name the place!'

But she was shaking her head. 'I want to go home. I want to be with our cats.'

SIXTY

After one look at Dulcie, Rogovoy had cleared her to leave, and she and Chris cabbed home. Over three bowls of Raisin Bran, Dulcie had managed to tell her boyfriend about her own morning. Chris, who'd grabbed his own bowl to be polite, was torn between anger and disbelief.

'Dulcie, you're a heroine. You saved that little guy. But – but how could you?' She had paused in her eating by then, and he reached out to take her hand. Esmé, who had jumped up on the table, sat and watched. 'How could you sneak off like that?'

'I thought those guys were long gone. They'd caught the other guy – Harris – at the train station.' Dulcie paused, remembering, and shivered. Chris saw her shudder and leaned over to gather her into his arms. 'If it weren't for Griddlehaus. And for Esmé . . .'

They both turned toward the cat. The little tuxedo had settled into her sphinx pose and looked quite pleased with herself.

'Rogovoy told me he'd been heading to Providence,' she said finally. 'I knew that had sparked something – I just didn't put it together. The Kiplinger.' She shook her head in disbelief and pushed her bowl back.

'I know,' Chris said. 'I could kill her. Not literally!'

'Not even metaphorically.' Dulcie turned toward her boyfriend.

'Hey, it wasn't a totally awful morning. I found something in the Mildon. Something Rollie pointed me to.'

'Rollie?' He looked at her quizzically. Esmé, no longer the center of attention, jumped to the floor.

'Real name Rodney Gaithersburg – aka Roland Galveston?'

He nodded.

'Anyway, he really had worked in restoration, and he steered me toward some letters. I've only read one so far, but I'm pretty sure it's about my author, Chris, the author of *The Ravages*. She had fans, including Thomas Paine. And he wrote about her enemies – about how plagiarists were aping her style to discredit her. It's circumstantial, but it's a start.'

She got up and started clearing. Esmé twined around her ankles, but Dulcie's mind was already back at work. 'I need to read more, though. I need to get into the conservation center, to see if there are other letters and, well, what else is being worked on. I may have a lead on something even bigger.' She stopped and turned toward her boyfriend.

'Chris,' she said, her voice dropping to a hush. 'I think I may have found something. I may have found evidence that she was working on another book.'

Chris was chuckling as he took the bowls from her and shooed her into the other room. 'Go, Dulcie. Get to work,' he called after her as he turned the tap. At his feet, the little cat paused. He looked down, into those green eyes, then nodded. And Esmé followed her into the living room, purring.

SIXTY-ONE

Since Jerry had forgiven Trista so readily, it seemed churlish to hold a grudge. So when her friend called that evening, Dulcie agreed to meet her. Sure, it looked like rain, but it was Saturday night. Besides, Trista was buying, she told Chris, and they'd be gathering at the People's Republik for the last pint of the semester.

'I'm so sorry, Dulcie.' Trista drew her friend aside as soon as she and Chris showed up at the bar. 'I really am. Right before we went into the meeting, I'd gotten a text – a text from Rollie – telling me not to say anything to anyone. That I would be putting them in danger.' She paused and bit her lip.

Dulcie nodded.

'And I did, didn't I? I got you involved.'

'*You* didn't get me involved.' Dulcie felt herself thawing. Besides, this was the truth. 'Rollie did. He's the one who swapped out my ID for yours and planted a fake blue ticket on you with my name – even though Coffin had made a ringer for you.'

Trista shook her head, confused. Dulcie filled her in on everything that had happened. 'Coffin had been planning this for a while,' she concluded. 'He'd seen you, and when he found that undergrad – Jessica – it must have all come together. He got her good jobs. Gave her all kinds of perks. I guess at some point, she felt she couldn't turn him down. Anyway,' she said finally, 'she didn't. But go on.'

'Well, he scared me. He told me what he thought about those two – the two bruisers – and he warned me to make myself scarce. I was freaking out, Dulcie. But from what he said I knew that they weren't the cops, and that meant I had no reason to hang around. I had the Kiplinger scheduled; I had a place to stay. I just booked a little early. I'm so sorry.' She was shaking her head again and trembling. Dulcie suspected she was going to cry. 'I was hoping you'd figure it out. That Jerry would— I called him, finally. After the lecture. I just couldn't stand not hearing from him.'

'He was frantic. He kept trying to call you,' her friend said gently. 'We all did.'

'I'd thrown my phone away. I didn't know if they could use it to trace me. It was stupid, I know. But I was so scared—'

'No, it wasn't stupid. Those men were killers. *Are* killers. But they're in custody now.'

That's when the waterworks started. Trista sobbed and, hugging her, Dulcie started to cry, too. When Jerry came over, holding two full pints, he looked confused. 'Everything OK?'

'Yeah.' Dulcie wiped her face. Beside her, Trista nodded. 'Everything's just fine.'

That night, Dulcie had a dream. She'd drunk too much, she knew. It had become a hot night, as humid as full summer, and following on all the stress and fatigue, she'd been downright tipsy when Chris had helped her into bed. She'd been talking about her plans. About how she wanted to get up early the next morning. Get right to work.

Chris hadn't argued with her, though he had switched the alarm clock off when he thought she wasn't looking. She could start on Monday, he'd figured. They all could use a day off.

The dream was as vivid as they always were. Maybe more so, with an immediacy that would stay with her for days to come. Dulcie tried to describe it when she woke, but the beer – and the preceding days – were too much for her, dragging her back into the deep, healing sleep she needed.

Writing, writing, writing, the words flowing like the rain beating against the window. She brushed a curl from her cheek as the thunder broke overhead, refreshing the earth, wiping the dull heat from the air. She was on the path now, moving ahead – toward something, toward someone. And she was not alone. On her desk, curled by the papers that piled up with a reassuring speed, a small friend slept. At her shoulder, a familiar spirit, purring and satisfied. The echo of love.